PRAISE FOR

Daisy Woodworm Changes the World

"Melissa Hart weaves the disparate people and actions of an eighth-grader's daily life into a warm, realistic, and compelling whole. I truly love this book."

—Nancy Gruver, editor of *New Moon Girls* magazine

"What a wonderful story about the power of determination! This novel expertly weaves a tale of inclusion, acceptance, and confidence. Everyone needs to learn this valuable lesson. Never let someone else's low expectations limit our success!"

—Abigail Adams, Down syndrome advocate, and father Steve Adams

"Readers will devour this funny and touching story about relationships—with classmates, family, teachers, and beyond. Track star and budding entomologist Daisy is the kind of friend readers will wish they had in their own lives."

—Mary Boone, author of *Bugs for Breakfast: How Eating Insects Could Help Save the Planet*

"Melissa draws upon her own life to craft a beautiful story that's equal parts witty and warm. Brave Daisy Woodworm will inch her way into your hearts as she discovers the power of her own voice. An inspiring read for young changemakers."

—Sarita Menon, editor of *Smore* magazine

"Melissa Hart writes with knowl[illegible]ng to be entertaining; that's quite a [illegible]ct matter. Why didn't this book ex[illegible]en a much different person. Daisy [illegible]ds, and—just maybe—the world."

—Amy Silverman, author of *My Heart Can't Even Believe It: A Story of Science, Love, and Down Syndrome*

"*Daisy Woodworm Changes the World* is a funny, moving novel with a serious question at its heart: if you love someone with a disability, how do you help them flourish? I loved this book for its twists and turns, for its diverse, finely drawn characters, and for the rare nuance Melissa Hart brings to her depiction of intellectual disability."

—George Estreich, author of *The Shape of the Eye: A Memoir*

"Daisy encompasses the magnificent complexities of being a teenage girl. Family, friendships, school, rules, expectations, and challenges all pose seemingly insurmountable roadblocks for Daisy. But in the end, she succeeds beyond her wildest dreams. *Daisy Woodworm Changes the World* is an uplifting, inspiring story of teenage triumph. It is packed full of lessons of love, determination, and forgiveness. I loved it!"

—Verna Wise Matthews, Executive Director, Ophelia's Place

"This delightful novel is told by the insightful and hilarious Daisy 'Woodworm' Woodward. Her tale delightfully blends laughs, thrills, and even fashion with the powerful bonds of family. And author Melissa Hart's unique talent for writing sparkling dialogue with heart and humor is on full display. So I urge everyone to postpone cleaning the terrarium and instead to find out just how Daisy Woodworm changes the world today!"

—Bart King, author of *The Big Book of Girl Stuff* and *The Big Book of Boy Stuff*

"This was such an inspirational and affirming story of how important it is to have your voice heard and how sometimes it's the small things that you do for someone that can make all the difference in the world."

—Alisha Emrich, author of *NerdCrush*

Daisy Woodworm
Changes the World
MELISSA HART

MELISSA HART

Mendota Heights, Minnesota

First Edition
First Printing, 2022

Book design by Karli Kruse
Cover design by Maggie Villaume
Cover illustration by Ofride

Jolly Fish Press, an imprint of North Star Editions, Inc.

Library of Congress Cataloging-in-Publication Data (pending)
978-1-63163-637-0 (paperback)

Jolly Fish Press
North Star Editions, Inc.
2297 Waters Drive
Mendota Heights, MN 55120

www.jollyfishpress.com

Printed in the United States of America

For My Brother, Mark

1

The night my mother volunteered me to pass out gingerbread rabbits to my brother and other athletes at the Special Olympics Moonlight Ball because she and Dad were too busy picking up dog poop, I knew my family would never be normal again.

It was Friday, Pizza-Movie Night. Mom stretched out on the living room couch and rested her bare feet on the coffee table. The tattoo of the daisy on her right ankle faced me. She had a tattoo of red sorrel flowers on her left ankle, in honor of my older brother, Squirrel. His name's really Sorrel—like the herb people plant in their gardens to attract bees and butterflies. But I couldn't say Sorrel when I was learning to talk. I called him Squirrel, and the name stuck.

"Dad and I have a last-minute gig tomorrow night, Daisy," my mother said with her brightest Mom smile. "So I volunteered *you* to help at the Moonlight Ball. You'll be supervising the dessert table."

My mouth dropped open. "But . . . I had plans!"

My tongue lisped the S. I bit the tip of it and fell silent. I knew better than to make plans now that my parents worked all the time. Other kids had time to themselves, time to relax. My brother and I had dinner to cook and dishes to wash, floors to sweep and mop, and the bathroom to clean—all the things Dad had done when he worked from home.

My father blinked at me from behind his round glasses. The brown bangs flopping over his forehead made him look like a kid, though silver strands peeked through to remind me he wasn't my age, but a father with a never-ending supply of dad jokes and reminders to take out the trash.

"Plans, kiddo?" he asked me. "What're you up to on a Saturday night. Got a hot date?"

Beside me, my best friend, Poppy, snorted and formed a heart shape with her fingers, which were rainbow-painted to match her toenails. "With Miguel Santos," she teased. "The hottest boy in middle school."

"Ew, never." I socked her in the arm. "Dad, Poppy said she'd be glad to volunteer at Squirrel's dance."

She fished the cherry out of her Shirley Temple and stuck it in her mouth. "Can't." She shook her curly ponytail. "My moms are making me and my sisters drive to San Diego to visit my ammachi and achachan . . . we're even taking the poodle. We won't be back till midnight."

I dropped my half-eaten pizza slice onto my plate and scowled at her and Dad. "Actually, I had plans to clean my terrariums," I began. "I was going to switch the millipedes and the cockroaches."

"Daisy!" Mom pulled her feet off the coffee table and folded her arms across her blinding yellow T-shirt, hiding the ridiculous picture of a dog squatting in the grass. A wrinkle appeared between her eyebrows. "Are you honestly choosing a cockroach over your brother?"

Squirrel leaned down from the love seat he shared with his girlfriend, Angelina, and peered anxiously into my face, so close I could smell his pizza breath. His eyes widened, the color of the ocean on a clear, sunny day.

"You're not going to the dance, sister?" he said, twisting his fingers together. The skin around his nails was red and swollen with eczema from the cleaning products he used when he worked as a janitor at his high school. Our parents kept offering to help him find another job, but he loved cleaning toilets—no joke. "I make them sparkly!" he'd say to anyone who asked.

I bent and tore off a piece of pizza crust for our giant white rabbit, Hasenpfeffer, so I wouldn't have to see my brother's face contorted with worry. But I could still hear him.

"Please?" He jumped up and draped his arms around my neck. "Please, please, please, please, *please*?"

I closed my eyes and clenched my teeth. Squirrel knew I couldn't resist his charms.

"Maybe," I muttered, and stalked into the kitchen for Shirley Temple refills. In the doorway, I paused with the liter of 7Up in one hand and the jar of cherries in the other. Everyone sat piled on the carpet and sprawled across the living room couches just like we had every Friday for years—Mom and Dad on the couch with their feet up on the coffee table, Squirrel and Angelina holding hands and whispering, Poppy busy eating my discarded slice.

Friday was always Pizza-Movie Night, even after my mother lost her accounting job last year and persuaded my stay-at-home dad to start their disgusting new business for dog owners too lazy to clean up their own pets' poop. Never mind that we didn't have a dog, that we'd never had a dog. Mom said the community had a need, and she and Dad were filling it.

They called their company "the Poop Fairies." They'd traded

in our Subaru for a bright yellow pickup and painted it with Dalmatian spots. Then, they mounted two blue fabric wings on the top, and painted the sides with black letters that spelled out *The Poop Fairies.* I tried never to ride in that truck, and I wouldn't let them transport pizza in it. No stinkin' way.

On this particular Friday, Mom and Dad had ordered a Pie of the Day with candied walnuts and feta cheese and peaches glowing like pieces of amber half-buried in mozzarella. But my stomach churned with frustration, and my appetite vanished. I refilled our glasses and passed Poppy another slice while everyone watched an episode of *Stephen Ming, Fashion King* on YouTube.

Squirrel and Angelina and a bunch of other kids at their high school were obsessed with Ming. Tonight, he was teaching men how to roll up their sleeves on a long-sleeved dress shirt. Apparently, it was an art form.

"You've got to roll them past the elbow if you're raking leaves or washing dishes!" Ming hollered into the camera, eyes wide like he was warning viewers about a tsunami. "But you better end that roll just *before* your elbow for parties and business-casual, or you'll find yourself answering to the fashion police!"

He held up one arm to the camera and showed off a perfectly rolled cotton sleeve, blue with an inch of orangish pink. "Bonus points if the color of the inside of your sleeve contrasts with the outside color, fashionistos!"

Angelina cheered and brushed crumbs off the front of her vintage yellow dress dotted with honeybees. It was a dress I wouldn't be caught dead in, but it looked perfect on her, especially with her curly red hair twisted up into two buns like beehives on top of her head. "I love this guy," she told us all just like she did every Friday night.

Squirrel preferred to get his fashion tips from Alina Petrov, a movie star his age who had her own YouTube channel, but Angelina flipped out every time he watched her. "You like Alina better than me," she'd tell my brother. "You think she's prettier than me, don't you?"

Angelina had a little problem with jealousy—one of many reasons I wanted nothing to do with romance. She wouldn't even let Squirrel *look* at another girl.

Poppy draped her legs over mine and wondered out loud for the millionth time: "How did Ming go from being a total nobody to getting six million followers on his YouTube channel just because he knows how to tie a stinkin' necktie?"

I barely heard her. A million angry words crowded my head—words about how Mom had volunteered me as a Moonlight Ball dessert waitress without even asking me first. Words about how no one had even thanked me for dusting and vacuuming the living room and unloading the dishwasher. But before I could launch into a full-blown protest, Ming's video ended and Squirrel started the movie.

It was his night to choose—and he went with a Pixar film, like always. He and Angelina cracked up at every single joke, but my brain barely registered the movie. Instead, I sat and fumed about how everything in my life had changed since the Outdoor Store had eliminated my mother's bookkeeping job and her paycheck. No more half-price running shorts and sports sandals. No more vacations to San Francisco and the Academy of Sciences with their incredible insect collection.

We couldn't even afford pizza delivery now. Poppy and I

had to jog a mile to Beto's on the Beach and walk the giant box back home. We set out plates and cups and napkins and made Shirley Temples and served my parents when they dragged themselves in from work at six and collapsed on the couch smelling like sweat and something else I didn't even want to think about.

Now, I had to keep track of whose turn it was to choose the movie and figure out how to find it for free online or at the library since we could no longer afford Netflix.

Now, I came home right after cross-country every day instead of hanging out on the field or at Serrano's Tacos with my friends, and I stayed home on weekends when my parents were working because they didn't want my brother to be alone.

Never mind that he loved being in the house by himself and blasted his music and cleaned every room and made dinner *and* dessert. #EligibleBachelor had happened four months ago, and just because he'd locked himself in his room to cry over Garth Brooks songs for a week, Mom and Dad had decided someone should always be with him just in case he got depressed again.

I hated having to be so responsible. Everyone else's needs seemed so much more important than mine, and I never got time alone anymore to do what I wanted to do. I tried not to complain. I didn't want my parents to worry any more than they already did about money or my brother. But giving up a whole Saturday night of solitude after five days of school and cross-country practice and homework and housework to volunteer at a dance? I loathed dancing, strangers, and Michael Jackson's music. The Moonlight Ball would be full of all three.

Poppy leaned her head against my shoulder and gave my hand a sympathetic squeeze. When the movie was over, Squirrel and Angelina leapt up to dance to the song in the closing credits. I envied them. They knew exactly how to move to the music while I could only shuffle in place searching helplessly for the beat.

"Your father's made his special gingerbread bunnies." Like a vulture, my mother circled back to the topic of the Moonlight Ball. "They just need to be frosted."

"Who hires someone to pick up dog poop last minute on a Saturday night?" I demanded.

"Oh! We're not just poop fairies tomorrow," Mom said. "Dad and I are taking clients on a neighborhood walk to look at holiday lights while their owners are at a party."

"Clients?" I muttered. "You mean dogs." I rolled my eyes at Poppy.

Dad stood up from the couch and began to gather plates. "Your mother and I are dressing up as elves! I'll have a chance to get some great photos, and we'll pass out stacks of business cards while we're out walking . . . er . . . jingling."

I cringed. My father, who had black-and-white photographs in an art gallery up in the hills, was going to spend his Saturday night walking rich people's dogs in a jingle-bell hat. Who even knew you could make a living doing such ridiculous stuff?

But when the Outdoor Store closed, my mother swore she'd never work in an office again.

She'd had cancer when I was in first grade, and ever since then, she'd been looking for a job outside in the sun instead of in an air-conditioned cubicle. After she got laid off, she jumped at the chance to create her own career.

Which was admirable, I guess, but did that career have to be picking up dog poop?

"What about the photo booth?" I asked Dad. "You always take the athletes' pictures at the Moonlight Ball."

"Someone's stepping in for me tomorrow." His voice held a hint of sadness, but he picked up the last piece of pizza and held it up in the air. "I would tell a joke about pizza, but it's a little cheesy."

Again, Angelina threw back her head and howled with laughter. She loved my father's dad jokes. I sighed and stomped on the empty pizza box to flatten it. At the sound, Hasenpfeffer leapt into the air and scampered toward his cage in the laundry room.

"Do dogs like to look at holiday lights?" Poppy asked my parents. "I mean, all our poodle wants to do is pee on the bushes. Moms say she's going to electrocute herself urinating on someone's Christmas lights."

My mother stood up and stretched her arms over her head. "The dogs' owners think they like to look at lights, and they're paying Dad extra money to take portraits of their pets. I can think of worse things than getting paid to take an evening stroll around the harbor!"

"Yeah. Volunteering at the Moonlight Ball," I muttered.

"So you'll do it, Daisy?" Mom took the flattened pizza box out of my hand. Up close, I saw that her eyes looked red and exhausted. Strands of hair fell out of her ponytail and framed her face like a limp, faded curtain. I almost felt sorry for her.

Almost.

"Fine," I snapped. "I'll go. But I'm not helping out at Special Olympics practice tomorrow morning. I've got a cross-country meet, even if Poppy's bailing on it."

"Take it up with my moms," Poppy said. "It's not like I want to go to San Diego."

Angelina high-fived Squirrel. "Bowling tomorrow!" she said. "I wanna be on your team!"

Angelina always wanted to be on my brother's team. Given the choice, she'd spend every waking minute with him, guarding him from every other girl in the entire world. Once, one of their classmates gave Squirrel a chocolate heart for Valentine's Day. Angelina upended a bottle of glue on her chair and ruined her shorts.

But Squirrel didn't seem to care about how possessive she was. He twirled around in a classic Michael Jackson move and beamed. "Daisy's coming to the ball!" he cried. "You're my best sister ever."

"I'm your *only* sister." I threw a couch cushion at him.

"Look on the bright side," Poppy told me. "My Bestie Intuition says you'll meet a prince."

"Not interested." Other girls had crushes. Not me. Romance appealed to me about as much as getting showered with the stinking spray of an angry darkling beetle.

"Wait. How are Squirrel and I supposed to get to the Ball?" I asked my parents. "It's at that banquet hall half an hour south, right?"

My brother's forehead furrowed. He twisted his fingers together again and shot Angelina a worried look.

"My dad can't take us," Angelina said. "He's gotta drive my big sisters to their tournament in Los Angeles."

As usual, my mother was way ahead of us all. "Billy's mother is going to take all three of you."

"Marlena?" I yelped. "She drives like a wild woman, and she smokes."

"She'll pick up Angelina first, and then you and Squirrel," Mom said calmly. "She's the one working the photo booth, so she can drive you home too."

"Yes!" Squirrel pumped his fist in the air, and he and Angelina wrapped their arms around each other.

"I don't have to dress up, do I?" I growled.

"Yes, you do!" Mom sang out, and disappeared into the kitchen.

"Dad!" I protested.

He swept pizza crumbs from the couch into his hand. "I think formal wear is appropriate tomorrow evening to show respect for Squirrel and the other athletes."

"Formal wear?" Squirrel's head shot up. "You gotta see the tie I bought at the thrift store today!" He jumped off the love seat and pounded upstairs to his bedroom.

Angelina clapped her hands, and her orange and silver bracelets jingled. "Oh, boy! Here comes Mr. America!"

When Squirrel returned, he was wearing his charcoal-gray pants and coat with black dress shoes and a white linen shirt. His blue necktie had clusters of little silver bells tied with red and green ribbons. He'd sprayed himself with Old Spice.

I waved my hand dramatically in front of my nose and coughed. "Geez, bro, did you marinate in cologne?" In commercials, guys slapped a little aftershave on their cheeks when they'd showered. Squirrel used half a bottle of the stuff.

He shrugged. "A man's gotta smell good."

Across the room, Angelina smiled so wide that her cheeks looked like strawberries. "Whoeee! My boyfriend's a hottie!"

Poppy whistled. "She's right, Squirrel. You look like a movie star." She tilted her head and studied him through narrowed eyes. "You'd be a great YouTube fashion celebrity. You're way more attractive than that Ming dude."

Angelina narrowed her eyes at Poppy, ever on the lookout for a potential rival for Squirrel's affections. My brother nodded. "I've always wanted to teach people about fashion on the computer. It helps people like my sister."

He winked at me and cracked up. Then he got a super-serious expression. "Michael Jackson said, 'Please go for your dreams,'" he told us. "My dream is to be a YouTube celebrity."

Poppy applauded. So did everyone else . . . everyone except for my parents. "No Squirrels on YouTube!" Dad said over a tower of empty glasses balanced on a stack of plates. "Not now, not *ever*."

When my parents had disappeared into the kitchen, Poppy snorted and tossed her ponytail. "Everyone else is on YouTube," she said in my ear. "Why shouldn't Squirrel have a channel?"

I left my brother and his girlfriend practicing their Michael Jackson moonwalks and pulled Poppy into the hallway. "Two words," I said in a stage whisper. "Eligible Bachelor."

"You mean that thing that happened *four months ago*?" she hissed. "When Squirrel's friends put his picture on Instagram and hashtagged it Eligible Bachelor?"

I nodded. "That thing scarred my parents for life. When Squirrel showed them his picture, and they read all those hater comments about how he'd never get a date, they went ballistic. No social media for Squirrel. Not now, not ever," I said, echoing my father.

Hasenpfeffer hopped into the hallway, looking for more pizza crusts. I scooped him up and draped him over my shoulder. "Honestly, it's a miracle Squirrel even has a flip phone," I told Poppy. "They're terrified he'll get trolled again."

She shrugged. "Haters gonna hate."

"Right?" I said. "Let Squirrel experience life. I mean, I've been bullied and lived to tell the tale."

"Barely." Poppy scratched Hasenpfeffer's soft white nose. The rabbit closed his eyes and leaned into her hand. "Anyhow, didn't a lot of girls see Squirrel's picture and ask him out on a date?"

"Right. I'm surprised Angelina let them live." I rolled my eyes. "She threatened to break up with him."

"But it wasn't his fault!" Poppy said.

"She can be a little . . . unreasonable where other women are concerned. Anyhow, the mean comments really got to him. He shut himself into his bedroom and didn't come out for a week."

My father walked back into the living room with bowls of chocolate ice cream for Squirrel and Angelina. I set Hasenpfeffer on the floor and pulled Poppy into the bathroom and shut the door. "He's so overprotective," I whispered. "When Squirrel was born, Dad's parents said to put him in a group home. Mom and Dad totally freaked out and stopped speaking to them for a year."

"Understandable," Poppy said. "But what's the big deal? He's *seventeen*. He's almost an adult."

"Tell that to my parents," I replied. "Mom and Dad proved to my grandparents that Squirrel's super-smart and capable, but they won't let him grow up. Angelina wants him to get an apartment with her after they graduate high school and go to community college, but Mom and Dad want him to stay here. They're scared he'll get beat up by some stink bug on the street if they aren't around to protect him."

Poppy glanced in the mirror and pulled off her ponytail elastic so her curls bounced free around her face. "If he wants an apartment and YouTube channel, he should get them!"

"I know." I peered into the mirror and tugged at the ends of my bangs, trying to flatten out the frizz. "You try talking to my parents. Remember what happened when I tried to get an evening to myself?" I asked. "Squirrel and I try to talk to them, but they just walk away like we haven't said a word."

Someone knocked on the door. "Everything okay, girls?" Mom asked.

"Fine!" Poppy and I chorused. We looked at each other in the mirror.

"I wish you could come to this dance with me tomorrow," I said.

She lay her head on my shoulder for a moment. "Me too. I've gotta sit in my grandparents' living room all day eating fried lentil balls and drinking chai. I hate chai. Last time, I asked if I could walk down to Starbucks and get everyone a vanilla latte. My aja acted like I'd spat on her."

"That's a bummer," I said. We walked back into the living room. Squirrel and Angelina sat at the dining room table, checking out Stephen Ming on the laptop as he taught people how to loop a necktie into something called a Windsor knot. "The *wide end* of the tie goes in front!" he yelled into the camera. "Not the *skinny end*, fashionistos!"

"I love this guy!" Squirrel slapped the table with his palms.

Angelina giggled. "He's so funny!"

"His voice gives me a headache." I glared at Stephen Ming's ear-to-ear smile. "I gotta get out of here," I told Poppy.

She glanced at the purple Fitbit on her wrist. "Me too. Moms are making us leave for San Diego at the butt-crack of dawn. Bye, Other Mom!" she yelled toward the kitchen. "Bye, Pops!"

"Bye, Poppy!" my parents said from the doorway. Dad wore a flowered apron. Mom waved a checkered dish towel. "See you next Friday!" they said.

"Bye, Squirrelgelina!" Poppy called.

"Bye!" Squirrel and Angelina called, eyes still glued to Ming on the laptop screen.

"I'm walking her home!" I said from the hallway. "Back in half an hour."

On the porch, we shoved our feet into our running shoes and shivered in the cold night air. "What is that horrible noise?" Poppy smacked her palms over her ears.

"That." I pointed at the neighbors' new inflatable holiday decoration on the lawn across the street—a carousel with elves instead of horses, spinning horror-movie slow. "'Cause nothing says Christmas like a merry-go-round that plays 'Jingle Bells' a thousand times a night."

"That's just wrong," Poppy said, and we took off jogging down the street. The neighbors' houses glowed under strings of holiday lights. On their front lawns, inflatable Santas and snowmen loomed out of the fog that drifted up from the ocean. I breathed in the salty air. I could almost feel my hot-ironed bangs curling into a mass of fuzz on my forehead.

"Yikes." I sidestepped some guy on a bike wearing dark clothing with no helmet and no lights.

"Look, Ma! No brains!" Poppy and I called after him at the same time, then fell silent so that all I could hear was the smack of our shoes on pavement. That was what I loved about foggy nights like this one—the quiet, draped like a heavy quilt around the city. For once, I didn't even mind the fact that my running shoes were about a hundred years old, and running on their sad, flat soles made my shins burn.

But Poppy didn't like silence. She said it made her nervous. Just as I began to relax into the mood, she dropped a bomb. "I wonder what Mr. Lipinsky meant about assigning us a 'life-changing' final project? I mean, won't high school be life changing enough?"

I didn't want to think about the social studies final project we'd be assigned as soon as winter break was over, and I definitely didn't want to think about high school. Poppy and I had gone to the same small charter school together since kindergarten—so small there was only one class for each grade. Most of us had known each other for nine years.

But after our final semester of eighth grade in June, Poppy was going to the public high school with its state champion cross-country and track teams. I was supposed to go, too, but every time I thought about all those people—*hundreds* of strangers swarming the halls and slamming their lockers and laughing at my lisp whenever I opened my mouth to speak—my stomach churned and the back of my neck prickled with dread.

"Wanna hike Lone Pine when you get back?" I said to distract Poppy now. "Not too early, though. It's gonna take me a while to recover from the Ball. What am I even s'posed to wear to this thing?"

"Too bad I'm six inches taller. Otherwise, you could borrow my sari," she said. "What you need is a fairy godmother!" She pushed open her front gate. Her moms had outlined it with little green and white and orange lights—the colors of the Indian flag. "Come in first place at the race tomorrow. I hope Miguel and Devon don't show up."

"You know they will." I sighed. "They'll get first in their races and spend the rest of the day gazing at themselves in the reflections from their trophies. Have fun in San Diego!" I called and jogged toward home. Poppy was right, I realized. I needed a fairy godmother, someone who could transform me from plain old Daisy Woodward in running shorts and sneakers into someone glamorous, just for one night, so that I didn't look like a total loser in front of my older brother and all his friends. While she was at it, maybe my godmother could throw some money my parents' way so they wouldn't have to pick up dog poop for a living.

The Poop Fairy pickup glowed yellow all the way up the street, lit up by the green and blue lights that Squirrel and I had risked our lives to hang because our parents were too busy to decorate this year, and my brother would have a heart attack if he didn't see the same lights and the same fake tree with the same goofy homemade felt ornaments they'd been putting out since he was born. I didn't even want to know what the neighbors thought of us when they saw that truck.

I walked past it, holding my breath so I wouldn't catch any leftover poop-stench, and collapsed on the porch steps to unlace my shoes. I sat there for a long time, staring at the palm tree that Squirrel and I had wrapped with lights as far as the ladder would reach. I knew I was lucky to have neighbors, lucky to have a house, unlike the girl I'd met at Thanksgiving when Mom volunteered us to serve food at the community dinner for people living on the streets. Complaining because I didn't get a night to myself felt suddenly ridiculous. Every honeybee had a role to play—whether worker, drone, or queen—to ensure the success of the hive. Why would a family of humans be any different? Right now, my role was to help around our house and be there for Squirrel while our parents built up their new business. Teamwork was how we'd survive.

I let myself into the house and pulled on a pair of wool socks. It was dark downstairs. Michael Jackson crooned softly from Squirrel's bedroom. Mom had hung her short, black lacy dress on the coat rack and placed a pair of low black heels below. *Daisy! Wear these tomorrow!* she'd written on a sticky note.

"Ick," I muttered, and stomped into the kitchen for a banana. Dad had left a note on the refrigerator . . . one of his weird little poems.

I'm early to bed, and early to rise.

Please frost the bunnies, and you'll win a prize!

I opened the fridge. Two cookie sheets full of baked gingerbread rabbits stood on the shelf. Rabbits, because my father always had to be original. No reindeer or snowflakes for him.

I shook my head, but I pulled out the cookie sheets, then got out powdered sugar and vanilla and began to mix up icing.

So I had to decorate cookies and pass them out at the Moonlight Ball. So what?

At least I had a kitchen, and my own bedroom to hide in once the ordeal was over.

3

Late Saturday afternoon, I paced the living room in my mother's black dress with my hair in curls. My calf muscles ached from racing that morning, and the one-inch heels made them hurt even more, but my only other options were sports sandals or my running shoes.

I hobbled to the bathroom and studied myself in the mirror. I looked like Squirrel and I had been playing dress-up again with the bin of our parents' old clothes and Halloween costumes. All I needed now was my grandma's silver wig from when she had chemo and my humiliation would be complete.

"Daisy!" Mom walked past me with an enormous box full of red and green biodegradable dog poop bags. "You say you came in second in your race this morning? Amazing work! And now, you look like a supermodel!"

"Right," I muttered, still angry about losing first place to a seventh grader from Santa Barbara.

"Thank you for volunteering tonight!" Dad told me from the door with his hands clasped in a prayer-position over his sparkly blue Poop Fairy T-shirt.

"I was volunteered," I replied, but stopped short of reminding him that I'd sacrificed a whole evening alone. "Hey, what's the prize, anyway?"

"Prize?" He frowned.

"Your poem said that if I frosted the gingerbread rabbits, I'd win a prize."

"Ah." He gazed up at the ceiling, then grinned at me. "It's the prize of knowing that all your hard work bought me an extra hour of sleep last night."

"False advertising! That's weak."

I wanted to remind him about how we'd always decorated the bunnies together, eating half of them while we frosted, so we had to bake more. But something sad in his eyes made me bite back the words before they spilled out.

"Hope the dogs are good for you," I said instead. "Get some great photos."

He slung his camera around his shoulder and picked up his tripod. "Honestly, I'd rather shoot photos at the Ball. But this gig tonight pays shockingly well."

My heart actually ached for him. Holiday lights and rich people's dog poop, when he wanted to take pictures of my brother and his friends.

Mom appeared in the hallway. She was dressed identically to Dad in a Poop Fairy T-shirt, knee-high rubber boots, and a red-and-green elf hat topped with little gold jingle bells. *Big yikes*, as Poppy would say.

Dad headed for the truck, but my mother paused to hug me. "You really are beautiful. I'm so sorry, Daisy. I thought this new job would mean we'd have more time to spend together. I didn't think we'd have to work so hard."

She blinked, hard, and her lips trembled. She covered her mouth with one hand.

It was impossible to stay mad at her for volunteering me tonight. I mean, it wasn't her fault that she'd lost her job. "We'll hang out tomorrow," I promised. "It's Sunday! We'll go for a walk on the beach."

In the driveway, Dad honked twice. He'd rigged the horn in the Poop Fairy pickup so it sounded like a barking dog. The sound echoed all the way down the street. "I'd better go." Mom kissed the top of my head and jingled out the door.

"Squirrel!" I called up the stairs. "Five minutes!" I wobbled into the kitchen to pack frosted gingerbread bunnies into tins.

The red cookies had green sugar sprinkles, and the green cookies had red sugar sprinkles, and some had blue icing and white sugar sprinkles for Hanukkah, though if you asked me what rabbits had to do with Hanukkah or Christmas, I had no idea.

I wrapped our blue platter in a dish towel so it wouldn't get broken on the way to the Moonlight Ball and looked out the window just as Billy's mom's silver Prius pulled up in front of our house. Taylor Swift blasted from the open windows.

"Squirrel!" I hollered.

"Ready!" My brother walked down the stairs like royalty in the thrift store suit and tie he'd bought with money from his janitor job. He lifted his chin the way he did when he was really proud of himself. "I look like a celebrity," he said, and hugged me in a cloud of Old Spice.

I coughed. "You're right." Squirrel looked like a model, and I looked like the black swimsuit Hasenpfeffer had chewed up last summer and left like a rag on the bathroom floor. At that moment, I would've given one of my millipedes to crawl back into my flannel pajama pants and lock myself in my bedroom. But Squirrel grabbed my hand and pulled me out the door. "You look gorgeous, sister."

"You're a good liar," I muttered.

He shook his head, and his face was serious. "I never lie."

Billy's mom, Marlena, stood beside her car with a cigarette in one hand and her red hair gathered in a sloppy bun on top of her head. I'd known Billy as long as Squirrel had. They'd met in first grade. He was practically a brother to me, but if I had to live with him and his mouth, I'd move into our treehouse and only come inside to shower.

Billy stuck half his body out the passenger window of the Prius. He wore a shiny red shirt and a white tie. The setting sun turned his yellow hair to gold. "Let's get this party started!" he hollered and high-fived Squirrel.

Angelina had plastered herself against the far seat behind Marlena. Squirrel squeezed in next to her. "You look beautiful!" he said. The blue satin in Angelina's dress matched the carnation he'd pinned in his lapel and the roses he gave her in a little plastic box. "We planned it!" he told me. "I bought the corsage on the way home from work. They gave me a discount because I'm so cute!"

Angela took the corsage, but she wouldn't look at Squirrel, and when he tried to take her hand, she yanked hers away and stared out the window.

"What's wrong with her?" I whispered in my brother's ear.

He furrowed his brow and said nothing. But Billy gave me the scoop. "Angelina's mad because Megan thinks Squirrel is *her* boyfriend! He got a strike in bowling today, and Megan kissed him! On the lips!"

I rolled my eyes, but Billy continued. "Tell Daisy what you said to Megan, Angelina!"

"Really, Billy, that's not—" Marlena began, but Angelina yelled over her.

"I said, 'I hope you go to hell and live there, stupid butt-head!" Angelina shook her fist in the air, and her blue and silver bracelets rattled together.

I would have laughed, but she looked so angry, and Squirrel looked so confused that I just scrunched down in the six inches of seat space they'd left me and said nothing. Let them figure it out. I didn't even want to be here.

Always before, Dad and I had driven Squirrel and Angelina the half hour to the Moonlight Ball. He'd blast Santana on his stereo, and we'd all blow bubbles out the window at stoplights. We'd laugh at the other drivers sticking their heads out their windows to see where the bubbles were coming from.

This drive used to feel like a party. Not anymore.

"Let's go, Mom!" Billy said. "I don't want to be late!"

Marlena started the Prius and a new cigarette. She dangled it out the open window, driving with her right hand flat on the steering wheel so she wouldn't stab herself in the palm with her long red-and-green fingernails.

Mist blew in off the ocean and ruined the half hour I'd spent with Mom's curling iron. I tugged on the ends of my bangs with my fingers, trying to keep them from fluffing up. Billy turned around in the front seat. "Basketball starts next week," he told me even though Squirrel had written the date in giant black letters on the refrigerator whiteboard months ago. "We're gonna win this thing!"

He and Squirrel bumped fists. Angelina tossed her head so her red curls swung silky against her shoulders, strong and broad from swimming practice. "I'm gonna win this thing too!" she said.

"This thing" was the Special Olympics Summer Games. They took place every year, all over the world. Athletes with disabilities got together to show off their stuff, same as in the Olympics people watch on TV. Some of the athletes had Down syndrome, like Squirrel and Angelina and Billy. Some of them were autistic, and some had cerebral palsy.

My brother and his friends trained all year for Summer Games. On the first of January each year, Mom and Dad presented him with a new Lakers calendar, and he immediately circled that weekend in June with red Sharpie and stuck little gold stars all over the squares.

Squirrel lived for Summer Games.

Every year, we drove down to L.A. to watch him compete. Last year, he'd won a gold medal for the 400-meter run and a silver for the 300, plus a team third-place medal for basketball. He hung the medals on the bulletin board in his bedroom along with his most prized possession—one of LeBron James's giant size 15 shoes, autographed. He'd won it in a Special Olympics raffle.

Now, Squirrel and Billy and Angelina yelled over each other, comparing notes about all the medals they wanted to win in June. I curled my toes in Mom's high heels and tried not to think of the evening I'd had planned, just me and millipedes and cockroaches and the Snickers bar I'd bought at the 7-Eleven—not runner's fuel, exactly, but still packed with peanuts and really satisfying.

"Oh my god. Billy just *loves* those Summer Games!" Marlena interrupted my thoughts with her high-pitched Valley Girl voice. She swerved around a pickup full of broccoli. "He's too modest to tell you, but he's totally playing field hockey and he's bowling this year too."

"And track and field!" Billy yelled. "I run the two hundred!"

"You do a little running yourself, don't you, Daisy?" Marlena met my eyes in the rearview mirror. "Darn it, there's the exit!" she said, and swerved across three lanes of traffic.

I pressed the blue platter against my stomach and prayed not to throw up. "I run on my school's cross-country and track teams," I said, trying not to breathe the mixture of cigarette smoke and broccoli-stench from the fields.

"Daisy got a second-place trophy in November!" Squirrel draped his arm across my shoulders. "She's the second-fastest runner in the world."

"The *county*," I corrected him. "Second-fastest middle school girl. And only in cross-country. We'll see what happens in track."

Squirrel gave me a squeeze. "You'll win a first-place trophy. You're the best."

"Miguel Santos is the best," I mumbled. "First in every one of his races, all season."

Miguel and I had been classmates since kindergarten, and he ran on the boys' team at school. He was a spoiled brat, always bragging about his race times and his million-dollar running shoes. Still, I envied his speed.

Marlena swung into a parking lot and pulled up to the front of the banquet hall. The doorway sparkled with strings of white twinkling lights. Billy leapt out of the car and opened the back door. He held out his hand to Angelina. "My lady?" he said with a bow.

It was no secret that Billy had a crush on Angelina. Until

tonight, she'd only had eyes for Squirrel. But now, she climbed out of the back seat and took his arm. Squirrel got out and smoothed down his suit jacket and reached for his fedora. In that moment, Billy and Angelina headed for the banquet hall without him. He looked after them with his mouth hanging open.

"Go!" I told him. "Go catch up. Tell Angelina it's not your fault some weird girl kissed you."

"Daisy, can you help me?" Squirrel followed the others, and Marlena lurched into an empty parking spot. "I need an extra pair of hands." She stepped out of the car and opened the trunk. "Here." She dropped a large pink box into my arms, right on top of my towel-wrapped platter. "Cupcakes from the grocery store. Who has time to bake?"

My father, I thought, balancing my tins full of his gingerbread bunnies under the platter and the pink box. Marlena hoisted a giant bolt of red velvet up over her shoulder.

"What's that for?" I asked.

"Backdrop for the photo booth," she said. "Red velvet's so Christmasy, don't you think!"

She pulled out a Santa made from tumbleweeds—red hat and a white-cotton beard stuck on one side of the thing. I bit my tongue to keep from pointing out that Dad had always let dancers choose their backgrounds for photos. He brought Christmas and Hanukkah and Kwanzaa and snowflake decorations. It was my job to switch out the pine branches and the gold menorah and the red-green-and-black Kwanzaa flag.

Marlena's tumbleweed Santa would've sent Dad into hysterics.

"Where's your camera?" I asked her.

She shrugged. "I'm just gonna use my iPhone. Good heavens, don't tell your daddy. I know he's forever lugging around lenses and lights and whatnot."

Whatnot, I thought. Otherwise known as the equipment that made the Moonlight Ball portraits look so professional that athletes' parents from all over the county hired my father to take their senior pictures every year. But not anymore. We'd miss the money he'd made, but he told me there was no time for side hustles when you were trying to start a business. Right now, he was probably walking six dogs at once while scooping poop in a jingle-bell hat and taking pet portraits alongside boats lit up at the harbor.

Marlena and I stepped under the lighted doorway and into the banquet hall. Chairs were set up around the edges of the room. Ropes of twinkling white lights sparkled on the walls. A big silver disco ball spilled glimmering triangles all over the floor. Angelina and Squirrel and Billy were already dancing together to Michael Jackson's "Billie Jean" cranked up loud over the speakers.

My arms were full, so I couldn't stick my fingers in my ears to block out his whiny voice. We all knew the singer had been accused of a whole bunch of horrible crimes, but Squirrel and his friends loved Michael Jackson's songs. They demanded that the DJ play them.

"Cupcakes!" Squirrel's friend Sam caught sight of the pink box I was holding and loped over to me in the tuxedo he'd been wearing to every dance for years. His wrists stuck out from the sleeves, and the hem of his pants hung two inches above his black shoes. He had a fluffy brown tail pinned to the back of his pants. As long as I'd known him, Sam had worn that tail pinned to his blue jeans, his track shorts, and even his basketball shorts as he ran down the court and made his famous jump shot. That tail was just Sam's thing.

"Can I have one, Squirrel's sister?" He lifted the lid on the pink box.

A sweet scent rose up, and my mouth watered. Sam and I gazed down at the cupcakes. Their two-inch-thick frosting swirls gleamed with sugar crystals. My stomach growled. Immediately, I felt guilty about cheating on my father's gingerbread bunnies.

Sam reached for a cupcake. Across the room, Marlena dropped her bolt of red velvet and screeched. "It's not time for refreshments yet!" She made a time-out T with her hands.

I rolled my eyes at Sam. "Sorry. I'll save one for you."

"Okay!" He set the cupcake back in the box. "Thank you, Squirrel's sister. You look pretty!"

He bounced away toward my brother and his friends with his tail swinging, and I headed for the long, white-clothed table with my boxes, instead of over to the photo booth where I'd always volunteered in the past.

For a moment, I missed Dad so much I thought I'd die. I squeezed my eyes shut to stop the sting of tears across my nose and concentrated on arranging the bunnies on the blue platter. I lifted Marlena's cupcakes out of the box one by one and set them on a silver tray next to the punch bowl. Someone had already filled it with red liquid and floated green sherbet over the top. It looked like gutter water, but I ladled up a glass and gulped it while I watched my brother on the dance floor.

Squirrel made dancing look like fun. Under the disco ball, he showed off a perfect Michael Jackson moonwalk. Billy twirled Angelina until her dress spun out like the petals of a flower. I had to admit that I was glad I'd showed up tonight, if only to watch my brother and his friends on the dance floor.

"Funny how these things look the same no matter what country you're in," said a voice beside me.

I turned. Miguel Santos—superstar runner and owner of what looked like a brand-new pair of ASICS GEL-NIMBUS running shoes—stepped behind the dessert table. My mouth fell open as he unwrapped a pan of brownies covered with chocolate frosting and sprinkled with crushed candy canes. Then, he arranged the brownies on a plate painted with a big red poinsettia. His shoulders, under a black coat, swayed to the beat of the music.

At last, he looked up at me. "What?"

"What?" I repeated, and my mouth went suddenly dry as Death Valley. I gulped my cup of punch and choked out a single question. "What are you doing here?"

4

Miguel finished arranging his peppermint brownies on the poinsettia plate and lifted one eyebrow. "So I'm not allowed to attend the Moonlight Ball?"

My cheeks flushed hot and my heart began to pound, just like they'd done every time he'd made fun of me when we were little. I grabbed a napkin and started polishing a silver tray like the Queen of England might show up and demand a gingerbread rabbit on a spotless platter. "You've never volunteered at these dances before," I mumbled. "I mean, why would you?"

"Why wouldn't I? I'm here to support my cousin Ricky. He just moved up from Mexico," he added, chatty, like there hadn't been this thing between us for nine years. "He plays Special Olympics soccer, and man, he's got the moves!"

I stared at him. Was it possible he actually understood what it was like to have a family member with a disability—how it made you want to help out in a way that my friends with nondisabled siblings and cousins just didn't get? I wanted Squirrel to have as good a life as I did. Could it be that Miguel wanted the same thing for his cousin?

Miguel pointed at a tall, skinny kid dancing near Squirrel in a green soccer jersey and black shorts. He shook his head. "Guess my cuz didn't get the message about formal wear."

I turned toward Ricky, but I checked Miguel out in my peripheral vision. He wore jeans with a brick-red shirt and a dark blue tie. I'd seen the outfit before. Our school made us dress up for holiday assemblies, and some of the girls whispered that when he wore that shirt and pulled his hair into a ponytail, he looked like Lin-Manuel Miranda from *Hamilton*. Still, even though he'd showed up to volunteer at the Moonlight Ball, we had a history, and I stayed immune to his charms.

In kindergarten, and all the way into third grade, Miguel and his best friend Devon had teased me nonstop because of my lisp. They called me "Daithy" and laughed every time I opened my mouth to speak. If I had to answer a question in class or walk up to the whiteboard to work out a math problem, I flushed bright red and my heart pounded in my ears. I couldn't even speak up to defend myself. Speaking up was what made them bully me.

Finally, I stopped talking altogether. It got so bad that I flat-out refused to go to school. I hid in bed with the pillow over my head until Mom pried the truth out of me. She and Dad called the principal and demanded a meeting with my teacher and Miguel's and Devon's parents.

In my head, I could still see Miguel sitting rigid in an orange plastic chair, staring down at his knees while his mother and father lectured him about the importance of showing kindness to his classmates. "It's cruel to make fun of people with differing abilities," his mom told him. Winter light streamed in through the window, and I thought I saw tears in Miguel's eyes.

Then again, I could've imagined it. Devon sat slumped in the chair beside him, kicking the principal's desk while his dad maintained a death-grip on the back of his neck like he was scruffing a puppy. His mom wasn't at the meeting. Devon's parents had just gotten a divorce, and she was overseas leading educational tours.

After that third-grade meeting, Miguel stopped teasing me. But Devon kept tormenting me when no adults were around.

And Miguel just stood by and let him.

In middle school, Miguel and Devon wore designer clothes and had confidence to burn. They bought the most expensive shoes from the running store downtown instead of the cheap Big 5 version, and they didn't mind telling the rest of the cross-country and track teams how much they'd spent on their Adidas or Nikes, or whatever.

"It's not just about the equipment," Miguel had gloated after he won State at the boys' meet last season. "But it helps."

Poppy and I had long ago dismissed him as a shallow rich boy, not worthy of our time. But now, I found myself watching as he ran onto the dance floor and slid on his knees under the disco ball, straight toward a girl in a wheelchair.

The girl—a shot-putter named Casey who'd won a gold medal at Summer Games last year—screamed with surprised laughter. Drool shined on her chin. Miguel ignored the drool. He grabbed her hands and began to dance with her.

I had to admit that he was a beautiful dancer. He looked like one of those guys from the old black-and-white movie musicals my grandparents watched—Gene Kelly, I think one guy's name was, and Fred Astaire.

The athletes circled around Miguel. Some clapped in time to the music. Others started copying his moves.

"Daisy!" Marlena rushed over with a stack of paper cups and yanked them apart with stiff fingers, trying not to break her nails. "There aren't enough glasses, and the buses are here!"

By buses, she meant the short orange shuttles that chauffeured older athletes from group homes all over the county. I used to think Squirrel would move into one of those group homes after he graduated from community college—he'd have a couple of roommates, and they'd all go to work, then cook dinner together and sit around watching TV and playing video games. But then Angelina wanted him to get an apartment with her after graduation, if their parents would let them.

Her mom and dad weren't the problem. It was my parents—my incredibly overprotective parents—who told Squirrel he'd be just fine living at home for the rest of his life.

"We're here!" a voice shouted, interrupting my thoughts.

Athletes from the group homes pushed through the doors. Suddenly, a dozen dancers became a hundred. Everyone yelled and hugged and high-fived each other. The DJ in the corner cranked up Michael Jackson's "Man in the Mirror," and dancers kicked off their heels and tossed their jackets onto chairs.

Squirrel ran over to me with his coat. "Keep this safe!"

"Got it." I draped his coat over the back of a chair. I couldn't help smiling, just a little. This was what Squirrel loved most—dancing with his girlfriend and their friends. And I got to be here to see him. Me . . . and Miguel Santos.

On the dance floor, my brother spun on his toes, Michael Jackson–style, and struck a pose. Miguel imitated the move, and Squirrel nodded his approval.

Poppy's not gonna believe this, I thought and reached for my phone to text her, then got to work passing out dessert to the dancers and ladling punch into paper cups.

Finally, Miguel returned to the table. "Sorry," he panted.

"I love dancing." He fanned himself with a napkin and turned to me. "Isn't it sad?"

"What's sad?" I mumbled.

"That Summer Games is canceled."

"What?" I cried. "No way! Why?"

"My tía just texted. Ricky's coach emailed her to say there isn't enough money this year." Miguel shook his head. "Money's tight everywhere, right? I don't think my cousin and the other athletes know yet. By the way, you look great tonight."

I barely heard him. My head spun with the news. I folded my arms tight against my chest and stared out at the dance floor. "They can't just cancel Summer Games," I muttered.

"They can if they don't have the money to pay for staff and a place to hold the event." Miguel picked up a peppermint brownie and handed me half, then shook his head sadly. "Ricky's going to be *devastated*."

"Squirrel too," I mumbled.

Sam appeared at my side with some red-headed girl I'd never seen before. She wore about a pound of makeup and enormous gold hoop earrings. "Where's that cupcake you promised me, Squirrel's sister?" Sam asked.

The girl flashed me an enormous smile and stuck out her hand. "I'm Megan. Your brother is sooooooo cute!"

"Let me guess," I said, turning away from Miguel so he wouldn't hear my lisp. "You bowled with Squirrel at Special Olympics practice this morning?"

"Yup!" The girl wrapped her arms around her own glittery gold dress. "I kissed him on his lips!"

I could see why Angelina felt threatened. Megan was over the top. Still, I chose the two largest cupcakes and put them on plates for her and Sam. They looked so happy. They had no idea Summer Games had just gotten the axe.

"Thank you, Squirrel's sister!" Sam said, and tugged on the sleeve of my dress. "Your brother is sad."

"Sad?" I repeated. "But he was just dancing."

"Not anymore. Look!" He pointed to the crowd of dancers. In the middle of them, right under the disco ball, Squirrel stood without moving. Tears shone on his cheeks. Had someone tipped him off about Summer Games? Had a friend spilled punch on his dress shirt? The dancers shifted, and I saw why he was crying.

Near him, Angelina stood with her arms wrapped around Billy, shuffling slowly to "The Lady in My Life." Billy rested his chin on top of her head. Then, he bent and whispered something in her ear and pressed his lips against her cheek. She lay her head on his shoulder and closed her eyes.

My brother's mouth dropped open. He ran over and snatched his jacket off the chair.

"Wait!" I blocked his way. "What's going on?"

He stared at me with wild eyes. "Angelina said I love Megan, and she doesn't want to be my girlfriend anymore."

"But Megan's just a friend!" I said.

"Angelina doesn't think so." Squirrel's face wrinkled up, and his lips trembled. "She says Billy's her boyfriend now." A single sob escaped him, and he ran for the door.

I spun to face Miguel. "Take over the dessert table!" I commanded, and grabbed my coat.

"Sure." His eyebrow shot up. "Everything okay?"

I rushed out the door without answering him and twisted my heel in Mom's shoe. I barely noticed the pain. My brother was somewhere out there in the dark with his heart kicked to the gutter. In one instant, he'd lost his girlfriend *and* Summer Games.

I couldn't call our parents; they were busy walking rich people's dogs half an hour up the freeway.

Which meant Squirrel had exactly one person in the world on his side right now: me.

5

I found my brother behind the banquet hall, standing in the middle of a cactus garden lit up by red and green lights. He stood near a sprawling prickly pear cactus with his coat slung over his shoulder, staring off toward the dark shapes of mountains on the other side of the freeway. The growl of traffic competed with the thump of drumbeats from inside the hall. The air smelled like sage and exhaust.

Squirrel looked alone and bewildered, like that *Bugs Bunny* cartoon we'd watched over and over when we were little—the one where Bugs is stranded in the desert, and he's so dizzy with heatstroke that he staggers over to what looks like a pond and dives in headfirst to find it's a shallow puddle.

Real life was like that sometimes. You dive headfirst into the Moonlight Ball with your girlfriend, and she leaves you for your best friend. Or you volunteer to supervise a dessert table and find yourself face-to-face with your sworn enemy. *Treacherous.*

I clomped over to Squirrel on my high heels, slipping on the gravel in the cactus garden. "Hey," I said, and bent to rub my aching ankle.

He said nothing. Just stared at the mountains. Fresh tears glistened in his eyes.

I swallowed against the ache in my throat. So often, I'd stood like this with Squirrel—both of us hurting, both of us confused. Our parents had always made us feel better—Dad with his silly jokes and goofy poems, Mom with her kind words and her hugs. But I couldn't call them now. They had to work.

"You okay?" I asked Squirrel, knowing he wasn't.

He heaved a shuddering sigh and turned to face me. "Angelina says I cheated on her with Megan," he mumbled. "I know she's just dancing with Billy to get back at me."

"Oh, Squirrel. She's not worthy of you." I wrapped an arm around his shoulder and leaned my head against his. "There are other fish in the sea."

"But *Angelina* was my fish." He turned and walked away toward the far end of the garden and stopped beside a three-armed cactus. He slumped against a boulder and buried his head in his hands.

I stayed where I was. My fingers found the pewter ladybug in my coat pocket—the half-inch lucky charm Mom had put in my lunchbox when I told her in fifth grade I wanted to be an entomologist. I rubbed the cold metal between my finger and thumb and the ache moved down from my throat to lodge in the pit of my stomach.

People who first meet me and Squirrel are surprised to find out that we're friends, and not just siblings. "You're really smart," they'll say, "and he's . . ."

They'd never finish the sentence, but I knew what they meant. He could read and write a little and do basic addition and subtraction, while I took second place in the middle school state science fair for using robotic cockroaches to locate misplaced pills and earrings. There was a 50-point difference between our IQs—not that either of us cared. We had the important stuff in common. We loved movies and bodyboarding in the ocean and Thrifty's Double-Chocolate Malted Crunch ice cream. We loved Hasenpfeffer and old David Bowie songs from before he got famous. We understood each other.

Squirrel never had to repeat himself the way he had to when he talked to other people. And I never had to choose my words around him—he didn't care that I'd had years of speech therapy and still lisped my Ss and Zs. Every time I sang along to *Hamilton* and *In the Heights* while we cleaned the house, he'd say, "My sister has a voice like an angel," and he'd mean it.

Most important of all, Squirrel and I shared years of history with our parents—with our practical, predictable mother and our spontaneous, hilarious father—until they went into business together and left us to figure out life on our own.

I wanted to race back into the banquet hall and tell Angelina she was being ridiculous. Megan had kissed Squirrel—not the other way around. I wanted to tell Billy he was being an opportunistic little vulture, and I wanted to call the Special Olympics office and demand that they find money to keep Summer Games for my brother and his friends.

But most of all, I wanted Mom and Dad.

I walked over to Squirrel and put my hand on his shoulder. "How can I help, bro?"

His hand reached out to cover mine. His palm felt rough and hot. "Angelina said she loved me. And now she's with Billy. I don't have a girlfriend. I don't have a best friend."

"You've got me." I wrapped my arms around him and squeezed my eyes shut. My head ached horribly anytime I cried. I tried never to go there, but now, even though I bit down hard on my tongue, my eyes filled.

"I'm going to make it okay," I mumbled. "I'm not sure how, but I'm going to make it better. You believe me?"

Squirrel looked up at me, tears and snot streaking his face. He nodded with his eyes fixed on mine. "I believe you, sister."

I sniffed, and then coughed. "We're a mess. I don't even have a napkin."

Squirrel reached into his jacket pocket and pulled out an ironed white handkerchief. "You should always carry one of these in case of emergencies," he lectured me, back in big brother mode. He wiped my eyes, and then his own. "Where's your purse, sister?"

"I don't *own* a purse," I reminded him for the millionth time.

Across the parking lot, the door to the banquet hall opened. A rectangle of light spilled onto the pavement, and music poured out.

Miguel stood in the doorway. I couldn't tell if he saw us. Just in case, I stood up straight and scrubbed at my cheeks with Squirrel's handkerchief. No way in H-E-double-hockey-sticks was I going to let him see me cry.

"Let's go dance!" I grabbed my brother's hand. "C'mon. We'll show Angelina what she's missing."

"But you *hate* dancing."

"Ha!" I scoffed. "I like dancing with *you*! Let's go, bro. The DJ's playing 'Thriller'!"

That did it. Squirrel ran toward the banquet hall, already working his best Michael Jackson moves. "Show 'em what we've got!" he hollered, and pushed past Miguel, dragging me onto the dance floor.

I kicked off my mother's shoes and joined the crowd of athletes in my bare feet. For once, I didn't care who was watching.

My brother needed me, and I would be there for him.

6

I walked to school the first morning after winter break with allergies plugging up my ears. I got them every year when some new flower or tree burst into bloom. The groundskeeper was speeding around the field on her riding lawn mower, and I sneezed five times in a row. Dizzy, I made my way to social studies and collapsed into my seat.

The classroom smelled like cut grass and armpits. Mr. Lipinsky's same old motivational posters and pictures hung on the walls. Bernie Sanders scowled next to Maya Angelou, who laughed beside Cesar Chavez. Jane Goodall and Greta Thunberg smiled grimly at one another in a photo over the whiteboard. A poster beside the open door said VOTE! in blue and red letters.

Mr. Lipinsky wasn't in the room, but music played from his phone on the stool beside the desk—the Beatles' "Revolution." Devon Smalley walked in, stared at the phone, and jumped up on his desk. He sang into his fist like it was a microphone.

Kristen Rockefeller flipped her long brown braid over her shoulder and laughed. Her braces caught the light. I wanted to tell her that the male peacock spider performed a way more thrilling mating dance, waving its front legs and displaying its super-colorful tail flap to females. But it wouldn't have made a difference. Kristen had been crushing on Devon—on his white-blond hair and the freckles across his sunburned surfer's nose—since seventh grade, even though he made fun of her and almost everyone else in our class all the time.

I sneezed again and looked across the circle of desks to Poppy's empty seat. Poppy was always late for everything—even for social studies, which she adored.

Miguel walked in and fist-bumped Devon, then sat down at his desk next to me. "Hey," he said, stretching his feet out in front of him so I could admire his running shoes—so new they practically sparkled. "How's your brother?"

I blinked at him. In the six years between our meeting in the principal's office with our parents and last Saturday's Moonlight Ball, Miguel hadn't said two words to me. It sounded ridiculous—I mean, there were only eighteen kids in eighth grade—but it really was possible to ignore someone for years and years, even when they sat beside you five days a week.

I'd been fine with our ignoring each other, but apparently, the arrangement wasn't working for Miguel anymore.

"How's your brother?'" he repeated.

"Okay," I mumbled with my cheeks on fire.

I didn't think Miguel had even noticed Squirrel after we'd come back in from the cactus garden. He'd spent the rest of the night passing out punch and cookies while I danced with my brother, and then he and his cousin Ricky had left without a goodbye.

Not that I expected Miguel to say goodbye. And I *definitely* didn't expect him to ask about Squirrel on our first day back at school.

"Ricky was bummed about Special Olympics canceling Summer Games," he told me over the clang of the first-period bell. "It's totally not fair."

I shrugged. On Sunday, my brother had shut himself up in his room all day to mourn Angelina, listening to the saddest country music he could find. So far, I'd kept him from finding out about the Games. And as far as I could tell, none of his Special Olympics friends had broken the news. The coaches had emailed my parents, but they hadn't said a word either.

For once, Mom and Dad and I agreed: Squirrel was so sad about Angelina dumping him for Billy that he couldn't handle any more disappointment. "Let's not tell him about the Games until we have to," Mom had told me. "My poor little boy."

"Mom, he's *seventeen*," I'd reminded her. "He's graduating next year."

Dad's face had clouded over, and he'd reached for his phone. "I'm gonna call Marlena right now and tell her what I think of her son."

I'd pulled the phone out of his hands. "People break up. I'm mad at Billy and Angelina too, but people get dumped all the time."

Except for me, I added silently. No one had ever showed the tiniest bit of romantic interest in me, which was just fine. I just knew that if I ever did develop a crush on someone and he rejected me, I'd turn Female Praying Mantis and bite off his head.

"Do anything fun for Christmas?" Miguel interrupted my thoughts now, tapping on my desk with his pencil. "I mean, if you celebrate Christmas. Maybe you're Jewish, or you celebrate whatever it is Poppy celebrates . . ."

Poppy burst through the door clutching her red coffee thermos, just in time to hear Miguel. "I'm Unitarian," she said. "My moms drag me to church on Christmas Eve, and we light the chalice and sing all these hippie songs, then go home and eat samosas."

"What's your family do, Daisy?" Miguel said, stubborn as a yellow jacket on a piece of watermelon.

I glanced at Devon, still standing on his desk. Were he and Miguel trying to get me to say a bunch of S-words so they could make fun of me for another entire semester?

"My dad makes tamales," I mumbled, quiet, so Devon wouldn't hear me. "We eat them on the twenty-fourth at mid-night and then open our . . . um . . ."

"Presents," Miguel finished with a smile. "My mom makes tamales too. Her roast beef's the bomb."

"And my wife makes incredible latkes with applesauce and sour cream," Mr. Lipinsky said, standing over us in his tie-dyed T-shirt and fleece vest. "But let's save the recipe exchange for recess and get to work. Mr. Smalley," he added, "get the heck off your desk, *this minute*."

Devon's running shoes smacked the floor. Mr. Lipinsky turned off the Beatles on his phone and perched on his stool in front of our circle of desks. He wore ancient-looking red-and-black running shoes instead of his usual Birkenstocks, and he'd pulled his curly silver hair into a ponytail.

"How was break?" he asked us. Behind his glasses with the nerdy black frames, his eyes searched ours like he really cared about our answers.

Kristen immediately told a story about the vacation she'd taken with her parents to the United Kingdom to visit her older sister. "The Christmas Markets in Cambridge are adorable!" she cried. "So many little gift shops, and there's hot chocolate, and we all went ice-skating in the middle of town!"

Devon snorted. "Right," he said, the single syllable dripping with sarcasm. The rest of us stayed silent.

We all knew that Kristen was making it up. She lived in the trailer park down the street and worked in her parents' food truck making sandwiches and rice-and-bean bowls. Poppy and I had seen her there all break whenever we ran down to the beach. But she'd gone to Cambridge in seventh grade, and now she acted like it was her second home.

I wiggled my pinky around in one plugged-up ear and tried not to look at Miguel, busy doodling a cat on the front of his Trapper Keeper. I'd always believed he was a grubby little larva not worth my time. But any entomologist worth her microscope would tell you that people—like insects—went through metamorphosis all the time. Just when you got used to them being, say, a boring accountant and a stay-at-home photographer, they metamorphosed into professional Poop Fairies.

Was it possible that Miguel had morphed into someone else over winter break?

I sneezed into the crook of my arm. Instantly, Miguel's hand shot out with a tissue. "Bless you. Allergies are killer right now."

"Uh . . . yeah." I stared down at the tissue in my hand. It was decorated with little pink pigs and the word "Oink!" printed over and over in red.

"They were in my Christmas stocking," Miguel said. "Guess Santa thought they were funny. But hey, they work."

"Thanks," I said, totally confused. Mr. Lipinsky had told us once that we each have a public persona and a private persona. He'd been talking about politicians, but also about ordinary people. Even little kids, he said, learn to hide their emotions so other kids don't make fun of them.

I got that. I was a pro. My classmates had no idea Mom had lost her job. Were the other kids keeping secrets too, scared of what we'd say if we knew the truth about them? Was Miguel Santos hiding something?

"We can never tell who someone really is just by looking at them," Mr. Lipinsky had told us.

When my classmates looked at me, they saw a girl with a brown ponytail and fluffy bangs in shorts and T-shirts, with three daisy earrings in each ear and a magnifying glass on a silver chain. They saw a straight-A student—a silent bookworm who carried *Peterson's Field Guide to Insects* under one arm and kept her eyes on the ground.

They thought I was shy, but they were wrong. I just loathed speaking up in class, and I kept my eyes down to look for beetles and caterpillars and millipedes.

I'd wanted to be an entomologist since I was little. Insects are way more interesting than people. Humans fight and yell and cry and get worked up about ridiculous stuff like having to pass out gingerbread rabbits at the Moonlight Ball. Not insects. They're too busy finding creative ways to survive.

Take the honey ant in Mexico. Some ants are workers, and some are what's called "repletes." The repletes store nectar in their abdomens and hang themselves upside down from the ceiling of their nest. When a worker gets hungry, it touches a replete ant's antennae, and the replete regurgitates the nectar.

Seriously awesome.

Or take the Australian stick insect. It defends itself against predators by giving off an odor that smells like peanut butter.

Also awesome.

But most people walk right by insects. They step over them without bending down for a closer look. Worse, they step *on* them.

Not awesome at all.

I doodled a fat honey ant on the front of my folder while Devon told the class about how he'd gone snowboarding at Big Bear over winter break. "I shredded all the black diamonds!" he bragged. "Got invited back to help with ski patrol."

"That's wonderful!" Kristen said.

Across the room, Poppy rolled her eyes at me. I rolled mine back and drew a beaded lacewing beside my honey ant. Lacewing adults are beautiful—black and brown, with delicate wings. They're super-smart too. They lay their eggs in termite nests, and their larvae hatch with this amazing superpower—they can fart a powerful toxin that immobilizes the termites. Then, the lacewing larvae eat them.

Someone should fart a powerful toxin on Devon Smalley, I thought, and smiled behind my hand.

"How was *your* winter break, Ms. Woodward?" Mr. Lipinsky asked suddenly.

My head shot up, and I looked at him wide-eyed, fire flaming across my cheeks. Devon cackled.

"Fine?" I mumbled, praying Mr. Lipinsky wouldn't ask me to elaborate.

For once, he didn't. Instead, he glanced at the clock, then patted his vest pockets and pulled out his purple whiteboard pen. He jumped off his stool, turned to the board, and wrote in big letters:

Project Change the World!

Instantly, Devon's and Poppy's hands shot up. "Yes?" Mr. Lipinsky's lips twitched in a smile under his silver mustache and beard.

"What's Project Change the World?" Poppy said, beating Devon to the question. "Is that our final semester project?"

"It is." He sat back down on his stool and folded his arms. "There's so much negativity all around us, my friends. Political polarization. Social unrest. Climate change. It would be so easy to give up and just bury ourselves in Netflix, you know?"

Poppy frowned. Miguel tapped his pencil against his teeth, laser-focused on everything Mr. Lipinsky was saying. "We *can't* give up," he continued. "In the final semester of eighth grade, before you head off to high school, I'm going to challenge you to change the world for the better."

"What?" Devon said. "How?"

Mr. Lipinsky looked around the room, letting his eyes rest on each of us a moment. "You'll each choose a project by Friday, and spend two months devoted to it," he said. "We spent the first semester learning about societies . . . why people do the things they do, and how—even though we're all different—we're connected by the common pursuits of food, water, shelter, and community."

"You forgot coffee." Poppy toasted him with her thermos.

"Coffee," Mr. Lipinsky agreed. "Or warmth, anyway. Comfort. When we strive for a common goal, we help each other succeed." He spread out his arms like he was trying to hug us all. He looked like the statue of Saint Francis that sat in front of the Catholic church downtown—the one surrounded by all the little stone birds and squirrels and rabbits.

"Today—right now, in fact—I want you to think about how you can be of service to those around you," he continued. "Your project needs to focus on one way you can make the world a better place—for one person, or for many."

Around me, kids groaned. I drew a fart coming out of a lacewing, stunning a stick figure of Devon into a stupor. Miguel took out a piece of paper and began to write.

"You've gotta be kidding, Mr. L.," Poppy said. "How are we supposed to change the world?"

He held up one hand. "You will. By the end of May, you'll give me a five-page written report on your project . . . and deliver a five-minute *oral* report to our class."

And then, he looked right at me. "I know some of you aren't fond of public speaking, but trust me, when you set out to change the world, it's critical to be able to communicate clearly."

He went on talking, giving us tips on how to start our projects, but I barely heard him. *Communicate clearly*. Easy for him to say. *He* hadn't spent years in speech therapy only to realize all those hours practicing S- and Z-words in front of the mirror were a total waste of time.

I glanced at Devon Smalley, sneering across the room at me. Maybe I'd simply refuse to do the oral report. Maybe I'd earn the first F of my life.

I sneezed three times in a row and sat dizzy at my desk with my eyes burning. *Then again,* I thought, *maybe my allergies will kill me before the report's even due.*

7

"How are we supposed to make the world a better place?" Kristen flipped her braid over one shoulder and splayed her hands out, palms up, on her desk. "I'm only thirteen!"

"You assume that a young person can't change the world," Mr. Lipinsky said. "But you forget that when you assume, you make an ass out of U and me."

Devon groaned. "That's so eighties. What do you even mean by 'change the world'?"

Around me, kids nodded in agreement. Only Miguel looked excited. He bent over a piece of paper, creating something that looked like a bullet list with red and blue markers. *He'd* change the world, no problem. He brought home as many As on his report card as I did, plus he was handsome and popular, and he and his best friend were the fastest runners in the county.

Mr. Lipinsky pointed his pen at the poster of Jane Goodall and Greta Thunberg over the whiteboard. "Ms. Thunberg was *fifteen* when she began the climate activism that earned her *TIME magazine*'s 2019 Person of the Year award." His face fell in pretend disappointment, and he shook his head sadly. "That's pretty old to start changing the world."

"What?" Poppy yelped. "That's young!"

"Not really." He walked over to the laptop on his desk and pushed a button to turn on the projector and drop down the screen.

"A PowerPoint, friends," he announced. "Especially for you."

"Not again," Poppy groaned.

Mr. Lipinsky was a PowerPoint ninja. He made slideshows at least twice a week, sometimes with pictures and videos and jokes that made us laugh even when he was giving us some ridiculous assignment like the one he'd just dropped on us.

The first slide had giant black letters on a blue background.

Teens Who Have Changed the World!

"Boring!" Devon said, disguising the word in a cough.

Poppy read the words on the second slide out loud. "Otherwise known as 'Stop Whining and Do the Assignment.' Ha ha!" she said, but she reached back and tightened her ponytail, then picked up her pencil. Her running shoes tapped the linoleum. I could tell that just like that, she'd figured out her project.

And obviously, so had Miguel. Beside me, he added another bullet to his list. Mr. Lipinsky clicked on the next slide.

"This is Mikaila Ulmer, from Texas." He pointed at a picture of a girl my age, with black hair pinned in two fluffy buns on top of her head. "Mikaila got stung twice by bees and decided to find out why honeybees are endangered. She started a lemonade stand and raised money for groups that plant bee-friendly landscapes and teach people how to cultivate their own beehives."

"Impressive," Poppy said, glancing up from her paper.

Mr. Lipinsky clicked on another slide and showed us a picture of four lemonade bottles labeled with the girl's photo.

"Mikaila called her product 'Me & the Bees Lemonade' and founded a nonprofit called the Healthy Hive Foundation. The Foundation donates money to help the Texas Beekeepers Association and Heifer International, which provides hives to families around the world. More than three hundred stores across the country sell her lemonade."

"Whoa," Miguel said. "That's big time."

Mr. Lipinsky peered over his glasses at Kristen. "Did I mention that Mikaila started her lemonade stand, with support from her family and her great-grandmother's lemonade recipe, when she was *four years old*?"

Kristen gasped and clapped one hand dramatically over her mouth. I sneezed. Poppy let out a surprised cough, spitting coffee all over her desk. Mr. Lipinsky pointed his pen at me. "Daisy, you like insects," he said. "You could start a project like this."

Everyone turned to stare at me. "Yeah, *Daisy*." Devon's lips curled into a sneer.

Blood rushed to my face. "Um . . . maybe," I mumbled.

Mr. Lipinsky clicked to the next slide—a picture of a boy in a stocking cap, a striped scarf, and thick gray gloves. "This is Jahkil Jackson from Chicago," he told us. "With help from his parents and friends, he made over three thousand bags filled with toiletries, socks, and snacks for homeless people, and delivered what he calls his 'Blessing Bags' to homeless shelters. Now, he organizes bag-stuffing parties with members of his community."

"That's wonderful!" Kristen's eyes shone, round as marbles.

Mr. Lipinsky nodded. "By the way, people . . . when he started this project, Jahkil was nine years old. Four years younger than all of you." He sat down on his stool again and clapped his palms together with a crack. "So I'll bet you can imagine how I might not be interested in your thoughts about how a thirteen-year-old has no power to make the world a better place."

"Sorry," Kristen mumbled.

"My bad," Poppy said, mopping up the coffee on her desk with paper towels.

Mr. Lipinsky clicked to the next slide—a column of bright red letters on a white background. They read:

B

A

R

A

T

"What's *BARAT*?" Poppy and Devon asked at the same time.

"Wait for it . . ." Mr. Lipinsky clicked to the next slide. It read:

BRAINSTORM

ASK

RESEARCH

ACTION

TRIUMPH

"These are the steps you'll take to ensure the success of your project," he said, and passed out big rectangles of paper. "Today, I want you to *brainstorm* your particular talents and skills and experiences. Think about how you might put them to use to change the world."

"Way ahead of you, Mr. L." Miguel tapped his bullet list with his pencil.

"Good on you, Miguel. The rest of you, get to work." Mr. Lipinsky started up the Beatles' "Revolution" again on his phone and walked to the open door. He stood with his hands clasped behind his back and studied the poster of Mahatma Gandhi smiling in white robes with sticking-out ears and a mustache. I propped my arm up on my desk and sank my chin into my hand. *Talents, skills, and experiences*, I wrote at the top of my paper.

1. Running.
2. Insects.
3. ???

And then, I stopped. How could either of those change the world for the better? The lemonade idea had already been taken by some four-year-old. Plus, all those inspiring kids had help from their parents. My parents were too busy picking up dog poop to help me change the world.

Across from me, Poppy scribbled down notes. So did Kristen. Devon tapped his pencil against his desk like a drummer, staring up at the ceiling until Poppy glared. "Will you please *shut up*?" she snapped.

Mr. Lipinsky tore his eyes away from Gandhi. "Mr. Smalley, save the band practice for after school."

I stared at my almost-blank page. Finally, I wrote down *housecleaning.* I could clean my family's whole house, top to bottom, in three hours, as long as I had a package of Twizzlers and Spotify cranked up loud. But I didn't see how that could change the world.

The bell rang, and everyone leapt up and rushed out the door to their lockers. They reminded me, always, of my Madagascar hissing cockroaches free from their terrarium and running around on my bedroom carpet in excitement.

Poppy cranked open her locker. "I think I have a project that might work!" She shoved her social studies textbook inside and pulled out her math book. "Mr. Lipinsky's weird, but he's kinda brilliant."

"Um, yeah." I twisted my lock and yanked open the dented metal door. A pile of textbooks fell out and landed on my foot. "Ow!" I yelped, and bent down to pick up the books.

"Looking for black widows, Daisy Wood*worm*?" Devon stepped around me with his upper lip curled like I was a stink bug who'd just sprayed him with foul stench. "You're blocking traffic."

"It's Wood*ward*." I glared up at Devon. A woodworm is a kind of beetle that hides in furniture and walls, chowing down on the pine or oak. Woodworm infestations are so powerful they can take down an entire house. Still, it was hardly a compliment. "Insects will outlive us all," I muttered to Devon.

"In*the*c*th*!" Devon yelled with his arms spread wide, the better to show off his brand-new Rip Curl T-shirt. Miguel stood beside him staring off in the distance, apparently fascinated by a Student Council poster about Pizza Day. Three questions hammered at my brain.

1. Couldn't he hear Devon tormenting me?

2. Why didn't he tell him to stop?

3. How could someone who'd been so nice to the athletes at the Moonlight Ball stand by while his best friend bullied me?

"Hey, Devon," Poppy snarled. "Why don't you go crawl in a hole and die?"

"Good one, Poopy," Devon retorted.

"Oh, *come* on, Dev," Miguel said at last, and yanked him by the arm toward the math classroom.

"Losers!" Poppy yelled after them.

I slammed my locker door. I *knew* Miguel hadn't metamorphosed. He was still the same old snobby brat. I followed Poppy down the hall, sneezing, with my ears plugged up and my eyes burning. For the rest of the day, I walked in an allergy fog with one question spinning in my head.

How on earth am I going to make the world a better place if I can't even improve it for myself?

8

Track and field practice started after school. Poppy and I, and the rest of the girls' team, changed into running shorts and T-shirts in our locker room. I smeared sunscreen across my nose and on the back of my neck and tossed the tube to Poppy.

She handed me half a sandwich. "Peanut butter and jelly on chapati."

I gave it back to her. "You know eating before a workout gives me cramps."

"I'd rather cramp than starve." She took an enormous bite. "Wonder who the new coach is," she said through a mouthful.

Ms. Bravo had been the girls' cross-country and track coach all through sixth and seventh grade, and during first semester of eighth. She was a two-time state champion in the women's mile, five feet of lightning-fast energy with killer quads. She ran ten-mile training runs with us, always at the head of the pack. But in December, she decided to stay home with her toddler for the rest of the year. Heartbreaking.

"Whoever the new coach is, she's gotta help us win State," I told Poppy.

State was the middle school track and field championships, held in May. Every year, athletes from all over California met to compete. Last year, our team had gone to the meet in a big bus and piled into two motel rooms, where we ate bucketloads of spaghetti and cracked up over Nick Jr. cartoons like we were five years old again.

First-place runners got trophies. Even more important, they got noticed by university talent scouts who promised full scholarships if athletes broke records in high school. I knew I'd need one of those scholarships if I had any hope of going to a university.

"What if the new coach is Miss Maynard, the home ec teacher?" Poppy grabbed my arm, her eyes wide with pretend horror. "She knits! She cooks! She runs!"

"Don't even joke!" I groaned, and headed outside.

Our team always stretched on the cement circle surrounded by grass in the middle of the track. The boys' team was already sitting there listening to Coach Wu lecture about how they needed to drink at least eight cups of water a day and lay off the soda. I didn't see our new coach anywhere.

Poppy and I sat down on the warm cement and began to stretch. The field was a graveyard of cut grass and decapitated dandelions. I sneezed.

"Bless you!" Kristen said, and took a hit off her asthma inhaler. She held it out to me. "Want some?" I held up one hand and braced for another sneeze.

Miguel jogged across the field. He dropped down to the cement beside me and stretched out his legs in red running shorts. I scooted away from him and turned my back so he and his new running shoes wouldn't be in my face.

"New kicks, Miguel?" Poppy nudged me with her elbow and rolled her eyes.

Miguel took the bait. "You know it! Everyone running

the boys' fifteen hundred this season better get used to me coming in first."

Poppy covered her ears with her hands. "Save it for your fans, rich boy," she said.

Miguel's face clouded. "I'm not rich."

"Check these out," Devon interrupted, and stuck one foot in the air. "My dad read about a million reviews and bought me the best shoes out there. Said if I don't come in first in the three thousand, he's gonna ground me for life." He grinned. "That trophy's already *mine*."

"So much hubris." Poppy clucked her tongue and reminded us of the Greek myth we'd studied in English that morning. "Watch out, boys. Icarus got shiny new wings too, but they melted, and he fell down to Earth and kicked the bucket."

"Mythology according to Poopy," Devon scoffed.

I looked away. Every workout in my year-old running shoes felt like pounding the pavement on soles made of cardboard. My shins burned no matter how long I stretched my calves and hamstrings. And my track spikes—the super-lightweight shoes we wore to grip the rubber track during races—were so small that my toes curled up at the top.

I needed money, and fast. Poppy had started babysitting, but between homework and cleaning and cooking, I didn't have time. I'd tried to start a pet-sitting business. So far, a couple of neighbors had hired me to walk their dogs and feed their cats. One paid me ten dollars to clean her goldfish tank while she was in Hawaii. I had two twenties and a ten folded into my ladybug bank, but that was a third of what I needed for decent running shoes.

Miguel's new shoes made me squirm with jealousy. Most

kids at my school seemed to get new stuff whenever they wanted. Their parents had good jobs, *normal* jobs like my mother used to have. Until last summer, I'd been one of those kids. I'd taken for granted the fact that my parents bought me running shoes twice a year, plus sports bras and shorts—even a third terrarium when I got two millipedes from an entomologist who was moving and had to downsize her collection.

But now, I knew what Poppy—with her house full of sisters, and one mom who stayed home—had always known. Money was a privilege, and most people had to work their butts off to get it.

For an instant, I felt a flicker of respect for my mother. When she'd lost her job, she'd figured out a need in our city and filled it. I wished that need didn't involve picking up dog poop. Still, it earned her and my father enough to keep our house and buy groceries and a pizza from Beto's once a week.

"So where's our new coach?" Kristen scooted over to Poppy and me and pulled her braid through the green ball cap she always wore—the one with the footprint on the front of it.

"Not here," I said.

"Absence on the first day of practice does not bode well." Poppy stood up. "We might as well go warm up until she gets here."

We stood up and jogged a lap around the track with the boys' team. We were working on another when Poppy stopped and grabbed my arm. Kristen crashed into me.

"Girls." Poppy pointed toward the field. "What is that?"

I shaded my eyes with my hand. Mr. Lipinsky strode across the grass in plaid shorts and running shoes and a purple T-shirt with our team name—the Sea Urchins—in white. A silver whistle bounced on a string around his neck. A wide-brimmed straw hat covered his forehead. His phone blared Queen's "We are the Champions."

"What the . . . ?" Miguel and Devon stopped beside us and stared.

"He looks like a farmer!" Poppy cried. She ran over to him, and we all followed. "Whatcha doing on our turf, Mr. L.?"

Mr. Lipinsky licked his finger and held it up, testing the direction of the breeze. He turned down the volume on his phone and nodded at Poppy. "Greetings, Ms. Banjaree. I'm the new girls' track and field coach."

"Ha!" Devon smacked Miguel on the shoulder. "Good one!"

Miguel rubbed his shoulder. I recognized the look on his face—total confusion. Our social studies teacher was our new coach? Impossible.

"You're kidding," Devon said, putting into words what all of us were thinking.

Mr. Lipinsky raised his eyebrows. "I assure you, Mr. Smalley, I'm not joking."

The smile fell away from Poppy's face. Her eyes met mine with a look of horror. I knew exactly what she was thinking: *How on earth is he going to lead our team to victory at State?*

The other girls crowded around us. Poppy scowled down at Mr. Lipinsky's filthy running shoes—a brand I'd never heard of. "Do you know anything about track and field?" she asked him.

He twirled his whistle on its string. "Once upon a time, I took first place at State for the mile."

"Like, a hundred years ago," Devon retorted.

"More like thirty. Girls' team!" He pointed at Poppy and

Kristen and me and the rest of our teammates. "Four laps to warm up. Then, we'll discuss today's workout."

"But Mr. Lipinsky," Kristen said, and paused to take a hit off her inhaler. "We already jogged two."

"Go. And it's *Coach* Lipinsky now." He strode over to talk with Coach Wu. They put their heads together and studied a piece of paper, then clapped each other on the back and laughed.

Poppy and I jogged our laps with the other girls, stunned into silence, and met him back on the cement pad where the boys were gulping water before their run. "Give me five miles," Coach Lipinsky instructed us. "Down to the beach and back. Slow enough that you can talk. But if you can sing, you're running too slowly."

"Got it, Coach." Kristen saluted him. "No singing."

"Who sings on a training run?" Poppy grumbled.

Miguel caught my eye. "Tough luck." He held out a pack of peppermint gum. "Want one for the road?"

I thought about how he'd stood by the lockers that morning while Devon made fun of me, how he hadn't said a word. "No," I said coldly, and turned and followed Poppy and the other girls out onto the sidewalk.

We jogged down the sidewalk beside the street noisy with cars and buses and trucks and emergency vehicles from the hospital nearby. "I guess we should give Mr., uh, Coach L. a try," I reasoned over the honks and sirens. "I mean, if he took first at State for the mile . . ."

"I thought you were mad about his project," Poppy reminded me. "Coach is making Daisy and me change the world," she added for the seventh graders in our pack.

"And me!" Kristen ran up beside us. "I've been tutoring

math at that center for homeless families downtown, and I'm going to start a math club. We'll have meetings and field trips and fundraisers and everything!"

Poppy punted a crushed soda can into an alley. "I'm gonna get my moms and sisters to help me put on a dance benefit for our relatives in India. A flood wiped out a bunch of their houses and schools." She swiveled her hands and held up her arms in a graceful pose. Her silver rings sparkled in the sun. "Might as well put all those dance lessons to use, right?"

"Right!" Kristen said.

Envy burned in my chest. Every Thursday evening, Poppy grumbled about having to take classical Indian dance lessons with her sisters at a local studio. But she'd just done exactly what Coach Lipinsky had asked—she'd identified one of her talents and figured out how it would help change the world.

Kristen appeared beside my elbow, her braid flopping side to side as she ran. "What about you, Daisy? What's your project?"

I looked away at the giant inflated gorilla on top of the mattress store with its mouth wide open to show two rows of sharp white teeth. "I'm not sure what I'm doing," I confessed.

Kristen flashed me a smile. "No worries. You'll think of something!"

"Yeah." We ran past a Mexican restaurant, a Thai food truck, and a pizza place. Each new smell drifting out from each kitchen made my mouth water.

"Whoa, Daisy, was that your *stomach*?" Poppy said at a red light. "Bet you wish you had my PB&J on chapatis now. Hey, look at those trolls!"

She pointed over at the high school, where Miguel scooped

up a basketball abandoned on the side of the court. He dribbled it and passed it to Devon, and then the entire boys' track team started a game instead of doing their training run. Poppy gestured for us all to surround her. "Coach Wu sent them out for a six-miler," she said. "On the count of three, let's all yell 'losers!' One . . . two . . . three."

"Losers!" we hollered across the street.

The boys looked over. Devon picked up the basketball and pantomimed hurling it at us. The rest of the team huddled around Miguel, then took off running and caught up with us. "Not a word to Coach!" Miguel said. "We're begging you."

Poppy's eyes narrowed. "One word," she said sweetly. "*Blackmail*."

We all ran together down the long hill to the beach and turned left on the cement path, away from the long pier that jutted out into the ocean. Ice plant grew all around us, leaves curving up like green french fries. Beyond the plants, sand formed low dunes. When we were little, Squirrel and I had slid down those dunes on flattened cardboard boxes.

"You never told me how your brother's doing," Miguel said beside me.

"Why do you care?" The words were out before I could bite them back.

But Miguel only shrugged. "He's a cool cat. He was nice to my cousin at the dance. I just wondered how he is."

With the back of one hand, I wiped sweat and sunscreen out of my eyes. "My brother's fine."

"For real?" Miguel looked unconvinced. "I saw his girlfriend dancing with that other guy at the Moonlight Ball. He looked pretty bummed."

"How'd you know Squirrel and Angelina were a couple?" I demanded.

"Who's Squirrel?" Miguel's face furrowed in confusion.

"My brother. And how'd you even know he was my brother?"

"You danced with him all night at the Ball, and I recognized him from school assemblies and plays and stuff." Miguel elbowed me in the side, tricky to do when you're running. "I notice things, you know."

"Oh, really?" I glared at him and picked up my pace. "Things like Devon making fun of me while you stand there and say nothing?"

"But I—"

"Gotta go!" I said, and ran to catch up with Poppy.

"What's up with Miguel?" she said. "He *never* talks to you."

"He volunteered at the Moonlight Ball, remember? He was asking about Squirrel."

"Ah. Squirrel still depressed?"

"Super sad. Yesterday, he barely came out of his room. And this morning, he missed the bus, so my parents had to drive him to school. He refused to get out of his Lakers pajamas."

"No," Poppy said.

"Yep. He went to school in them."

"Whoa. He must be really depressed."

We jogged toward the fancy mansions on the beach. Sometimes, we played games of Let's

Pretend, imagining ourselves sunbathing on ocean-view balconies, and playing volleyball in the sandy courts beside gardens full of flowers and fountains. But now, as we ran toward the three-story houses, I froze.

"Oh no." I grabbed Poppy's hand. "*Look!*"

In the driveway of the mansion closest to us stood a yellow truck—a pickup painted with black Dalmatian spots and topped with giant sparkling blue wings. A black vinyl dog tail waved from the back of the truck. Flies buzzed around the garbage bags piled in the bed. "The Poop Fairies," Poppy and I said together.

I squeezed her hand and whispered a single world. "*Run!*"

9

Poppy and I ran, but not fast enough. Devon sprinted past us and stopped in front of the spotted yellow pickup, throwing out his arms to block the sidewalk. A street sweeper roared past us, its brushes spinning and shrieking again the asphalt.

"The Poop Fairies!" Devon shouted over the noise, and pointed at the truck. "Epic, people!"

"Don't say a word," I hissed in Poppy's ear.

The rest of our team jogged up behind us and stopped to check out the Poop Fairy pickup. The house that belonged to the driveway was a blue three-story with bushes trimmed into dolphin and seal shapes. An iron gate led to the backyard . . . and to my parents.

"Ick!" said a seventh grader. "What's a poop fairy?"

"It's someone who makes a living picking up dog poop." Kristen passed out gummy bears from the package she kept in her shorts pocket. We all took one, and none of us pointed out the little orange price tag that read *The Dollar Store*. "People make a lot of money doing that job," she told us.

I almost snorted. *Tell that to my mom and dad*, I thought.

Miguel jogged in place. "Maybe you can make bank, but who wants to pick up dog poop . . . especially a stranger's? You've gotta be pretty desperate to do *that* as a job."

I thought of Mom coming home the day she got laid off

and breaking into tears at the dinner table. "I'm forty-five years old," she'd wailed. "Who's going to hire me?"

"Or me?" Dad had replied. "Not a lot of full-time photography jobs out there. Especially jobs with health insurance."

Miguel was right. My parents *were* pretty desperate.

The Poop Fairy pickup swam in front of my eyes. I wanted to run before my parents emerged from the backyard, but my feet felt immobile, stuck, like the time I'd waded into Lake Cachuma and mud sucked off my flip-flops, threatening to sink me along with them.

"Gross!" Devon hollered. "Picking up cold poop's the worst!"

Poppy smacked him on the side of the head with her palm. "They use shovels."

Devon rubbed his head. "What makes you the big expert, Poopy?"

"I own a giant poodle." She shoved past him on the sidewalk and pulled me along with her. "Let's get out of here."

For an instant, I thought the danger had passed. And then, right as we all began to jog, the iron gate swung open, and my parents walked out in their jeans and sparkling T-shirts and knee-high rubber boots with shovels and plastic-lined buckets that could be full of only one thing.

"Daisy!" Dad broke into his widest smile and waved his shovel at me. "How's it going, kiddo?"

"Hi," I said, praying my teammates would think he was just a family friend.

But Mom hoisted her bucket into the back of the pickup and called after me. "Daisy, don't forget to turn on the Instant

Pot at five and take the bread out of the freezer. And make your brother clean the rabbit's litter box!"

Humiliating. I sprinted after Poppy. But Devon was on me like a fly on . . . well . . . you know.

"Why, Daisy Wood*worm*." He ran backward in front of me, stretching his lips into a mocking smile. "Your parents own a dog poop company? I thought your mom was an accountant."

"She was," I growled. "She got laid off last year."

Suddenly, I felt protective of my mother, a way I hadn't felt since I was little and she'd had to stay in the hospital a week after cancer surgery, and then on the living room couch—so weak that Dad and Squirrel and I had to bring her milkshakes and Chinese egg drop soup and extra blankets until she was back to being her super-energetic self again.

"My mother is an entrepreneur," I told Devon now.

He snickered. "You're taking that pickup to eighth-grade prom, right?"

Miguel shoved him with his shoulder. "Lay off her, Dev."

Devon's mouth formed a surprised O. "What'd you say, man?"

"*Lay off her*," Miguel repeated slowly.

Devon stared at him. I stared too. "Well, that's a first," I muttered, and kept running.

Back on the beach path, Miguel matched his pace to mine, so our shoes slapped the pavement at the same time. "Actually," he said, "that truck's pretty cool."

I couldn't look at him. He'd stood up for me in front of Devon, but he'd called my parents desperate.

And he was right.

Shame washed over me. Seeing Mom and Dad in public

in their glittering shirts, with their shovels and their buckets, felt like seeing them naked. My teammates had seen them naked too.

I jogged back to Poppy with my face on fire. "I gotta go. Drop my backpack at my house?"

"Totally." Her eyes shone with sympathy. "See you in an hour."

I bent and retied my shoes, waiting until the group had run far ahead of me. Then, I turned left to sprint up the hill to the city. My heart thudded in my chest. I forced my breathing into a rhythm, sucking in air and blowing it out, crowding out thoughts of my teammates and my parents. At the top of the hill, I stopped and bent over, panting hard. My shins burned. I limped the rest of the way home and kicked off my shoes on the porch.

Music blared from upstairs. "Squirrel?" I called, wrinkling my nose at the litter box smell. "Did your bus get here early? Mom says to clean Hasenpfeffer's toilet!"

My brother's big white rabbit hopped out and stood on his hind legs, sniffing my hand to see if I had any food. I walked into the kitchen and quartered an apple. I gave Hasenpfeffer a piece and sliced up the rest and put it on a plate with a spoonful of peanut butter.

"Bro?" I called up the stairs. "You alive? I made you a snack!" I carried the plate up the stairs and knocked on Squirrel's door. "You in there?"

No answer—just the wail of a country western singer. "Ugh," I groaned. Usually, Squirrel listened to Michael Jackson. Country was for when something horrible had happened.

I pushed the door open. My brother lay on his bed in his

purple-and-yellow Lakers T-shirt and flannel pajama bottoms in front of our laptop, watching Stephen Ming, Fashion King while Garth Brooks wailed out "The Dance" on his phone.

I didn't remind Squirrel that he was supposed to leave the computer on the table in the dining room so we could all use it. Instead, I sat down at the foot of his bed and handed him the plate of apples and peanut butter. "You okay?"

He grunted and moved closer to the laptop as Ming yelled into the camera. I sighed and looked around the room. The framed dance photos of him and Angelina lay facedown on his dresser. The pictures of him and Billy in their Special Olympics basketball jerseys and track singlets had disappeared. Jagged glass and broken frames stuck up from the trash can under his desk.

He'd left a single photo on his bulletin board. It was a picture of him and me dressed up as beetles—the insects, not the band—from a Halloween when Dad still had time to make us awesome costumes. Both of us were grinning, holding up our favorite candy bars: me, dark Milky Way; Squirrel, M&M's.

I reached over and paused Stephen Ming. "Did something bad happen at school today? How come you didn't go to work?"

"Called in sick," he muttered to his bedspread. "Billy told me the Games got canceled."

Freakin' Billy. I loved my brother's best friend, but any opportunity to bring the drama, and he was right there, center stage. He'd always been that way. When I was six and he and Squirrel were eleven, I fell off the monkey bars at the neighborhood playground and broke my arm. Squirrel carried me home, and Billy told everyone he saw on the half-mile walk from the park to my house that I'd had a horrible accident and I was about to die.

I don't know why I was surprised that he'd told my brother about Summer Games; he'd probably told every single athlete in Special Olympics, thrilled to be the first to break bad news. *Like stealing Angelina wasn't enough*, I thought.

Squirrel lifted his head. Tears streaked his pink cheeks. "Now, I have no girlfriend, no best friend, and no Games."

I put my hand on his shoulder. "Oh, Squirrel. I'm sorry. I wish I could change things for you."

He jerked his shoulder away. "No one can change things." He balled up his hands into fists. His knuckles were red and chapped from the cleaning supplies he used at work.

"I'll get your lotion," I told him. In the bathroom, I fished around in the cabinet for his eczema cream. Then, I glanced up at the mirror and met my own eyes.

I hated that, how you could be going about your business, and then you caught sight of yourself—not just your reflection, but your *eyes*—and it was like meeting up with your conscience, or something. Creepy.

All day I'd been thinking about my pathetic life . . . my parents and their work, Devon making fun of me, Coach Lipinsky's mandatory oral report. But now, my conscience, or whatever it was, glared at me from the mirror.

Stop whining, it commanded.

"How?" I asked it.

"Ask yourself how you can be of service to those around you." Coach Lipinsky's voice rang out clear as if he stood in the bathtub behind me. *"Make the world a better place—for one person, or many."*

I heard again the words Squirrel had said on Pizza-Movie

Night, the evening before chaos erupted at the Moonlight Ball. "My dream," he'd said, "is to be a YouTube celebrity."

I stared into my eyes in the mirror. In that instant, I knew exactly what my Change the World project would be. Somehow, I was going help my brother make that dream a reality.

10

I didn't tell anyone about my plan. It felt too big, too important. Too impossible, since we'd all been in the living room the night Dad laid down the law: *No Squirrels on YouTube.*

I'd never flat-out disobeyed my parents before. I did my homework, got straight As, and kept my room clean (hard to do with three insect terrariums), and Squirrel and I shared housecleaning and cooking duties. I was—as my parents and teachers kept telling me—a "good girl," a "team player."

Going behind Mom's and Dad's backs felt like betraying the hive, our little four-person family team. I hadn't forgotten #EligibleBachelor and the way my parents had reacted to the cyberbullying posts about my brother on Instagram.

I didn't *ever* want to be on the receiving end of their anger.

But now that I'd decided to change the world for my brother, there was no going back. Maybe Mom and Dad no longer knew what was best for him. Oh, they'd been great when he was a baby and they put him in therapy to help him learn to roll over and crawl. They found him good schools and got him into Special Olympics so he could make friends and play sports.

But they didn't seem to understand that he was almost an adult—an adult who had the right to do whatever he wanted to do, as long as he wasn't hurting anybody.

If they wouldn't help Squirrel follow his dreams, *I* would.

On Friday, Coach Lipinsky passed out iPads and told us to find the same news story on three different websites around the world so we could see how different journalists wrote about the same topic. I found a story about cricket farms.

People all over the place raise crickets to sell to restaurants and food carts and markets because insects are packed with protein, and they don't produce as much greenhouse gas as cattle raised for beef—a no-brainer if you've ever compared cricket poop to cow pies. Cricket farms were no big deal according to newspapers in Indonesia and Canada, but a journalist from the U.S. said that most citizens were still pretty freaked out about crunching down on mealworm tacos and cricket cookies.

Myself, I was cool as long as no one tried to cook up my cockroaches.

While we were researching, Coach Lipinsky called us up to his desk one by one to discuss our Change the World projects with him privately—as privately as we could with everyone eavesdropping from their seats. Like always, Kristen volunteered to go first. She walked over to Coach Lipinsky in her red-and-white-checked sundress and red sandals, her braces flashing silver.

My stomach churned. What did it feel like to be that confident? Then again, if I'd chosen to tutor kids in math, I'd be confident too. Kristen's parents wouldn't disown her if they discovered her social studies project. She'd probably already told them about it, and they'd gone and bought pencils and flash cards from the Dollar Store for her to take to the kids. *Lucky.*

Deep in my backpack, my phone buzzed. I glanced at Coach

Lipinsky. His eyes were fixed on the paper Kristen handed him, so I flipped my phone open. Poppy had texted me from across the room.

What project U doing?

I dropped my phone back into my pack and stared down at a picture of hundreds of roasted crickets in a pan on my iPad. Poppy and I told each other everything. No secrets. But the fewer people who knew about my project, the less likely someone would slip up and tell Mom and Dad. Still, she *was* my best friend. And she was stubborn as a fruit fly on a bunch of bananas.

She texted me again.

What project U doing????

I texted back quickly, typing with my hands inside my backpack.

Tell U ltr. U doing the dance thing?

Devon let out an enormous, dramatic cough. In the middle of it, he choked out, "Stop texting, Daisy!"

Coach Lipinsky glanced up from Kristen's paper. His eyes went from Poppy's phone half-hidden under her desk to my hands plunged into my backpack. "Your insurrection has been noted," he told us. "Four extra laps at practice today." He went back to reading.

Poppy's mouth fell open. "What about the separation of church and state? School and track? Whatever!"

Coach Lipinsky raised an eyebrow at her. "My castle, my rules, Ms. Banjaree."

He called Poppy up to his desk then and read what she'd written and gave her a thumbs-up. "This is a splendid idea." She sat back down at her desk and beamed at me.

Devon went next. He stood up and sauntered over to Coach Lipinsky with his head high and his mouth set in a tight, angry line.

Coach Lipinsky studied the crumpled piece of paper he held out. "You sure about this?" he asked Devon in a low voice.

Devon shrugged. "Best I can do, Coach. My dad says this project's a waste of time. It's taking my energy away from track practice."

Coach Lipinsky stroked his beard. He read the paper in his hand a second time and met Devon's eyes. "I think you can do better," he said gently.

Devon swiveled his head toward the open door. I recognized the expression on his face. He wanted to run out of the room and never return.

Good, I thought. *Now you know what it feels like every time you bully me in class.*

"I'm just really busy with track and stuff," he mumbled to his feet.

"Well." Coach Lipinsky smoothed out the paper and handed it back to him. "Let's be on the lookout for a slightly more ambitious project, okay?"

"Whatever." Devon dropped back into his chair with an exaggerated sigh.

Poppy passed me a note, old school. I unfolded it in my lap.

Devon's Change the World Project = cloning himself to make the world a better place.

I stifled a snort and shoved the note under my leg before Coach Lipinsky could see it. "Mr. Santos!" he called from his desk, and Miguel walked up to the front of the classroom. Coach Lipinsky read his project description and beamed. "Perfect!" he said. "Let me know how I can help."

Poppy and I rolled our eyes at each other. *Miguel Santos, perfect, as usual.* Devon pumped his fist in the air. "You're gonna win this thing!" he said like he was talking about an NFL game instead of a social studies project.

Poppy tossed her ponytail. "There's nothing to win, Devon. The point is to make the world a better place, which you're obviously going to fail at."

Coach Lipinsky stood up from his desk and clapped his hands. "Silence, friends! Ms. Woodward, approach!"

I bit the tip of my tongue. For an instant, I was terrified I'd throw up. But I made myself stand and pick up my folded piece of paper and walk over to his desk. He unfolded it and read. I watched his eyes shift back and forth behind his glasses. "Ah," he said at last. "This is gonna be a tough one."

Tears sprang to my eyes. I ducked my head so people couldn't see my face. Coach Lipinsky nudged my arm with his elbow. "Let's discuss this outside," he said.

"Ooh, the woodworm's in trouble!" Devon sneered as I stumbled out the door.

Coach Lipinsky walked a little away from the classroom, toward a shady spot under a pepperberry tree. "Let's give this some thought. I know you want to turn your brother into a YouTube celebrity, but it's hard to build up thousands of followers in just a few months."

I twisted my fingers together and looked up at him. "He *needs* this, Coach. He just lost his girlfriend, and Special Olympics canceled their Summer Games. He's seriously depressed."

"I see." Coach Lipinsky folded his hands behind his head and gazed up into the tree. A starling hopped around, squawking between the clusters of little red berries. "There are millions of channels on YouTube," he said at last. "You'll have to help your brother find a platform of some sort. He needs a shtick—something original to offer people. Have you thought about what that could be?"

"Um . . . no." Even though we were standing in the shade, sweat trickled down my back and pooled in the waistband of my shorts. I'd tried my whole life not to attract attention—to do everything my parents and teachers asked, to keep my mouth shut and be good. I could tell Coach Lipinsky wanted me to choose a different project. Everything in me wanted to agree.

But I had to do this for Squirrel.

"I see that you've got your heart set." Coach Lipinsky smiled at me. "Okay, you figure out his shtick, and I'll help promote your brother's videos. By the way," he added. "You might want to help Miguel with his project, and get his help on yours."

"Why?" I couldn't help wrinkling my nose. "I guarantee he doesn't want help from me."

Coach Lipinsky laughed. "You might be surprised. Ask him what he's planning when you have a moment. You'll see."

We walked back inside. I sat down fast and bent my head over my iPad. Coach Lipinsky perched on his stool. "Most of your ideas look superb. Who can remind us of what BARAT stands for?"

Poppy waved her hand. Her silver bracelets jingled. "Brainstorm, ask, research, action, triumph!"

"Excellent!" Coach Lipinsky smacked his big palms together. "We've reached the *Ask* section of the project, my friends. Write down two questions you have about your endeavor—questions you must answer in order to make your project amazeballs. For instance . . ."

He looked at Poppy. "May I?"

She nodded and raised proud eyebrows at Devon, who snorted.

"Ms. Banjaree is planning a dance performance to benefit flood victims in India," Coach Lipinsky explained. "Questions she might ask are . . ."

He grabbed his purple pen and wrote on the whiteboard. "Where should she hold the event? How much should she charge? Live music, or recorded? Refreshments, or no refreshments? Where can she post pictures of flood damage in Kerala so the audience can better understand the need for financial assistance?"

"Slow down!" Poppy hollered, scribbling notes like crazy.

"See what I mean? Her project's stupendous!" He turned his attention to Miguel. "May I?"

Miguel gave him a thumbs-up.

"His plan is to save the Special Olympics Summer Games, an annual event for people with intellectual disabilities. It's canceled this year, for lack of money," Coach Lipinsky explained. "Miguel needs to ask what types of fundraisers he can organize, and whether he knows anyone who might sponsor the event. But first, how much money does he need to raise?"

"The Special Olympics director said they need another ten thousand dollars," Miguel said.

Devon whistled. I stared. "You've got to be kidding," I said. "That's so much money!"

Miguel shrugged. "We've gotta do something."

"*We*?" I echoed.

"Yeah." He shot me an annoyed look, like my participation in his project was a no-brainer. "I mean, you'll help, right?"

"I have my own project." I gripped my pen and looked down at my paper. No way could Miguel raise that much money in just a few months, with or without my help. I hunched over my paper and focused on my questions.

1. How do you make a good YouTube video—camera? Lights? Microphone?
2. How you become a YouTube celebrity?
3. What is Squirrel's shtick?

Coach Lipinsky was right. My brother had to offer people something they hadn't already seen a billion times on YouTube. Maybe he could teach them how to dance like Michael Jackson, or how to clean toilets like he loved to do at his high school. He'd have a million ideas—he always did.

Whatever he chose, it had to be stupendous.

11

That afternoon after track practice, I jogged home, showered, and shredded up lettuce for my cockroaches and millipedes. The millipedes—each ten inches of serious awesomeness—crawled up my hands and my arms. "Hey, Millie. Hey, Pete," I said. I stroked their striped brown-and-black backs with one finger and checked their legs, all 200-plus of them, for any injuries.

"Looking good," I said, and placed them back on their bed of leaves so I could put new branches in the stick insect terrarium. Inside, Sprig sat motionless, so still that if you didn't look for her little bulging eyes, you might think she was part of her branch. Twig dangled upside down from the lid of the terrarium. He hadn't been eating, so I knew he was getting ready to molt. I sprayed him with water so he wouldn't get stuck in his old skin and lose a leg. That had happened last molt, and it took months for Twig to grow his leg back.

I gave the cockroaches fresh water and sat down to start my homework. But I couldn't concentrate. Trisha Yearwood wailed through Squirrel's bedroom door like she was about to die.

I leapt up from my desk and banged on his door with one fist. "Squirrel!" I hollered over the music. "Mom says it's your turn to vacuum!"

"Vacuuming gives me eczema!" he yelled. "You do it!"

I knocked again. The door flew open, and he appeared. "What?" he growled.

I stepped back. Squirrel had gone feral. His hair stuck up all over his head, and his lips were super chapped. His Lakers T-shirt was wrinkled and stained, and his pajama pants sagged, showing off the waistband of his boxer shorts—a look he normally hated. His eyes were red and crusty, and he smelled like he hadn't showered or brushed his teeth in about a year.

I peered around him and saw the laptop open on his bed. Stephen Ming was frozen on the screen, in the middle of setting a black hat at a ridiculous angle over his forehead. "I need the laptop for homework," I told Squirrel.

He folded his arms across his chest. "I'm using it."

"Homework trumps YouTube." I'd never had to remind him of our parents' rule before. He was the one who always reminded me to do my homework, and he did his chores and mine whenever I had a big project due. But now, he wasn't budging.

He gripped the sides of the doorway, blocking me. "Nope. You're not taking it."

"Come on, Squirrel." I dug my fists into my hips. "If Mom finds out I couldn't do my social studies assignment, she'll—"

"Fine!" He slammed the laptop closed and shoved it into my hands. Then, he kicked the door shut behind me.

"Stink bug!" I yelled, and instantly regretted it.

I didn't know what it was like to be dumped. I'd never been in love, unless you counted me marrying Hasenpfeffer in a ceremony Poppy and I filmed when we were nine. But I did love running, and I knew if my track meets had been canceled—if State this year got obliterated like Squirrel's Summer

Games—I'd probably hole up in my room with country music and Stephen Ming too.

I pressed my face against his door. "I'm sorry," I said, and walked down to the kitchen. I poured him a glass of milk and made him a peanut butter and graham cracker sandwich before walking back up the stairs and opening the door. He lay facedown on his bed.

"I brought you a snack," I said.

"I said I'm *not* hungry," he muttered into his pillow.

"All right, all right." I left the snack on his desk and took the laptop down to the dining room table with a half sleeve of graham crackers. It was Friday, Pizza-Movie Night, so I had time to research instead of starting dinner. Hasenpfeffer hopped over and stood on his hind legs and stared at me out of one pink eye until I handed him a square of graham cracker. He snatched it from my fingers and hopped off to eat it under the coffee table.

I had no idea what to research. I'd watched hundreds of YouTube videos about everything from how to pick the perfect running shoe to DIY toys for Madagascar hissing cockroaches. You could find videos about anything in the world on the site. So where did Squirrel fit in?

Coach Lipinsky had made us brainstorm our talents and skills and experiences. "So do that for Squirrel," I said to myself. I opened up a word doc and typed: Dancing. Michael Jackson. Basketball. Fashion.

I studied the list for a moment, looking for anything that might make Squirrel unique among the millions of other people trying to make it as YouTube celebrities. What made him unique was Down syndrome.

I thought of #EligibleBachelor and how my parents worried about someone hurting my brother because of his disability. But it was a part of who he was, just like his love of sports and nice clothes. Maybe if he shared that love with the world, people would start to see kids with Down syndrome as just . . . well, *kids*.

I Googled "Down Syndrome + Fashion."

Instantly, dozens of pictures appeared on the screen—children and teens and adults in fancy clothes with gorgeous hair and makeup. Most of the pictures featured the same model. She had long red hair like Angelina's, full lips, and eyes as blue as my brother's. In one picture, the girl leaned against a pier piling in a fluffy white dress with the beach spread out behind her. In another, she wore a black lace dress and dramatic eyeliner with her hair styled in an enormous swoop on top of her head. One photo showed her in a pink bikini on sand surrounded by shells. One showed her walking down a runway in a silvery dress at something called New York Fashion Week.

I clicked on a link and watched an interview with the girl. Her name was Madeline Stuart. She sat on a couch beside her mother in a silky brown dress decorated with big roses and answered the interviewer's questions. She beamed at the audience and laughed in her perfect makeup with her perfect hair.

Madeline had become a fashion model thanks to social media. Her mom had posted photos that went viral, and modeling agents saw the pictures and contacted her. "Maybe Squirrel could be a model," I told Hasenpfeffer, who was back for another graham cracker. "He could show off his wardrobe on YouTube."

Voices rang out at the front door. I cleared my browser history and put the laptop to sleep. Poppy walked in with my parents. "TGIF!" Dad said, carrying the giant pizza box into the kitchen. "Mom and I got off early, so we picked up the pie and Poppy on the way home."

"Thank God." She collapsed in a chair beside me. "My legs are killing me. I can't believe Coach made us run fartleks for an *hour*. Ms. Bravo would never have been that evil." She rolled her eyes at me. "By the way, Coach says you've gotta run extra fartleks on Monday to make up for skipping out on practice."

I shrugged. I liked running fartleks—jogging, then sprinting all-out for a minute, and then jogging again. "They're way more interesting than quarter-mile repeats," I reminded Poppy. "Those are so boring."

"Plus, they're fun to say," Dad observed.

"I beg you, please do *not* start with the fart jokes." Mom sat down at the table and put her feet in pink poodle socks on the empty chair. "Squirrel upstairs?" she asked me. I nodded.

"Michael Jackson or country?" Dad cupped an ear, listening.

"Country," I said.

"I was afraid of that." Dad shook his head and took off his glasses to clean them on his Poop Fairies T-shirt. "You know, if your mother broke up with me every time some girl kissed me in a bowling alley . . ."

"He's joking, Poppy." Mom waved Dad away and glanced at the laptop. "Homework?"

"How was your day?" I asked Mom before Poppy could tell her about Coach Lipinsky's Change the World Project. I was a terrible liar. If Mom and Dad asked me whether I'd chosen a project yet, I'd turn bright red and start stammering, and they'd know something was up. Then, my plan to put Squirrel on YouTube would be ruined before it even got started.

"It's such a gorgeous day to be outside!" Mom told Poppy

and me. "The weather was perfect. Dad and I got an unexpected lunch break because the truck had a cracked oil pan, so we took a walk on the beach and picked up a couple of driftwood pieces for your terrariums. That storm last week tossed up a lot. So many shells!"

"Great," I said, and walked into the kitchen. Poppy followed me, and we took out glasses—five instead of six because, for the first time in years, Angelina wasn't coming to Pizza-Movie Night. I missed her laugh, her dancing, the way she gazed at Squirrel and held his hand when they sat together on our love seat. How could she be so jealous when my brother obviously adored her?

"Love is ridiculous," I muttered, and searched the fridge for 7Up and cherries. "Dad!" I popped my head into the living room. "Where's the soda?"

Mom answered. "The truck cost a lot to repair," she told me. "We can't afford extras for a couple of weeks."

Heat spread across my face. Were we really too broke to afford a liter of soda and a jar of maraschino cherries? "Guess we're drinking water tonight," I said, way more cheerful than I felt.

Poppy shrugged and pulled out place mats and napkins. Her family shopped at Grocery Outlet—the Gross Out, she called it—and ate generic ice cream and drank water instead of soda. Her one splurge was coffee; she spent all her babysitting money on Starbucks.

"Coach told me at practice that I need twice as much water as everyone else because of all the caffeine I drink," she said. "He's such a dictator."

"He told me to eat more vegetables." I rolled my eyes. "He says I look *peaked*. Is that even a word?"

"He tells everyone to eat more vegetables. He must live on broccoli." Poppy got out the ice cube tray and clattered ice into glasses. "He seemed concerned about your Change the World project. What are you doing, again?" she asked for the tenth time today.

I dropped my voice. "I can't tell you with my parents in the next room."

"Why not?" Poppy hated mysteries and magic and anything else that didn't offer an instant explanation. She'd refused to read the Percy Jackson books when the rest of us were wild about them, and if a birthday party included a magician, she wouldn't go. "What's the big deal?" She handed me the glasses to fill with water. "They can't hear you over the TV."

I was dying to tell her about the fashion model I'd discovered, and about putting Squirrel on YouTube. But if Dad heard me, I'd be toast.

"I'll tell you later," I promised. "Did your moms and sisters say they'd dance at your benefit?"

"I know you're just trying to distract me," she said, but she took the bait anyway. "Mom's at some psychology conference this weekend, and Mama's got her hands full chauffeuring everyone around. When we're all home Sunday night, I'll give them the scoop about my project. Unlike some people," she added, punching me in the arm.

We carried the water glasses out to the table and set up the TV trays. Poppy peered up the stairs. "Squirrel's still up there?"

I nodded. "He only comes out to go to school and use the bathroom."

She smacked her fist into her palm. "I swear, the next time I see Angelina . . ."

"She's just confused," I said.

"Bestie, if Angelina had her way, she'd marry Squirrel and keep him locked in her house so no other girl could look at him!" Poppy shook her ponytail at me. "You're too nice."

"Maybe." I pulled out a slice of pizza—basil, feta, and circles of roasted squash. "I'll see if I can tempt him out," I said, and headed upstairs with a plate and napkin. Poppy followed on my heels.

I pushed open Squirrel's door without knocking. He lay on his bed with his head bent over a magazine. The spicy smell of basil on the pizza competed with his BO. Usually, he showered and shaved twice a day. But now, stubble darkened his chin and cheeks, and he smelled like death.

"Jeepers, friend, take a shower already!" Poppy said.

He glared at her. "Shut up, Poppy!"

"Kids! Chill." I pushed back the curtains and slid open the window to let in a breeze. I set the pizza on Squirrel's desk beside the untouched graham crackers and milk and sat down and picked up his magazine. "That the new *GQ*?"

"Yeah," he grunted. He flipped through the pages until he came to a photo of some guy in plaid pants, a yellow turtleneck, and a navy blue peacoat and lavender scarf. "I need this outfit."

"Um . . . if you say so." I sat down on his bed and put a hand on his shoulder. "I have a secret," I whispered. "But you can't tell Mom and Dad. And neither can *you*." I narrowed my eyes at Poppy.

"Yeah, yeah." She waved her hand impatiently. "Is this about your Change the World project?"

I nodded.

"I hate secrets," Squirrel said, and buried his face in his magazine.

I clenched my molars and sucked in a breath through my nose. "I'm going to help you become a YouTube celebrity." I thumped the magazine cover to get his attention. "Maybe you could model clothes, or teach people to moonwalk, or something."

Poppy's eyes widened. "That's a great idea!" she cried and clapped her hand over her mouth. "That's a great idea!" she stage-whispered.

Squirrel put down his magazine. "I'll be a celebrity?" he said, and a hint of a smile twitched at the corners of his mouth—the first I'd seen since the Moonlight Ball.

I thought of all the times he'd trusted me. When I was ten and he was fifteen, I'd convinced him to jump off the roof with me, both of us holding umbrellas like Mary Poppins. He'd sprained his ankle, and I'd helped him inside and wrapped up his foot with a bandana. I felt so guilty that I brought him snacks and drinks and magazines for a week until he could walk again, just like he'd done for me when I broke my arm.

Another time, I got him to run away with me to a "desert island" with a backpack full of Dad's chocolate chip cookies and a box of matches. A neighbor spotted us hours later in the rain. We were trying to start a driftwood bonfire under the concrete bridge on the beach. When our parents found us wet and shivering, surrounded by screaming seagulls and a pile of soaked matches, I told them it was my idea, so they only grounded me and let Squirrel go free. He snuck me his flip phone that whole week so I could text Poppy.

He had my back, and I had his. I was the one who made him ask Angelina to dance at their first Moonlight Ball. I'd been helping Dad with the photo booth, and Squirrel couldn't take his eyes off this girl in a green lace dress and black knee-high boots. "Go dance with her," I'd said, and walked with him to where she stood all alone.

He literally got down on one knee in his suit and offered his hand, like a Disney prince. "May I have this dance, madam?" he asked the girl who turned out to be Angelina.

She laughed and pulled him onto the dance floor. They'd been a couple ever since.

Until now. "You still want to be on YouTube, right?" I asked Squirrel.

He pressed his hand against his heart. "It's my dream."

"Well, you know what Michael Jackson says," Poppy reminded him.

Together, we recited, "Please go for your dreams!"

Squirrel rubbed his eyes and leapt off the bed. He reached for his pizza and took a huge bite. "I'm going to give fashion advice on YouTube, just like Stephen Ming," he said through a mouthful. "I'll call my channel . . ." He paused and scrunched up his face in thought. "I'll call it 'Young Spice Squirrel Advice'!"

Poppy wrinkled her nose. "What's a Young Spice Squirrel?"

"Young Spice, like my aftershave, only I'm young instead of old. Get it?"

"I like it!" I said, and stood up. "Hey, why don't you bring your pizza downstairs? It's not a party without you."

"Okay, sister."

I stopped him at the door. "Remember—not a word to anyone. It's our secret." I pressed my finger against my mouth.

He blew me a kiss, and I nearly passed out from the smell of his unbrushed teeth. "My lips are sealed," he promised.

"Yours too," I reminded Poppy.

"Not a word," she said.

We headed down to the living room, where the movie was just starting—Dad's choice—about a photographer who walked every single street in New York City. Sitting there eating pizza with my family and Poppy, my chest felt tight with hope and fear. Hope, because even on the worst days, you can always wish for something. Fear, because when you decide to change the world, there's a lot to worry about. In my head, I made a list of everything that could go wrong:

1. What if my parents found out about my plan to make Squirrel a YouTube celebrity?

2. How was I going to survive giving a five-minute oral report in front of Devon Smalley?

And the most terrifying question of all:

3. What if I failed my brother?

12

On Sunday morning, I walked downstairs to make oatmeal and found Dad at the dining room table, looking at photos to post on the Poop Fairies' Instagram page. Squirrel couldn't be on social media, but dogs in party hats were apparently fine.

"You and Mom actually have a day off?" I asked him.

"Yup. Just catching up on some publicity," he said. "Squirrel and I are going thrifting later. He hasn't touched his latest paycheck. I thought shopping might cheer him up."

What would cheer him up is you and Mom taking his dreams seriously, I thought, but I kept my mouth shut. Instead, I peered over his shoulder at a picture of a Labradoodle in a tiara with rhinestone letters that spelled out "Happy New Year!" Dad had typed a poem below the picture. I read it out loud.

"Are you sick of picking up poop?
We can help you! Here's the scoop:
Daily cleaning. Dog walks, too!
The Poop Fairies deal with all your poo!"

I groaned. "You gotta be kidding, Dad."

He looked up at me and grinned. "Everyone's a sucker for rhyming poems. And cute dogs in tiaras."

"If you say so," I said, and headed for the kitchen.

Dad followed me into the kitchen with his coffee cup. "What's on the agenda for today, kiddo?"

"I thought I'd hike Lone Pine." I refilled his mug and handed him the carton of half-and-half. "Want to come?"

We'd hiked the two-and-a-half-mile trail up to Lone Pine on Sundays ever since Squirrel and I were little, to stand in the shade of the pine tree high above the city with the ocean stretching out forever. It was our family's special place.

Dad yawned and stretched his arms above his head. "What's Poppy up to? I'll bet she'd like to go hiking."

I measured water into a pot and added oatmeal and a pinch of salt. "Holy crickets, can't I ask my own father to go for a hike with me?" I joked. "We haven't hiked in months."

I miss you, Dad, I added in my head.

He took off his glasses to rub his eyes and ran his fingers through his hair. "Give me ten minutes to down another cup of coffee and get dressed," he said.

"I'll let you eat breakfast first." I got out two bowls and the brown sugar and raisins. I put a banana and a handful of Costco blueberries and kale and orange juice into the blender and whipped them into a smoothie, then poured it into two glasses.

"You're the best." Dad passed me his phone, open to a picture of a fluffy white poodle in a pink tutu decorated with little red hearts. "Think she'd look good on the Poop Fairies' website?"

"No," I said. "Just no."

I bit my tongue to keep from reminding him that he was an artist with photos for sale in a gallery up in the hills. I concentrated instead on filling a jar with water and lemon juice from our tree out back, plus a teaspoon of salt and sugar. In another jar, I shook up almonds and chocolate chips and leftover Christmas hazelnuts from my aunt in Oregon.

I tucked both jars into my backpack and drank my smoothie. Sunlight flooded the kitchen. The house felt quiet, peaceful. I loved Mom and Squirrel, but I couldn't help being happy that for once, only Dad and I were awake and getting to share the morning together.

We finished our oatmeal and headed for the Poop Fairy pickup. Already, flies buzzed around the back, smelling what had been there the day before. I held my breath and climbed into the blazing yellow truck.

Dad drove down the street. The Snoopy bobblehead on the dashboard wobbled, startling a spider on its web in a corner of the windshield. I had to admit it was a great place to build its trap. My parents' business attracted a lot of flies.

We headed for the park. At the trailhead, I put on my backpack, and Dad slung his camera over one shoulder and grabbed his monopod walking stick. He pulled on his camo baseball cap—the one with the big black letters that read WOOF—only slightly less ridiculous than his glittery blue Poop Fairies cap.

Dad and I stopped, as we always did, to check out the chewing gum mosaic on the dead oak near the trail. The colorful wads stuck to the trunk reminded me of the kookaburra song he used to sing to Squirrel and me when we were little—the song he sang now, in his deepest, loudest voice. "Kookaburra sits in the old gum tree!"

"Dad!" I glanced at the people around us—mostly early morning joggers and hikers. A couple of boys in shorts and red and gold singlets—the high school's track team colors—ran by and stared at my father, who was still singing. They burst out laughing.

He threw up his arms, pretending despair. "No one appreciates my melodious baritone!"

"Can we just *hike*?" I pulled him toward the path, wishing for the millionth time that he could be a little less charismatic.

After a few minutes of hiking, we left the hum of the freeway traffic behind. Our shoes crunched on the dirt. My calf muscles pulled tight as we began to climb, and I inhaled dust and ocean and new grass. Dad turned his cap backward and took photos of the oak trees and boulders along the trail. "I'm glad you hauled my butt out here this morning, kiddo," he said, and ruffled my hair. "I get stuck in a rut and forget to go outside in nature."

"Me too." I gnawed the tip of my tongue. Now that we were finally out alone together, I wanted to ask him why he wouldn't let my brother be on social media even though #EligibleBachelor was ancient history—but I didn't dare ruin the moment. Safer to just keep my mouth shut and hike.

We made it to the top in half an hour and leaned against the pine tree. The long sharp needles smelled spicy when I crushed them in my palm, like Christmas. A flock of crows flapped around us, and their caws filled the air. I took out the jar of lemon water and handed it to Dad. "Homemade sports drink," I said. "Saved us three bucks!"

"Nice work." He took a long swallow, then leaned down and picked up a skinny bone as long as his finger. "Chicken?" He widened his eyes at me. "Or . . . *human*?"

"*Dad*." I rolled my eyes. "You're such a weirdo."

Still, I loved being up at Lone Pine with him. It felt like old times.

We sat side by side for a while, looking out over the city and the ocean beyond. The mission bell downtown began to ring—ten metallic bongs that echoed all the way up to where we stood. Dad exhaled a deep, satisfied breath. "'The breeze at dawn has secrets to tell you. Don't go back to sleep,'" he recited. "That's from Rumi, a thirteenth-century Persian poet."

"You should read Mom some Rumi," I said. "I'll bet she's still in bed."

His brow furrowed. "She needs her sleep. She's exhausted."

An icy shiver spread across my shoulders, and I remembered the week my mother lay in the hospital after surgery—only a mile away, but Squirrel and I weren't allowed to see her. When she finally came home, she lay on the couch so pale and weak that I thought she was going to die. "Is Mom okay?" I asked.

Dad only shrugged. "Your mother's fine. Owning a business is hard work. She's up in the middle of the night, you know, worried about stuff."

"Money," I sighed.

"And Squirrel," he replied. "He's been so depressed since the dance."

He stood up and screwed his camera onto his monopod walking stick and began to shoot close-ups of pinecones. I watched the monarch butterflies fluttering around us. Their black-and-orange wings glowed above the brown grass flecked with new green blades from last week's rain.

Thousands of monarchs usually roosted in the eucalyptus grove at the park near our house. They hung upside down from branches with their wings closed, looking like dead brown leaves. But last year, there were only a few. Scary, since monarchs are both pollinators *and* food for birds. Entomologists freaked out, sure they'd disappeared because of climate change. They worried the butterflies would never come back. But this winter, the monarchs returned. The grove was full of them. They drifted across the freeway, fluttering above cars and trucks, and hovered over the sand on the beach.

I studied the monarch closest to me. It sat on a low bush opening and closing its wings, drying off in the sun. I looked for a tag. YouTube videos showed you how to tag a monarch so scientists could track its migration. You had to hold the body between your fingers carefully as a snowflake and press a tiny sticker onto one wing.

Tagging butterflies could help change the world, I thought. But I'd already promised to help my brother go for his dreams.

I just wished I had my father's blessing.

He aimed his camera at the monarch on the bush. "That's a male." I pointed with a blade of grass. "You can tell them from females 'cause males have black spots on their back wings."

Dad adjusted his lens. "I see them now. Cool fact!"

"Entomologists used to believe birds don't eat monarchs 'cause they taste bitter. But then, scientists ate some, just to see for themselves. They said monarchs taste like toast."

"Dry or with butter?" Dad quipped. "Can you butter a butterfly?"

I groaned.

"It's a legitimate question." He patted his stomach. "All this talk of toast is making me hungry."

I pulled the jar of trail mix out of my backpack and passed

it to him. He crunched a handful of chocolate and nuts. I leaned against the shady side of one tree, and something sharp poked me in the head—a yellow sticky note thumbtacked to the trunk.

"Gross," I muttered. Were people really so desperate to prove their love that they had to post it on innocent trees?

I wondered if M.S. was Miguel Santos. I remembered how he'd danced at the Moonlight Ball with the athletes falling all over him just like kids did at school dances.

Some male insects dance to attract females. The jumping spider can perform three different moves to charm women. Miguel struck me as slightly more intelligent than a spider. Then again, he *had* vowed to save Summer Games.

A weird new feeling of jealousy poked at me. *Who's S.R.?* I wondered. *And did they date Miguel?*

I ripped the note off the tree and crumpled it into my pocket. "Ridiculous," I muttered.

"Hey, it's better than carving their initials into the tree trunk." Dad crunched another handful of trail mix. "Thanks for bringing snacks. You're a good kid."

"I'm not that good," I said. And then, my brain listened in horror as my mouth shaped a question. "Can I ask you something?"

"Of course." He passed me the trail mix. "What's up?"

Don't say another word! my brain shouted. But my mouth refused to listen.

"Um . . . do I need professional lights and stuff to make a video of Squirrel, or can I just use my phone?" I asked.

He patted his ear with a cupped palm. "Sorry, not sure I heard you. Did you say 'video'?"

I nodded. "Um . . . yeah."

His eyebrows bunched into a question. "What *type* of video?"

"Actually, it's a lot of videos," I said. "It's for a project I'm working on at school."

Dad's voice went from warm to cold, like the shower water in our house whenever anyone started washing dishes or put in a load of laundry. "What project?" he asked.

"Um . . . fashion advice videos," I mumbled. "It's for social studies."

I didn't say a word about YouTube. Still, a cloud passed over my father's face, and he shook his head. "Sorry, Daisy, but no."

All the happiness drained out of my body and puddled into the dust at my feet. "What do you mean, *no*?"

"I mean, *no*," he repeated. "I don't want your brother on video."

A tiny flame of anger flickered in my stomach and began to spread through my body. "Why not?"

He clapped the lens cap onto his camera and slung the strap over his shoulder. "I don't want you showing videos of your brother at school."

"But Dad . . ."

He interrupted me. "You remember what happened when Squirrel's friends put him on Instagram. Those trolls made him cry for weeks. He's vulnerable. What if one of your classmates films your videos at school with a phone and posts them online?"

"They wouldn't!" I argued. "They're not like that."

He put his hands on my shoulders. "I'm sorry," he said gently, "but I'm not going to let you exploit your brother just to get a good grade in social studies."

"Ex . . . exploit him?" I turned away and stared out over the ocean, seething.

Coach Lipinsky had told us once how some farm owners exploit migrant workers, paying them just a little money to work overtime in blazing fields full of pesticides. He told us how clothing companies exploit people in other countries, making them sew shirts and shorts and dresses fourteen hours a day in freezing warehouses for a dollar a day.

"I don't want to *exploit* Squirrel!" I told Dad. "I want people to see that he's awesome!"

"I said no," my father said again, so sternly that a hiker who'd just made it to the top gave him the Stink Eye, then turned and headed back down the path.

I put my hands on my hips and frowned at Dad. "You shelter him too much! You should let him become a YouTube celebrity, if that's what he wants. There's this Australian model, Madeline—"

"I told you, Daisy, I'm not discussing this." My father turned his cap around so that the brim shaded his face. "Putting Squirrel on video leaves him wide open for haters. He's already depressed enough over his girlfriend and Summer Games."

"But Dad!" I cried. "If we help him follow his dreams, maybe he'll be happy again!"

Behind his glasses, his eyes narrowed. "I told you, Daisy, no social media!" he snapped. "And not a *word* of this to your mother. She feels exactly like I do, and she doesn't need one more thing to worry about right now!"

Then, he turned and stalked down the path without another word.

13

I stared after Dad with my mouth hanging open. Anger blazed through my body and howled in my ears. How could he be so closed-minded? Why couldn't he and Mom see that Squirrel was practically an adult—an adult who had the right to get on YouTube and talk about fashion if he wanted to? Why wouldn't he listen to me?

"What an ass!" I yelled, and instantly felt guilty. I'd never even thought such a thing about my father. I'd always worshipped him. But now, he was flat-out wrong.

Footsteps pounded toward me. A boy laughed and someone whistled.

"Kick it in!" a voice yelled.

I knew that voice. *Devon Smalley.*

He and the rest of the boys' track team raced past me bare chested and collapsed under Lone Pine, panting and dripping with sweat. The butterfly on the bush took off. I took off, too, but not before Devon pinned me with his sneer.

"Why, Ms. Woodworm!" He waved his shirt at me with a big fake smile and pushed his sweaty bangs off his forehead with his fingers. "How delightful to see you!"

The other runners ignored him, gulping water from their bottles and stretching against the tree trunks. "Hey, Daisy." Miguel nodded at me with his cheeks pink from exercise or embarrassment. He put his shirt on, fast.

"Hey," I grunted, praying he and the others wouldn't see that I'd been crying.

"Nice day for a workout." He took off his baseball cap and tilted his head up toward the sun. "Hot this morning. You been running?"

I shook my head. "Not on the weekend." I edited out as many S-words as I could. "Coach told our team to go for a bike ride or a hike, or lift at the gym. No running."

Miguel grimaced. "He knows nothing about cross-country and track, am I right?"

I shrugged and slung my backpack over my shoulders. I couldn't explain that Coach Lipinsky made us cross-train to strengthen our whole bodies, because no way in H-E-double-hockey-sticks was I saying "cross-train" in front of Devon.

"I better go follow my father," I mumbled.

"Is he the guy booking it down the trail with a camera?" Miguel asked. "The one with the cool dad cap?"

"*Woof*," I sighed.

"He looked kind of upset."

I nodded. "He is."

"Parents can be the worst," Miguel said, and for a moment, it was almost like he could look inside me and see the flames that had replaced the blood and oxygen in my veins.

But how could he understand? Miguel's mother and father, when they came to school assemblies, were perfect—tall and stylish and smiling. I'd bet my millipedes they'd never even raised their voices to Miguel, much less accused him of trying to exploit one of his siblings.

Miguel tipped his water bottle up and took a long drink.

When he came up for air, he looked at me, then looked away fast. "Hey," he began. "Any chance you'd want to—"

Devon walked over and slung a sweaty arm around his shoulders. "What's up, bro?"

I didn't stick around to hear the rest of Miguel's question. "Gotta go," I said, and turned and stumbled down the trail to find my father.

The next day at track practice, I collapsed on the cement pad in the middle of the field and began stretching with the girls' and boys' teams. The only bright spot in the afternoon was that Devon had injured his IT band running down from Lone Pine and had to leave early for physical therapy.

Coach Lipinsky cranked up music on his phone—Tom Petty's "Runnin' Down a Dream."

"Your dad loves this song." Poppy nudged me with her knee. "He and Coach should hang out. I mean, they're probably the same age!"

I scowled down at my running shoes. The last thing I wanted to think about was my father: my father who thought the worst of me, who believed I'd exploit my brother to get a good grade.

In the Poop Fairy pickup, heading home from Lone Pine, Dad and I had sat silent and cold, like two strangers forced to share a bus seat. Sitting next to him felt like sitting too close to an overfull Instant Pot ready to explode.

His anger—and mine—followed me into Monday, through all of my classes, so I couldn't concentrate on anything my teachers were saying. And then, it followed me to track practice.

Miguel sat down beside Poppy and me and began to stretch. "Changing the world, girls?"

Poppy took a swig of coffee from her thermos. "Go away, Miguel!" she commanded, and turned to me. "Wait'll you see my moms do the serpent dance. They practiced last night, and it's seriously cool."

"Save me a ticket," Miguel said to Poppy. He tapped one of my running shoes with his. "How's your project going, Daisy?"

I bent down over my legs and grabbed the tops of my shoes. My hamstrings pulled tight. "I sort of hit a roadblock," I mumbled.

A roadblock the exact size and shape of my father.

He took a pack of gum from his backpack and held it out to us. "You should just join my project. I set up a website so people can donate to Save Summer Games. Now, I've gotta find someone to be the face of the campaign."

"The face of the campaign?" Poppy grumbled. "What does that even mean?"

Miguel's hands waved in the air like my cockroaches' antennae whenever they explored new territory in my bedroom. "The best fundraising campaigns use a single person—or an animal—to represent the group they're trying to help." He tucked one leg under him, stretching his quad. "People get overwhelmed when you ask them to save a whole species or whatever. Instead of lots of polar bears, campaigns use pictures of just *one* polar bear. Instead of lots of athletes, I want pictures of—"

"Just one athlete," Poppy sighed. "Fine. I get it. Now, will you please let Daisy and me stretch in peace?"

"There's a baby food company that works that way," I heard

myself telling Miguel like he wasn't my sworn enemy. "Every year, for their ad campaign, they pick one toddler to represent all toddlers. In 2018, they picked a kid with Down syndrome. Squirrel was stoked."

I pulled a stick of gum from his pack and unwrapped it, put it in my mouth, then folded up the wrapper into a tiny silver square. The smell of peppermint rose up around me. "What about your cousin?" I asked. "He'd be a good face for your campaign."

"Ricky?" Miguel laughed. "The second someone points a camera at him, he screams that it's stealing his soul. He hates having his picture taken."

I could relate. In photos, my eyes were so big that I looked like a housefly—only, houseflies were way cuter.

Miguel stretched his other quad. "Your brother, on the other hand, totally rocks in front of a camera. I saw the way he posed for that photographer at the Moonlight Ball. He's got style to burn."

Poppy narrowed her eyes at Miguel. "You want Squirrel to be the face of your campaign, don't you?"

"I do," he said, and looked at me with something like pleading in his eyes. "Think he'd do it, Daisy? I've got an aunt who's a professional photographer in L.A. She said she'll drive up and do a photo shoot for free."

"Hmm. That could be useful for your project too," Poppy told me.

"What'd you decide to do?" Miguel asked with his eyes still locked on my face, waiting for my answer.

"No one's supposed to know," I muttered, glaring at Poppy.

She clapped her hand over her mouth. "Sorry," she said through her palm. "Pretend that didn't happen."

I clenched my molars and turned away to stretch my back muscles. Now I knew why Miguel was being so nice to me; he needed my brother for Save Summer Games. Still, a professional headshot would make Squirrel's YouTube profile look legit.

I moved into a butterfly stretch and knocked over Poppy's thermos. Coffee flowed from the spigot into the grass. "Yikes!" I cried. "Sorry!"

Poppy picked up the thermos. "My bad. Should've put the lid on."

Coach Lipinsky blew his whistle. "Ms. Banjaree," he said. "Please join me on the field for a moment. I'd like to discuss your interminable caffeine consumption."

"Big yikes. I just know he's gonna tell me to eat more kale." Poppy rolled her eyes and followed him to the grass near the long-jump pit.

The rest of the girls' team stood up and headed for the track. I waited until they were gone, and then leaned toward Miguel so the boys' team a few feet away wouldn't hear. "I'll ask Squirrel after school. If he says yes, can I . . . can I have one of the photos for social media?"

"Take as many as you want," he said. "So what's your project? I really want to know."

I almost told him. But what if he told Ricky, and Ricky told the other athletes, and Billy's mom called my parents and told them? What then?

A fire ant crawled across the top of Miguel's running shoe.

"Must be a nest nearby." I pointed to the ant with a blade of grass. "They can feel the vibrations of our feet underground."

He studied the red ant scurrying around on his shoe. "That's cool. I mean, until it stings me. Their bites *hurt*."

"That's 'cause first they bite, and then they sting," I explained. "They inject a venom that can actually kill people." I moved the ant off his shoe with the blade of grass and set it on the field.

"You saved my life!" Miguel laughed. "You sure know a lot about insects."

Over at the long-jump pit, Poppy made a chattering motion with her hand behind Coach Lipinsky's back and waved me over to the track.

"I better go run or Coach'll make me do a million push-ups," I said to Miguel.

"Wait!" He tore a piece of cardboard off his gum package and wrote his phone number on it. "My cell," he said. "Text me Squirrel's answer tonight, and we can get started."

"Um . . . okay." I stuffed the cardboard into the little waistband pocket of my running shorts. I'd never texted a boy before, and I'd never dreamed Miguel would be the first.

The whole time I ran laps around the track, I felt that piece of cardboard in my pocket. The corner gouged my hip, sharp as an ant bite. What if it was a trick to get my cell number, so Miguel and Devon could send me evil texts?

Still, I needed a professional photo of Squirrel for his YouTube channel, and no way was I asking my father. I'd just have to take a chance.

As soon as I got home, I told Squirrel about Save Summer Games and asked him about the photo shoot. "I'd love to!"

he said, and threw his arms around me. "Thank you, sister! You're the best."

"Not a word to Mom and Dad," I reminded him. "Remember, your lips are sealed."

I went into my room and texted Miguel before I could talk myself out of it. I didn't send any words. Instead, I found an emoji of a bright green worm and hit *send.*

Let him figure it out.

14

Miguel texted me on Friday during Pizza-Movie Night. We were chowing down on the Pie of the Day—roasted apples, squash, and hazelnuts—and watching *Bend It Like Beckham* while Poppy criticized the Indian family on-screen the whole time even though she'd picked the movie. My phone buzzed beside me. I flipped it open to read Miguel's message.

Photo shoot 7:30 AM Sunday at pier?

I snapped the phone shut and glanced at my parents. They were holding hands on the couch, leaning toward the TV and totally engrossed in a soccer game scene. Squirrel balled his hands into fists. "Make this goal!" he commanded the girl on-screen. "Do it, now!" The girl made the goal, and my brother and Poppy cheered.

I slipped into the kitchen and texted Miguel back, three words.

We'll be there.

After the movie ended and I walked Poppy home, I read Miguel's text about a million more times, looking for clues. What if it was a setup? What if he and Devon filmed Squirrel and me wandering around on the beach and searching for a photographer who didn't really exist? What if they posted the video online? Or what if Miguel decided to sleep in on Sunday morning, laughing in his dreams about Daisy Woodworm with her head full of bugs?

Still, Save Summer Games was the real deal. He'd told our whole class, and he'd made a website with a PayPal donation button. When people saw a photo of Squirrel, they'd get inspired to give even more money. So maybe, just maybe, Miguel's invitation was real too.

For my brother's sake, I had to believe it.

On Sunday morning, I dressed and hung my magnifying glass around my neck, then tiptoed down to the kitchen to make peanut butter toast, muffling the pop of the toaster with a dish towel so my parents wouldn't wake up. I tiptoed back upstairs and opened Squirrel's bedroom door. Sweat, unbrushed teeth, and dirty clothes mingled into a stomach-twisting stench. I set a piece of toast on his dresser and opened his blinds and his window.

He turned over and blinked up at me. "School day?" he mumbled, reaching for his Lakers calendar.

I shook my head. "Remember? That photographer's meeting us down at the pier."

"I forgot!" Squirrel leapt out of bed and threw open his closet door. "I have the perfect outfit!"

"Shh!" I hissed. "Don't wake up Mom and Dad. We've gotta keep this a secret."

"Okay, sister." He disappeared into the bathroom with his arms full of clothes.

I ate my toast downstairs, praying our parents wouldn't wake up and ask why Squirrel was up so early, scrubbing and brushing and spraying Old Spice like his life depended on it.

In a way, maybe his life *did* depend on this photo shoot. He'd been depressed for weeks, holed up in his reeking room with country western music blaring 24/7. But now, he appeared in the doorway freshly shaved, dressed in a short-sleeved blue polo shirt and khaki shorts with a backpack over his shoulders. "I'm ready!" he said, and hugged me in a cloud of toothpaste and soap.

I handed him a piece of toast and a banana, and we let ourselves out the back door. The sun was just rising, and the trees and houses glowed gold in the cold light. I strode down our street toward the road that led to the beach. Squirrel jogged to keep up with me.

"Why can't we tell Mama and Daddy about the picture?" he panted.

"Because it's for your YouTube channel," I reminded him, "which has to be a secret."

"Got it, sister." Squirrel nodded. "But I can tell them I'm saving Summer Games with your friend, right?"

"No! I mean . . . they'd better not see your picture on his website either. And Miguel's not my friend. He's just a boy in my class."

Squirrel stopped to check himself out in the mirror of a VW bus parked on the street. "I look gorgeous!" he said, and smoothed back his hair with one hand.

I pulled him down the hill to the beach. "You're not a celebrity yet. C'mon! We don't want to be late!"

A chilly breeze blew off the ocean, and I shivered in my purple Sea Urchins sweatshirt. Squirrel reached into his backpack for his windbreaker. The pier loomed ahead of us in the fog, and the dim lights from the seafood restaurant on top made it look like a UFO. I didn't see Miguel or his aunt anywhere.

Squirrel nodded hello to joggers and bicyclists like he was already a celebrity. My peanut butter toast sat like a rock in my stomach. I bit the tip of my tongue until it stung. Under the pier, a hawk sat on a wooden beam with its eye on a flock of pigeons on the bike path. I felt like one of those pigeons, sitting in the path of a predator, oblivious to impending doom.

But then, two people appeared on the other side of the pier—a tall woman in jeans and blue fleece and a rainbow-knit cap, and Miguel with his arms full of tripods and circular silver light reflectors.

So it wasn't a setup. I let out a breath and squeezed Squirrel's hand. "That's them."

"Hi." Miguel waved a tripod at me. "Sorry we're late. This is my tía Tammy. Tía Tammy, this is my friend Daisy and her brother Sq—Sorrel Woodward."

Friend? I thought. Who was Miguel kidding?

"So sorry about being late." Tía Tammy interrupted my thoughts with her low, gravelly voice. "Two accidents on the freeway coming up from L.A. Traffic was horrendous."

Miguel shook Squirrel's hand. "Good to see you, man," he told him. "You killed it on the dance floor at the Moonlight Ball."

I winced, but my brother grinned like he'd forgotten all about being dumped in front of everyone on the dance floor.

"Why, thank you!" Squirrel said to Miguel. "You're a great dancer too."

Tía Tammy pointed to a pier piling on the sand, lit up by the early morning light. "I thought we'd start with some photos of you leaning against the pier."

"That model I told you about, Madeline Stuart, posed like that," I told Squirrel.

My brother pulled a tube of Vaseline from his backpack and rubbed some on his front teeth. "For my smile," he explained.

I wrinkled my nose. "Ick. Doesn't it taste gross?"

"Standard modeling trick," Tía Tammy said. "You see it in a lot of beauty pageants."

She positioned Squirrel against the wooden pier piling and told him to look off over her shoulder. Miguel and I held up reflectors, bouncing the light off his face. Tía Tammy clicked the shutter again and again while Squirrel gazed out at the water or looked directly into her camera.

My shoulders began to ache from holding the reflector up high. The smells of cinnamon rolls and bacon drifted down from the restaurant above us. "I'm starving," Miguel groaned, clutching his stomach.

"Me too," I admitted. "All I had this morning was toast and a banana."

Tía Tammy collapsed the lights and headed toward the ocean. The three of us followed. She placed the reflectors carefully on a towel. "I'd like to take a few pictures without all the equipment. Squirrel, you okay wading barefoot for a few minutes? I brought an extra towel."

"Sure!" he said, already pulling off his shoes and socks.

Tía Tammy checked the focus on her camera, then waved Miguel and me away. "Go take a walk. I concentrate better when it's just me and the model."

When she said the word *model*, Squirrel's smile grew even wider. He looked over his shoulder and into her camera lens with his hands stuck into his pockets like a *GQ* model.

Why not? I thought. Once he got famous on YouTube, editors would be dying to feature him in their magazines.

"Let's go," Miguel told me, and kicked off his shoes and socks, so I did the same. We started off down the beach, stopping when we came to a weird-looking piece of driftwood or a shiny blue-and-purple mussel shell covered in barnacles. I picked up a piece of green beach glass to add to my family's collection in the jar on our kitchen windowsill.

"Squirrel acts like he's been modeling for years," Miguel told me.

"He loves fashion." I lisped the S and clamped my lips together. A wave broke near us and soaked my feet. I shivered and splashed through the white foam left behind on wet dark sand.

Miguel pulled a foil-wrapped rectangle from his sweatshirt pocket. "Want half a granola bar?" he asked. "My dad makes them. Peanut butter, oats, and chocolate chips. Probably flax seeds too. He's kind of a health nut."

"Um . . . okay." I held out my hand for the bar. We chewed in silence for a moment until the awkwardness threatened to kill me. "These are way better than the granola bars I buy in the . . ." I paused, searching for a word without an S.

"Store," Miguel finished, and turned to face me. "Daisy, you've gotta chill. We've been in the same class since kindergarten. I know you lisp. It's no big deal!" He put his hands on my shoulders for an instant and looked into my eyes. "Relax!" He bent down to pick up a flat gray stone and skipped it into the waves.

My cheeks flamed. *Relax?* I wanted to shout. *You're the one who tortured me for years, you and your stink-bug best friend!*

But I had to admit that the last time Miguel had teased

me was in third grade. How long was it okay to hold a grudge? Especially when the subject of that grudge was going to give you a professional portrait for your social studies project?

Still, he'd never apologized for all those years standing by while Devon bullied me.

I turned away and started walking again. Miguel hurried after me. "We've got to save Summer Games," he told me. "Before Ricky moved up to live with us, I went down to Mexico with my family every year and helped out with their Games. They're super fun. Hey, who's Squirrel's friend with the tail, by the way?"

"Sam."

"He's cool. I love that he wore that thing with his tuxedo."

We laughed, and I actually did find myself relaxing, just a little. Miguel picked up another stone and tossed it into the water. "A lot of Ricky's new friends live in group homes around here without parents. The Special Olympics athletes are their *family*. So are the coaches."

"You're right." I closed my eyes and pressed my fingers into my eyelids. When I opened them again, Miguel looked different—clearer, somehow. He reminded me of a beetle—specifically, of the Panamanian golden tortoise beetle, which can change its color from gold to red. With his feet in the water and his eyes dark and serious, Miguel seemed changed too.

"I . . . I guess I should tell you about my project . . ." I began.

But suddenly, he frowned at something behind me. "Oh, no," he muttered. "That's just great."

I turned to see Devon Smalley walking across the sand in a wet suit with a surfboard under one arm. He looked like a model in a sunscreen commercial. Even his freckles were perfectly spaced.

"*She's* why you bailed on surfing?" Devon's lips curled in a sneer. "Dude!" He yelled so loudly that a family setting up their umbrella for the day turned to stare at him. "You stood me up for Daisy *Woodworm*?"

15

I bent down and searched for sand crabs so I wouldn't have to see Miguel walking away with Devon toward the other side of the pier where the cool kids—mostly surfers and volleyball players—hung out.

But Miguel didn't walk away. Instead, he stepped closer to me.

"Daisy's helping me with Coach's project, Devon," he said. "And so is her brother."

He pointed down the beach at Squirrel, who stood ankle-deep in salt water with his arms thrown up over his head.

Devon stared. "No way, man. Your project's the wood-worm's little brother?"

"Older brother," I muttered to my feet.

"Squirrel is going to be the face of Save Summer Games," Miguel said slowly, patiently, like he was talking to a five-year-old. "*Some* of us are taking Coach's Change the World project seriously."

"Yeah, but why do you wanna work with her?" Devon said.

Miguel's mouth bunched up hard and angry. "You know what, Dev? Never mind."

He turned and grabbed my hand, pulling me up and away. "C'mon, Daisy. We've got business to discuss."

I almost laughed at the sight of Devon standing there in

his wet suit with his mouth open like a beached fish. But he got the last word, as usual.

"Suit yourself, dude!" he yelled after Miguel. "If you want to hang out with the woodworm, be my guest."

"Slimeball," Miguel muttered, still holding my hand.

I yanked it out of his grasp and stuffed my hands into the pockets of my sweatshirt. "Why do you hang out with him?" I demanded.

"I barely ever hang out with him anymore. I didn't want to go surfing with him this morning." He sighed, and I smelled his mint gum. "Our dads are best friends."

"Ick." I wrinkled my nose. "Really?"

"Yep." He sat down at the border of wet sand and dry. "They play poker together every Saturday night. They have since we were little. They used to bring us along to entertain each other. We were sort of forced to hang out."

"But you're almost in high school now." I reached for a small blue stone and rubbed it between my thumb and fingers. "You can choose your own friends."

"True that," Miguel admitted. "The thing is, I've got a lot of good memories of him."

"Memories like torturing *me*?" I countered, and pressed my knuckles against my lips. I'd never dared to speak up about the way he and Devon treated me. But now that Miguel needed my brother's help, I couldn't stay silent.

His face flushed red. "I'm sorry," he said, looking into my eyes. "For how I teased you when we were little, and . . ."

"And . . . ?" I prompted, waiting.

"And for not defending you when Devon was a jerk. Until now."

"Until now," I repeated. I walked to the edge of the water and dug beneath one of the little bubbling holes in the sand to scoop out the crab I knew would be hiding there.

"Buried treasure," Miguel said beside me.

I nodded. "They live in wet sand. Did you know, they can only crawl backward?" I lifted the quarter-sized gray-and-white crab to my eyes and studied it through my magnifying glass. "They stick their head and antennae out of the sand when a wave breaks over them, to feel what's around them. Then they pop out a second set of antennae and use them to pick up plankton for food."

"Huh." Miguel held out his hand, and I set the crab carefully on his palm. "Looks like it's wearing armor," he said.

"Exoskeleton. Remember biology? It's like armor."

I wished *I* had an exoskeleton. Maybe then Devon's insults wouldn't hurt so badly.

I stood up and brushed sand off my legs. "Scientists are studying the way sand crabs use their tails and legs to burrow." I looked out at the ocean instead of at Miguel. "They're trying to build a robot that can burrow into the ground and tell whether soil is healthy or not."

"Wow," he said. "Hey, can I borrow your magnifying glass a sec?"

I pulled the chain over my neck and handed it to him. He held it up to one eye and peered at the crab on his palm. "It's got eye stalks like a snail."

I couldn't tell if he was really interested, or if he was just being nice because my brother was helping him. But when he set the crab down, he dug it a hole first, then buried it carefully in wet sand. "Know what, Daisy?" He handed me my magnifying glass. "You're pretty cool."

I flushed from my bare toes to the top of my head. "Um... thanks," I mumbled. "I better go check on Squirrel."

My brother and Tía Tammy stood by the pier. "Check out these pictures!" she said, and held her camera out to me.

I looked at the images of Squirrel leaning against the pier, wading in the ocean, and sitting on the sand. He looked every bit as professional as Madeline Stuart.

Miguel's aunt fished a piece of paper out of her backpack. "Model release." She gave it to Squirrel. "I just need your parents' signatures. You can take a picture of it and email it back to me. I'll send you a couple of pictures, and you can use them for whatever you want. Write down your email for me?"

Squirrel handed me the model release. I'd have to forge their signatures—something I'd never even attempted. I slipped the piece of paper into my backpack.

"I don't like email," Squirrel told Tía Tammy. "Can you text the pictures to my phone?"

"I can send you thumbnails," she replied. "How 'bout I send your sister the high-res images, and she can download them for you?"

I gave her my email address. Miguel and Squirrel headed for the playground and tossed around a dog-chewed yellow Frisbee. Tía Tammy shrugged off her fleece jacket. Tattoos of women's faces and rainbow-striped flags covered her arms. She had three silver hoops in each ear... seriously fashionable.

I cleared my throat. "Um... do you know how someone might go about becoming a YouTube celebrity?" I asked her.

Her eyebrows shot up. "Wow. Well, some of it's luck, I guess.

And probably, some of it's who you know, like if you're friends with someone on social media who has a bunch of followers and promotes your channel." She zipped her camera into its case and folded up the light reflectors. "I mean, I know you've gotta come up with something original to grab people's attention."

"A shtick," I said.

"Exactly," she replied. "So what are you going to talk about?"

"Oh, not me." I held my hands up and shook my head. "I don't want to be on camera. That's my brother's dream."

"Huh." Tía Tammy thought about that. "Maybe he could make videos for Miguel's fundraising campaign. I'll bet he'd get tons of attention."

She was right. If Squirrel made videos for Save Summer Games, he could get a bunch of followers, plus help Miguel raise $10,000. And then he could take all his followers over to Young Spice Squirrel Advice.

My phone chimed in my back pocket. I pulled it out and read the text. "My parents," I said. "We've got to get home."

Tía Tammy nodded. "Let me take a quick picture of you and Miguel, since you're here. Hashtag Besties!"

"I'm not really photogenic," I began, "and Miguel and I aren't . . ."

"Nonsense." She waved him over from the playground. "Pose against the pier, where Squirrel was standing," she told us.

Miguel sighed dramatically and pulled me over to the pier. "She's always taking pictures of us. Resistance is futile."

I grimaced into the camera as Tía Tammy fired off shots. I just knew I'd come out looking like a giant housefly. Finally, she put her camera down. "You two are adorbs. Daisy, tell your parents thanks for letting me keep you a little longer this morning."

"No problem," I mumbled, because *problem* didn't begin to describe what would happen if Dad found out what Squirrel and I had been doing on the beach that morning. It would be more like a *catastrophe*.

I called my brother over. He wrapped his arms around Tía Tammy, and then Miguel. "I had fun!" he said. "Thank you!"

"Anytime, bro. I like hanging out with you." Miguel hugged Squirrel, then took a step toward me.

For an instant, I froze, and then I grabbed Squirrel's arm. "Okay, well, bye!" I called, and jogged away fast, before Miguel could get any ideas about hugging me.

16

Squirrel and I kicked off our sandy shoes on our porch and pushed through the front door. The house smelled like onions and bell peppers and potatoes fried with herbs from Dad's garden. "He's making his famous Killer Spuds!" I said.

Squirrel patted his stomach. "He hasn't made them in *so long*," he said. "C'mon!"

We rushed into the kitchen, where Dad was stirring up biscuit dough in his Kiss the Cook apron and bopping around to music on his headphones. Outside, Mom set the picnic table with place mats and a jar of her homemade strawberry jam. Red and yellow roses from our bushes bloomed in a vase in the middle of the table. I stepped onto the back porch. "What's going on?" I asked her.

Mom gathered her hair into a ponytail and straightened her pink Poop Fairies tank top. "Dad and I have to work all next weekend, so he thought he'd cook Sunday brunch, and maybe we could all hike Lone Pine afterward. We haven't eaten out on the patio in so long. It's fun to have a few minutes to make it look pretty."

She glanced at my sandy ankles. "Did you two go to the beach? How on earth did you get Squirrel up so early?"

I bent and brushed the sand into the grass so she couldn't see my face. "He was awake," I said.

"I'm surprised." She lit two of the hand-dipped candles I'd

made in school last year, their ends jammed into soda bottles. "He's been so depressed, poor guy."

Squirrel appeared in the doorway looking anything but depressed. He'd slicked back his hair with gel, and I could practically see the fumes rising up from his aftershaved cheeks. His face glowed pink and smooth. "Today is a great day!" he cried, and threw out his arms.

Dad walked up behind him balancing a bowl of scrambled eggs. "Oh, yeah? Why's that?"

"It's great because we got up early and walked on the beach," I said before Squirrel could tell him about the photo shoot. "The early bird gets the sand crab."

My brother's phone chimed, and he looked down at it, then held it out to me.

"It's a text from Tía Tammy," he said.

"Aunt . . . Tammy?" Mom cocked her head and bunched her eyebrows together.

Dad set down the bowl of eggs and looked at her. "Do the kids have a Tía Tammy?"

I froze. And then I grabbed Squirrel's hand and pulled him into the living room. "Tía Tammy and her pictures are a secret, remember?" I hissed in his ear.

"But I want Mama and Daddy to see them." He showed me a thumbnail of him posing against the pier. "I look gorgeous!"

"Not yet," I pleaded. Out back, Mom and Dad stood with their heads together, talking and looking into the house. "Give me your phone until after brunch, okay?"

"Okay, sister." He surrendered his phone. I turned the ringer to silent, and we walked back outside to the patio.

The yard smelled like lemons from our trees and biscuits

from the basket Dad brought to the table. Sun replaced the early morning fog. I pulled off my sweatshirt and adjusted the overhead umbrella so it shaded all four chairs. "Killer Spuds, Daisy?" Dad passed me the bowl. "I made a double batch, thinking you were out on a run and might be starving."

I took a huge serving of potatoes and passed the bowl to Mom. "So who's Tía Tammy?" she asked, pointing the big silver serving spoon at Squirrel.

He gulped audibly and looked at me. Under the table, I stepped on his foot. "She's just this woman we met on the beach this morning." I scooped eggs onto my plate. "There were so many crabs out there. I'm gonna call the aquarium and find out if there's more than usual."

"But why would a stranger refer to herself as your aunt?" Mom persisted. "And why is she calling Squirrel?"

"How'd she get his number?" Dad raised a suspicious eyebrow.

I clenched my jaw and stared down at my potatoes. It was all over: Miguel's project, my project, Squirrel's celebrity . . . we were washed up.

And then, Squirrel saved us.

"Tía Tammy is my friend's aunt," he said with a big fake smile. "I gave her my number. Uh . . . yard work. She needs yard work." Under the table, he stepped on my foot.

He was a terrible liar. Our parents looked at each other, and then at him. "You already have a job and school," Mom said.

"I don't want you taking on any more work," Dad added. "Not with a full load of high school classes."

They believe him.

Maybe that was one of the perks of being truthful all the time. If you never told a lie, then when you did, people bought it.

Squirrel took a huge bite of his biscuit. "Okay, Daddy," he said through a mouthful. "I won't take the job." He curled his fingers into a heart shape and winked at me. I practically choked on my potatoes.

"Why're you working next weekend?" I asked Mom and Dad when I could talk again. I pretended to be disappointed, but not too disappointed. With our parents out of the house, Squirrel and I could make videos for Save Summer Games. That is, if Miguel thought it was a good idea too.

Mom explained. "We landed a contract from a production company that's in town to shoot a movie. Some of the actors and crew have dogs, so the company hired Dad and me to walk them."

"And pick up their poop," I groaned.

"Never thought I'd have a job picking up Alina Petrov's poodle poop." Dad forked up a potato and waved it in the air. "She pays extraordinarily well for the privilege!"

"Alina Petrov?" Squirrel stared at him. "I *love* her. She gives fashion advice on YouTube!"

"She probably provides her own solid-gold poop bags," I told my parents.

"Her poodle probably *poops* solid gold." Dad grinned, and Squirrel snorted with laughter.

Mom held up her hand. "No poop talk at the table!" she begged, shaking her head and smiling. For an instant, we felt like a normal family again. But then, her phone rang in the kitchen, and she stood up to answer it. When she walked back out, a frown had replaced her smile.

"That was Melody Olson," she said. "She said her two Newfoundlands got into the trash last night, and threw up and had diarrhea all over the yard. She'll pay us double to do an emergency clean-up this morning before a party she's throwing tonight."

"What happened to 'no poop talk at the table'?" I said. "And what about our hike?"

Dad opened his mouth to tell Mom not to take the job—I could see it on his face.

Tears welled up in her eyes. "We need the money," she said in a small voice.

Money. Always money.

"Go," I told her, stuffing my disappointment down into the pit of my stomach. "Squirrel and I will clean up the kitchen. No worries."

"Thank you, both," Mom said, blinking hard. She brushed tears out of her eyes and walked back into the house to call the dogs' owner back. Her head hung low, and her shoulders slumped.

Dad cleared his throat. "Sorry about that, kiddos."

Squirrel shrugged. "That's okay. I hate hiking!" He finished his biscuit and reached for another.

"Seriously." I looked across the table. "It's no problem. BTW, Pops, these are the best spuds you've ever made."

Dad stood up and lay his palm against my cheek. His hand smelled like garlic and oregano. "You're a good kid, Daisy. The best." He picked up his plate and the egg bowl and walked into the house.

I looked after him and bit the tip of my tongue. I didn't even want to think about how many lies I'd already told my parents that morning, and how many more I was going to tell . . . right after I forged their signatures on Squirrel's model release.

Poppy texted while I was cleaning my cockroach terrarium.

What's up, woman??

I sent her a picture of my cockroaches crawling around on my desk. She sent a scared-face emoji. And then:

Devon told Kristen he saw you and Miguel on the beach this morning. She's totally freaking out!!!

Gossip. Kids in my class needed it like they needed air, food, and water. I texted Poppy again.

Coincidence. I was out for a walk.

My phone rang.

"Liar!" Poppy shouted. "Devon said a photographer was taking pictures of Squirrel. Come clean, woman!"

"Fine. But stop yelling!" I said. "Squirrel and I were helping Miguel with his social studies project. His aunt's gonna give us a picture for Squirrel's YouTube channel."

"No way," Poppy said. "You hung out with Rich Boy all morning?"

"Hey, it was *your* idea to make Squirrel the face of his

campaign." I set a dish of shredded carrots and lettuce in the cockroach terrarium. Gregor and Samsa immediately crawled over and started investigating with their long black antennae. My mother had named them after some character in her favorite novel—this guy called Gregor Samsa who wakes up to find that he's become a giant insect.

"Tell me you didn't hang out with Devon," Poppy groaned.

"Ick!" I said. "Of course not."

"But he was there."

"For about a minute," I said. "And then he and Miguel had a fight, and he left. Hey, did you know Alina Petrov's coming to town to make a movie?"

Silence. And then, Poppy screamed. "Alina Petrov's coming here?! To our city?!"

"Yep." I put the phone on speaker and set it on my desk.

"Why aren't you excited?" she shrieked. "Oh my god! She was the lead in *Beetle Boy*, remember?"

"You tricked me into seeing that movie," I reminded her. "It wasn't about beetles at all."

"Whatever, Daisy." I could practically see Poppy hopping around her bedroom decorated with all her running trophies and strings of purple lights. "Alina Petrov's amazing! And she's gonna be here! Wait. When?"

"Next weekend," I said.

Her fingers clacked across her laptop keys. "OMG, you're right! We've got to go see her!"

"I have plans." I looked around my room, thinking about where to position Squirrel for the Summer Games videos.

"What plans would keep you from meeting Alina Petrov?" Poppy demanded.

I barely heard her. I'd borrow Dad's photography lights and a reflector umbrella, and mount one of his cameras on a tripod like he'd taught me when I made a video about my cockroaches for the science fair. While he and Mom were gone, I'd turn my bedroom into a movie studio.

"So you're coming to the movie set?" Poppy asked me.

"Uh-huh."

"Daisy! Are you even listening to me?"

"Uh-huh."

"Did you tell Miguel about your Change the World project?" Poppy said suddenly.

"Of course not," I said. "The fewer people who know, the better."

But it wasn't just that. What if he made fun of my project? It was one thing to save Summer Games. Turning my brother into a YouTube fashion celebrity was a different story. What if Miguel thought my project was ridiculous?

Still, before next weekend—Filmmaking Weekend—I'd have to tell him.

17

"Whoa. Your parents let you have insects in your *room*?" The weekend after his aunt took Squirrel's photos, Miguel walked into my bedroom and headed straight for my cockroaches. Right away, I saw that I shouldn't have stayed up half the night worrying about what he'd think of my shelves full of terrariums, or my posters of magnified fly eyes and thirty different species of beetles.

"These are so cool!" He bent down and peered through the glass, checking out the three-inch cockroaches with their gleaming black and brown shells. "What are they?"

"Madagascar hissing cockroaches." I knelt down next to him. "They're eighteen months old. That one's Gregor, and that's Samsa."

"Hissing cockroaches?" Miguel turned to me with his eyes wide. "For real?"

"They hiss if they're threatened," I explained. "They've got these little breathing holes called spiracles, and when they force air out, it makes a hissing sound. Want to hold one?"

I thought he'd say no. Poppy refused to get within three feet of my cockroaches. But Miguel held out his cupped hands. "Sure!" he said.

I reached into the terrarium. "I'll let you hold Gregor. He's the one with a bent antenna. He's a little calmer than Samsa."

I set the cockroach in his hands. Gregor sat still, letting us admire his shiny brown-and-black carapace. Miguel laughed. "Its legs tickle. But it's pretty cool."

"*He's* cool," I corrected him. "This is why I want to be an entomologist."

Miguel stroked Gregor's back with one finger. "That's great that you already know what career you want. I have no idea."

Squirrel appeared in the doorway. He wore last year's blue-and-white Summer Games T-shirt. He'd styled his hair and shaved. "I'm ready to be famous," he cooed, and batted his eyelashes.

Miguel handed Gregor back to me and fist-bumped Squirrel. "Looking good, man."

"I try." He patted the top of his styled hair. "Where's Ricky?"

"Shooting hoops with neighbors at the park," Miguel said. "You should join them."

"But not now," I said. "We've got to film."

Mom and Dad had told me they'd be Poop Fairying on Alina Petrov's movie set until dark. Still, anything might happen. What if they ran out of poop bags and came home? Dad's camera sat on a tripod across from my desk chair. I'd set up his studio lights and umbrella with my bulletin board in the background, covered with Squirrel's Special Olympics medals and programs from Summer Games.

"Nice." Miguel nodded, approving the scene. "So you said on the phone we'd do three short videos about Summer Games and post them on our YouTube so people could donate, right?"

"*Our* YouTube?" I repeated.

"Sure! You're helping me, right?"

"Right," I said. "Hopefully, people will follow Squirrel over to his own YouTube channel."

"It's Young Spice Squirrel Advice," my brother told Miguel. "I'm gonna be a fashion celebrity!"

"Cool!" Miguel said.

"That's . . . that's sort of my project for Coach Lipinsky's class," I heard myself admit. "I'm helping Squirrel with his channel."

"Great idea!" Miguel said. "Hey, Squirrel, I just heard a fashion tip. You can get wrinkles out of your clothes without ironing. Just throw 'em in the dryer with a couple of ice cubes."

Squirrel nodded, deadly serious. "And use a drop of lotion instead of gel so your hair doesn't get crispy."

"You know it, bro! Hey, and if one of your T-shirts shrinks? All you have to do is put it in a—"

I held up my hand. "People?" I prompted. "We have work to do."

"Oh. Yeah. I made a list of potential topics for Squirrel's videos." Miguel reached into his pocket and unfolded a square of paper. "Number one: What is Summer Games? Number two: Why is it important? Number three: What's Squirrel's favorite sport?"

Squirrel clapped his hands. "Basketball's my favorite! I can wear my jersey and show everyone LeBron's shoe!"

He ran out the door and pounded down the hall to his bedroom. "Um . . . LeBron's *shoe*?" Miguel shook his head.

"For real. LeBron James autographed a shoe for a Special Olympics raffle, and Squirrel won it."

"Size fifteen!" Squirrel held out a plastic case with an enormous basketball shoe inside. Miguel stared at it like Squirrel had just handed him a backpack full of gold.

"Cool," he breathed. "LeBron's the best."

"His shoe's the perfect prop," I said. "Let's tag LeBron on YouTube. Maybe he'll see it and donate to Save Summer Games."

"Smart." Miguel set the shoe on my desk. "In the first video, maybe you could tell people how sad you're gonna be if the games stay canceled. I mean, that is, if you *are* still sad. I don't want to bring up bad feelings."

Squirrel gazed at him. His face crumpled, and he fell down across my bed. "I'm so sad!" he cried. "Boohoohoo!"

Miguel's eyes grew wide. "I'm sorry," he whispered to me. "I didn't mean to make him cry."

Squirrel leapt to his feet. "Fooled you!" He socked Miguel in the arm.

Miguel blinked. He shook his head like a wet dog. And then, he burst out laughing. "You're an amazing actor, Squirrel!" he said. "You totally had me fooled."

My brother beamed. I rolled my eyes. "Can we get started already?"

I sat Squirrel in my desk chair in front of the bulletin board and adjusted the lights and the umbrella to smooth out the shadows on his face the way I'd seen Dad do at the Moonlight Ball. "Sit there," I told Miguel, and pointed to the head of the bed next to my stick insect terrarium.

"Whoa . . ." He looked at the skinny green insects perched on branches. "Those are cool!"

"Shh!" I crouched in front of Dad's camera. "Hitting record in three, two, one. Squirrel, tell us about Summer Games."

I knew my brother was a pro at modeling. But I wasn't sure how he'd do in front of a video camera. What if he froze up, went silent, or mumbled so we couldn't understand him?

Instead, he looked into the lens and chatted away like he'd been making videos his whole life.

"Summer Games gives me and my friends a chance to compete," he explained. "We play basketball, baseball, and badminton. We do swimming and bowling and track and field."

Behind the camera, I gave him a thumbs-up. He bent toward me slightly and furrowed his forehead. "Without Summer Games," he said slowly, "my friends and me will be so sad. We need them. Can you help us?"

He paused a moment and stared into the lens like he was looking straight into the eyes of millions of YouTube viewers.

"Cut," I said softly, and stopped recording.

"Dude!" Miguel gazed at him with my stuffed toy tarantula pressed to his chest. "That was incredible."

Squirrel beamed. "I know. I've been practicing!"

I reviewed the recording on Dad's camera. "This is gonna get thousands of views!" I cried.

Miguel tossed the tarantula into the air and caught it on top of his head. "Hey, after we make these videos, maybe I can help with the ones for your fashion channel," he said.

"Yes!" Squirrel pumped his fist in the air. "We're partners!"

I twisted my fingers together. The silver scarab ring I'd slipped on that morning cut into my pinky. "I guess," I said slowly, "but you can't tell anyone about my project. For now, it's gotta be a secret—I mean, a surprise."

My phone buzzed. Poppy.

Downtown looking for Alina with my sisters.

WHERE R U???

I texted back.

B there soon!

Miguel and Squirrel and I filmed two more videos. When we were finished, I turned off the camera and collapsed Dad's umbrella and lights. "Help me put these back in his office," I told Squirrel.

Miguel followed us downstairs with the tripod, and I put all the gear back in Dad's closet. "I'd better head downtown," I said. "Poppy wants me to meet this actress who's making a movie. She's over on Main Street. It's all blocked off because they're filming today."

I didn't add that our parents were there as Celebrity Poop Scoopers.

Miguel smoothed back his ponytail. "Alina Petrov, right?" he said.

Squirrel pretended to swoon over the stair railing. "I love Alina," he said. "She's got the best fashion tips. She showed me how to pluck my eyebrows!"

"They looked like inchworms when you got done," I teased him.

Miguel laughed. "I saw Alina in *Beetle Boy*. I'll come too. It's fun hanging out with you."

I couldn't tell if he was talking about me or Squirrel. "You don't have to," I said. "I mean, there's thousands of people down there." I pictured the look on Poppy's face if I showed up downtown with Miguel. "It's a mess. We probably won't even see Alina." Knowing my luck, we'd see the Poop Fairies going about their business, instead. Correction: going about Alina Petrov's *poodle's* business.

Miguel shrugged. "I don't care. Let's check out the scene. You're coming, right, Squirrel?"

My brother checked his hair in the hallway mirror. "You bet! After I meet Alina, let's get ice cream! I got paid yesterday."

"What's your job?" Miguel asked.

"I'm a janitor at my school." Squirrel giggled. "I make the toilets all sparkly!"

"Nice!" Miguel said. "What's brown and sits on a piano bench?"

"What?" Squirrel asked. He loved a good joke.

Miguel cleared his throat. "Beethoven's last movement."

At first, Squirrel didn't get it. But when I explained the punchline, he fell on the ground laughing. "Beethoven's last movement!" he howled.

"That joke's the best," Miguel agreed.

"Boys," I muttered.

Hasenpfeffer hopped out and stood up on his hind legs and put his white front paws on Squirrel's knee. "Um . . . shouldn't that be in a cage?" Miguel asked us with his eyes gone wide again.

"He's litter box trained." I reached for a banana from the fruit bowl on the table and gave Hasenpfeffer a piece. He snatched it from my fingers and scampered off under the coffee table. "He can stay out as long as the power cords are up," I explained. "He chewed up some when we first got him, so we put them up high and gave him pieces of wood to chew on instead."

Miguel whistled. "Cockroaches *and* a litter box–trained rabbit? Cool!"

"Don't you have pets?" I asked him.

He shook his head. "My mom's allergic. She'd flip if I asked for a cockroach. She's . . . well, you know all those fancy home magazines they sell at the market? Our house is like that."

"Must be hard being rich," I observed.

Miguel shook his head. "We're not rich. My mom's just obsessed with thrifting."

"For real?" I asked, but before he could explain further, Squirrel grabbed our hands and pulled us out the front door. We walked down the street together and headed for the road that led downtown. On the way, we talked about how to turn Squirrel into a YouTube celebrity.

"You're great on camera," Miguel said. "People just need to find out about you. You could do a whole bunch of videos about how the athletes train for the Games all year—stuff like what you eat to stay in shape, how you balance school and work and exercise—"

"And fashion!" Squirrel reminded him.

"Young Spice Squirrel Advice. I remember." Miguel bumped me with his shoulder. "You're gonna get an A+ on your project."

I should've been flattered, but I wasn't. Because no matter how hard we all worked on Squirrel's channel, I was going to flunk the oral report part of Coach Lipinsky's assignment. There was no way in H-E-double-hockey-sticks that I could survive speaking up in front of Devon.

Otherwise known as Miguel's best friend.

18

Downtown, Miguel and Squirrel and I waded through a sea of people on Main Street. They crowded together on the sidewalks and in the street, trying to get a glimpse of Alina Petrov.

"There's Kristen and some of the girls from track." Miguel pointed. "And our principal!"

I spotted one of the librarians from the teen section, and a cashier from the grocery store. Everybody talked at once, yelling and bumping into orange traffic cones and white cement barriers. I didn't see my parents anywhere.

"Any sign of Alina?" I asked. But Miguel was my height, which is to say, vertically challenged.

He shook his head. Squirrel headed for the ice cream shop next to the movie theater.

"I can't lose him!" I grabbed Miguel's hand and pulled him through the crowd toward my brother. Just then, a figure stepped in front of us and stopped, blocking our path. *Poppy.*

Her eyes went from me to Miguel, and her mouth fell open. She looked just like Devon when he saw us on the morning of Squirrel's photo shoot at the beach.

"*He's* why you couldn't meet me downtown this morning?" she demanded.

I dropped Miguel's hand and folded my arms across my chest. "We were working on his project videos with Squirrel."

Poppy's ponytail swished, and all her little curls bounced like angry snakes. "Where is Squirrel? He should meet Alina Petrov. She's about to go on break."

I turned toward the ice cream shop, but Squirrel had disappeared. Poppy climbed up onto a low wall. "There he is!" she shouted, and jumped off onto the sidewalk. "Follow me!"

We got to a fenced-off area just in time to see a security guard waving my brother through a gate. A few feet away, Alina sat like a queen in a canvas folding chair, barefoot in ripped skinny jeans. Her toenails glowed a deep red. A white poodle sat beside her. She beckoned with her finger for Squirrel to come closer, and they shook hands.

Poppy and I watched as Alina Petrov leaned in close to hear something he was telling her. She laughed, and even from where I stood, I could see that her teeth were incredibly white and her hair was incredibly shiny. She said something in Squirrel's ear and handed him a little piece of paper. Then she kissed him on the cheek.

"Next!" the security guard yelled.

"Over here!" Poppy cried, hopping up and down and waving. Squirrel walked toward us with his cheeks bright pink. "I can't believe she kissed you!" Poppy crowed. "Angelina who?"

Squirrel's hand flew to his cheek. "She kissed me!" He giggled. "She said I'm cute!"

"Let's go get that ice cream," I told him. In the shop, we'd be less likely to run into our parents and their poop bags.

"I'll come too," Poppy said. "I've got babysitting money."

"Miguel's gonna be there . . ." I began, but she was already five feet in front of me, pushing through the crowd. And Miguel had disappeared.

The woman behind the counter looked up as we walked into the shop. Her eyes stopped on Squirrel. "Haven't I seen you somewhere?" She cocked her head, and one of her cow-shaped earrings grazed her shoulder. "You're a model, right?"

Squirrel turned to me, confused. "Am I?"

"Totally!" The woman held out her phone.

I looked down at an Instagram picture—Tía Tammy's photo of my brother leaning against a pier piling, gazing out toward the ocean.

Poppy hovered over my shoulder, so close that her curls tickled my cheek. "Hashtag SaveSummerGames," she read. "He's got a hundred fifty-two likes already?"

A fist clenched my stomach, squeezing my guts. Miguel never told me he was going to put Squirrel on Instagram. My *parents* used Instagram to build up their business.

"That's amazing!" Poppy cried, so that people sitting around us looked up and stared.

Squirrel high-fived her. "I'm famous!"

"Oh no," I groaned, and clutched my stomach.

There's an insect—the bombardier beetle—that shoots a boiling, stinging mixture of chemicals out of its abdomen when it's upset. That beetle had nothing on my parents if they saw Squirrel's photo on Instagram.

"This is Sorrel Woodward, the face of Save Summer Games," Poppy was explaining to the woman behind the counter.

"Right on!" She handed Squirrel a double scoop of chocolate fudge brownie. "On the house, sweetheart. Where do I donate?"

"SaveSummerGames.com," Squirrel recited, just as he had in the videos.

Poppy ordered a scoop of coffee chocolate chip. "Anything for you?" the woman behind the counter asked.

"I'll buy." Poppy waved a ten-dollar bill in the air.

My stomach churned, empty as a washed-up clamshell. "Mint Oreo," I mumbled. "In a waffle cone."

Might as well go big, I thought. It was probably the last ice cream I'd ever eat, because when my parents realized what I'd done, they were going to ground me for life.

As we turned away from the counter, Poppy frowned at me. "What's the problem with Instagram?" she demanded. "I mean, Squirrel's gonna be on YouTube, right?"

"My parents don't use YouTube. But they're on Instagram constantly. I've got to make Miguel delete that photo before they see it!"

Poppy licked her cone. "Don't do it. Squirrel deserves a chance. Hey, I'm gonna get back in line for another autograph. Maybe this time, Alina will kiss *me* too!" She grinned. "You coming?"

I shook my head. "I've gotta find Miguel."

She shrugged. "Suit yourself. Text you later." She walked out the door and disappeared into the crowd with her ice cream.

On the walk home, I swore Squirrel to secrecy. "You can't tell Mom and Dad about Instagram. Promise!"

"Why not?" He jogged beside me, his chin smeared with chocolate ice cream. "I want to tell them I'm a model!"

I handed him a napkin. "Squirrel. Remember the last time your picture was on Instagram?"

"People wrote mean things about me. I cried." He sniffed dramatically, then giggled. "Miguel said they're the losers 'cause they don't know I'm gonna be famous like Stephen Ming."

"Still, if Mom and Dad find out about your picture, *they're* gonna cry!" I reminded him.

"They won't," he argued. "No one's written mean things."

Not yet, I thought. Out loud, I said, "Let's just keep it to ourselves, okay?"

"Okay, sister." He pressed a finger to his lips. "My lips are sealed."

We walked into the house. Up in my bedroom with the door closed tight, I didn't waste time texting Miguel. I called him.

"Oh. Hey, Daisy," he answered. "Sorry I lost you downtown. Way too crowded. I had to get out of there."

"Who said you could put Squirrel's picture on Instagram?" I gripped my phone in sweaty fingers.

For a moment, Miguel didn't say anything. I heard music in the background, the *Hamilton* soundtrack.

"This *is* Daisy . . . right?" Miguel asked.

I heaved an enormous sigh. "Why is my brother on Instagram?" I said, practically yelling.

Miguel made a sound between a cough and a snort. "Amnesia much? My tía drove up from L.A. to take his picture for our project, remember? It's on Instagram and Facebook."

"*Facebook?*" I slapped my palm against my forehead. The Poop Fairies had a Facebook page. Dad posted photos to it every weekend.

"What's the big deal?" Miguel asked.

Outside, a dog barked. No, not a dog. A dog *horn*. My parents' bright yellow pickup pulled into the driveway.

"Meet me at the pier in fifteen minutes," I hissed into the phone.

"Um . . . okay," Miguel said. "Is this . . . is this a date?"

A date? I stared at my cockroaches. They stared back at me, looking equally shocked. What did it mean that Miguel thought I was asking him out on a date? And what did it mean that he'd told me "okay"?

"It's not a date!" I said with my face on fire. "Just meet me there!"

I hung up and pulled on a sweatshirt. Mom and Dad met me on the front porch as I was shoving my feet into running shoes. "Hi!" I cried, fake-cheerful so they wouldn't get suspicious. I looked away from their glittery T-shirts and rubber boots. Almost everyone I knew had been downtown that day. Which meant almost everyone I knew had seen them picking up Alina Petrov's poodle's poop.

"Going for a jog?" Dad patted the top of my head. I squirmed away, not wanting to think about where his hand had been an hour earlier.

"Yep!" I replied. "Just a quick three-miler."

Mom kissed my forehead. Her lips felt warm and sticky with lip balm. "How was your day, sweetie? How's Squirrel?"

"Good. He's in his room listening to Michael Jackson," I said. "We took the lentil soup out of the freezer and put it in the Crock-Pot. Salad's in the fridge."

"You're amazing." Mom pulled off her boots and rolled her head around on her neck. Something—bones or tendons or ligaments—popped. "Wow, I need a shower."

"Me too." Dad put his arms around me. "I tell you, there's nothing like picking up poop all day, then coming back to homemade soup!"

"You're right," I muttered. "There's nothing like that. Back in half an hour."

I pulled out of his grasp and jumped off the porch, then sprinted down the street. I had half an hour before my parents finished showering and sat down to check their phones. Half an hour to persuade Miguel to delete Squirrel's photo. If he refused, I'd have to steal his phone and do it for him.

19

Miguel met me at the pier in running shoes, shorts, and a sweatshirt.

"Wanna go for a jog?" he asked like I hadn't just yelled at him over the phone. "I didn't get a workout today. Had to babysit my sister when I got home." He held out a pack of gum.

I ignored it. "Why didn't you tell me you were putting Squirrel's picture on Instagram and Facebook?"

"It's on TikTok too," he said.

"No!" I howled. A flock of seagulls on the sand beside us took off squawking. "You told me you were putting his picture on your *website*. You can't put him on social media!"

He stared. "What do you think YouTube is?"

"That's different!" I pressed my palms against the sides of my head and squeezed my eyes shut.

"Daisy. Whoa. You need to chill out. Let's run." He turned and began to jog toward Surfer's Point.

"*I* need to chill out?" I yelped, but I fell into step beside him. I had to. Otherwise, I'd never convince him to delete Squirrel's picture from Instagram and Facebook and TikTok, and probably Snapchat too.

We jogged in silence, warming up as the setting sun sank toward the ocean. The air smelled like coconut sunscreen and sweat from people walking and wobbling all over the path on those ridiculous four-wheeled bike surreys.

"Please delete his picture," I begged Miguel when we reached Surfer's Point. All around us, people in wetsuits stood on the sand watching surfers catch waves. They hung out in the backs of their trucks and vans, talking and eating. Music—Tejano, pop, eighties, rap—blasted from phones and car radios. "Can you do it right now?" I asked.

Miguel shook his head. "Are you crazy? He's up to two hundred sixty Instagram likes. People are donating to Save Summer Games because of him."

"Too bad," I said.

Miguel spoke slowly, like I was three instead of thirteen. "Our plan includes a website and social media to drive viewers to our website with a donation button. You never told me I couldn't put Squirrel on Instagram."

"It's not *our* plan! You keep saying '*our* project,' and '*our* fundraiser,' but it's yours—not mine!"

He stepped backward. "Whoa," he said again. "Sorry. I should have asked before I put his photo out there."

"You should've." I ducked my head, feeling like the lowliest of woodworms. "But you're right," I said. "I never told you *not* to put Squirrel on social media."

He didn't say anything. He just looked at me with a confused expression. I thought about how we'd talked all the way downtown that day, and how we'd laughed with Squirrel in my bedroom. We were practically strangers. Still, sadness washed over me. I'd blown any chance of a friendship with Miguel. Any second, he'd turn and sprint back toward his mansion or wherever he lived, leaving me alone in the sand.

But he didn't run away. "Let's keep jogging," he told me. "I'm getting cold."

We ran up the path along the river. Fog drifted in off the ocean, turning the fairground streetlights to gold. The smell of horse manure rose up from the stables, thick and grassy. We passed the RV campground and stopped at the water fountain to drink.

"C'mon." Miguel started across the sand to an empty blue-and-white lifeguard stand. I followed. I climbed up the ladder after him, gripping the cold metal rungs, and sat down against the rough wall with my legs stretched out. My mouth felt dry and stale. I wished I'd gulped more water at the fountain.

"I'll take that piece of gum now," I mumbled.

Miguel reached into his pocket and held out the pack. The smell of mint rose up around us, mingling with the scents of dead fish and drying kelp. "So why don't you want Squirrel on social media?" he asked, and his voice was kind and curious.

I stared out at the ocean. "My parents don't want him exposed to haters."

"Haters? Have you seen the comments? People are talking about how cool he looks."

"Doesn't matter. Remember when that actor with Down syndrome, Zack Gottsagen, spoke onstage at the Academy Awards? The guy from *Peanut Butter Falcon*? People were jerks. They said things about Zack on Twitter that you wouldn't believe."

And then, I told him about #EligibleBachelor. "People wrote under Squirrel's Instagram picture that he'd never get a date. One person called him Shrek. Someone else wrote that he was about as eligible as Groot."

"From *Guardians of the Galaxy*?" Miguel rolled his eyes. "The alien that looks like a plant? That's just stupid."

I nodded. "Yeah, but it wrecked Squirrel. If you're gonna keep doing social media, you've got to find a new face for your campaign."

He threw up his hands. "But people make comments on YouTube all the time!"

I shrugged. "My parents don't use YouTube. They'll never see our videos."

Miguel dropped his head into his hands. "I don't get it, Daisy. Your brother wants to be a celebrity. Why deny him?" He pulled out his phone and typed something into his browser. "Look, show your parents this documentary. Ricky's obsessed with it. It's about a famous swimmer who has Down syndrome . . . Karen someone."

He passed the phone to me. I looked down at a picture of a woman with short blond hair and a high-necked wet suit. "Karen Gaffney," I read.

"She swam across Lake Tahoe. Ricky's watched her movie about a million times. He's totally in love." He nudged my knee with his. "If Karen Gaffney can swim across Tahoe, Squirrel can be a YouTube fashion star. Your parents need to get with the program."

I tucked my knees up to my chest and wrapped my arms around them. "I'm telling you, they'll disown us. They'll send us to military school . . . or a convent."

"Oh, get real." Miguel raised his voice slightly. "They're not seeing him for who he really is. They're standing in the way of his dreams. That's *so* not cool."

"Agreed," I said. "But what can I do?"

"Stand up for him!"

Out over the ocean, the sun sank into a crimson pool. I

thought about how Squirrel had sparkled with excitement at the ice cream shop earlier that day. He'd autographed a napkin for the woman behind the counter who'd pinned it up on the wall, and he'd strutted home like the sidewalk was a fashion show runway.

Miguel was right. Squirrel deserved to be happy. But standing up for him, instead of going behind our parents' back, felt absolutely terrifying.

I stretched out my legs again and studied my sad, flat running shoes next to Miguel's still new-looking ones. Maybe he was rich, but he really cared about my brother. "I have your back," he told me. "And Squirrel's."

"Okay," I sighed at last. "You can leave the photos up. I mean, they're gonna help you change the world. And maybe . . . well, maybe my parents won't see them."

There was something else too . . . something I hated to admit, but I couldn't ignore.

I wanted Miguel to admire me.

More than that, I wanted him to like me. As Poppy would say, *like me* like me.

Romance was ridiculous. If a kissing scene came on during Pizza-Movie Night, I groaned and closed my eyes, or left the room. But my heart was betraying me up here on the lifeguard stand. Miguel's running shoe bumped mine, and heat rushed to my face.

I climbed down the metal ladder, fast. "I better get home for dinner," I said.

Miguel climbed down after me, and we jogged back past Surfer's Point, under the pier, and toward the road that led to our houses. "Race you up the hill," he said.

The light turned green, and we took off sprinting. Drivers sped past us, honking their horns. One guy cheered. My heart began to pound, and my lungs ached, the thump and burn erasing everything in my brain except air and speed.

I loved that feeling.

Miguel won the race, but only by a foot. "Dang . . . you're fast," he panted, bent double.

"I'd be faster if I had those." I nodded at his shoes.

His cheeks flushed redder than they already were. "I guess I can be pretty obnoxious about my kicks."

"Uh-huh."

"It's just . . ." He looked at me, and his face was suddenly serious. "I worked so hard to earn the money for these shoes. All winter break, I babysat and mowed lawns and took care of our neighbor's cats and chickens."

I frowned. "Wait, your parents didn't buy them for you?"

He looked away from me. "They don't make that much money. I don't like to ask them for stuff, you know?"

"But . . . you always act like you're so wealthy," I said. "I mean, you're wearing a *Billabong* hoodie. And doesn't your family live near the racquet club?"

"Yeah, but our house is really small," he said. "My mom goes to yard sales and thrift stores on weekends, and she finds great stuff for just a few dollars. She found me these running shorts."

I glanced at his black-and-red shorts. I'd assumed he'd bought them at the expensive running store downtown. "So you're not rich."

He snorted. "Not even close."

"But Devon is."

"Oh yeah, his family's loaded." Miguel frowned down at

his shoes. "My house could fit in his living room. He's always telling me it's gross to wear yard sale clothes. He has no clue how much that hurts."

In my head, I heard Coach Lipinsky's voice: "When you assume, you make an ass out of U and me." I'd assumed Miguel was rich because he was proud of the shoes he'd worked hard to earn. And I'd assumed he was a jerk just because his best friend was. But now, I knew better.

At the top of the hill, with all the cars and trucks rushing past and the sky darkening over the trees, I realized something.

It wasn't Miguel who'd metamorphosed. It was me.

We started walking again. When we came to my street, Miguel stayed beside me. "Do your parents really have a business picking up dog poop?"

"They do," I admitted. "My mom lost her job when the Outdoor Store closed last year, so they had to get creative."

"That's creative." He fell silent a moment, then reached out and touched my arm. "Hey, don't tell Devon we're helping each other with our projects, okay?"

The happiness I'd felt at the top of the hill plummeted into the pit of my stomach and turned into shame. "Collaborating with Daisy Woodworm equals social life destruction," I muttered.

"No! That's not it at all! Devon's been asking me to help with his project, but I told him I was too busy. Then he asked if he could help with mine, so he could put his name on it too. That's just wrong."

"But it's okay if I help you?" I said.

"You've got your own project too."

"Hmm," I grunted, not convinced. I walked up to the Poop

Fairy pickup and braced my hands against one side to stretch my hamstrings. Miguel ran a finger over the hood ornament my father's artist friend had made for the truck—a yellow steel sculpture of a squatting dog.

"That's cool," he said.

I looked toward my house. Light shone behind the curtains. Through the screen door, I could hear the clank of pots and pans in the kitchen. I lowered my voice. "I won't tell Devon about your project, but you can't tell Poppy anything either, okay? I mean, she knows Squirrel and I are helping you, but—"

"She thinks I'm a spoiled rich jerk," he finished.

I winced, guilty. "Something like that."

The smell of frying garlic drifted through the screen door. I could see Dad setting the table. Mom carried the big blue soup pot over. I bit my lip and looked away. For thirteen years, I'd trusted them to know what was best for me and my brother.

But this time, they didn't know what was best. Miguel was right. We had to stand up for Squirrel. We had to help him find his voice.

"Soup's on," I told him. "Literally. Gotta go."

"Yup. My dad's making chili verde. I love that stuff." He stuck out his hand. "Thanks, partner." He drawled the words out like a cowboy.

"Partner," I echoed, and shook his hand. It felt warm and a little sweaty, and the touch of it sent a tingle through my body.

If anyone had told me a few weeks ago that I'd be shaking hands with Miguel Santos over *two* projects that might actually change the world, I would have called them crazier than an outhouse fly.

But now, we were partners.

Poppy came over after school on Monday so we could make a Facebook invitation for her dance concert. The people at the Buddhist temple across from the grocery store were letting her use their space for free, and she'd already sold a bunch of tickets to family members and her moms' and sisters' friends.

"I'll sell the rest to kids and their parents at school," she said and opened up her ancient, beat-up laptop on my dining room table. "All that's left is to figure out refreshments and decorations. Oh yeah, and we've gotta rehearse the dances, like, a million times."

My chest tightened with envy. Poppy's project was already a success, and it hadn't even happened yet. Meanwhile, Squirrel and I hadn't made a single video for Young Spice Squirrel Advice. We'd been busy helping Miguel with his project, and our parents hadn't worked weekends for almost a month, so we couldn't film anything.

"I'm gonna make a Facebook page to post pictures of rehearsals and what we're serving for refreshments and stuff," Poppy told me. She dug into her backpack and pulled out a round gold tin. "My sister made nankhatai. She's experimenting with different recipes before the show."

I reached for the tin. "I'll be her guinea pig." I loved the crunchy shortbread cookies spiced with cardamom—Poppy's oldest sister's specialty.

Poppy set the tin beside the laptop. "We need some Indian music to get us in the mood. OMG, Spotify's got a channel called 'Indian classical music for studying'!" She clicked play, and tabla drums and stringed instruments filled the room. She lifted her arms and moved them in an elegant snakelike movement.

I sighed. "Friend, you've got more grace in one finger than I have in my whole body."

She danced her finger like a caterpillar, and I laughed. We crunched nankhatai and chose photos of Poppy and her sisters and her moms in jewel-colored saris to post on the Facebook invitation.

I reached for another cookie. "You could also post pictures on TikTok and Instagram with a link to the Facebook invite."

Poppy socked me on the arm. "Whoa. When'd you go pro?" She dipped a cookie into her coffee. The sweet, spicy smell of cardamom rose into the air. Hasenpfeffer hopped over and stood on his hind legs. She handed him a piece of nankhatai, and he sat still for a moment, chewing and letting her scratch his head.

"Miguel's got a fundraising website for Summer Games," I told her.

"Hmm." She wrinkled up her nose. "It's probably a total joke, but we could look at it for ideas."

I'd seen his website. It wasn't a joke.

Poppy did a search, and Miguel's site popped up on the screen. "He's got Squirrel front and center on the home page! Check out the cartoon of the weight lifter showing how much money people have donated. Wait . . . *eleven hundred fifty-two dollars*! How'd he raise that much money so fast?"

"People love Squirrel's videos. But we need a lot more than that to save the Games."

She raised an eyebrow. "*We?* Don't tell me you're friends with Miguel Santos."

"You know I've been helping him a little with his project," I reminded her. "I mean, it's mostly to help Squirrel get YouTube followers."

"Right." She clicked on the "About Us" link. "Here's a bio of Miguel, and a picture of him with his arm around some tall kid—"

"That's his cousin Ricky."

Her eyebrow shot up again.

"What?" I rolled my eyes. "He's a Special Olympics athlete. I met him at the Moonlight Ball."

"I see," Poppy said. And then, she shrieked. "There's a picture of you . . . with Miguel!"

She jabbed her finger at the screen, pointing at the photo Tía Tammy had taken of us at the pier. We stood side by side, Miguel grinning and me not looking quite so much like an insect as I usually did in photos.

Seeing it, I remembered that morning—the cold ocean water, Squirrel's excitement, and Miguel examining the sand crab through my magnifying glass and telling off Devon.

"I didn't know he was putting that picture on the website," I said.

"He's done more than that. He's put your bio on his website! Listen to this: 'Daisy Woodward is a future entomologist and championship runner. Her brother, Squirrel, is the face of #SaveSummerGames. You can find him on YouTube at *Young Spice Squirrel Advice*!'"

Future entomologist? Championship runner? My heart did a tap dance in my chest.

Poppy kept reading. "You're not going to believe this, Daisy. He's listed you as co-chair of his fundraiser." She reached for her phone. "Just because you let him use Squirrel's photo, he thinks you're gonna help him with his whole project. I'm totally calling him."

"Don't," I said, and grabbed the phone away from her. I didn't love that he'd used my photo without my permission. I was going to have to tell him, but not in front of Poppy.

She peered into my face. "Daisy Woodward. Do you *like* him?"

"No!" I cried, but my cheeks flushed red.

She stared at me for a long minute. Her lips pressed together, so tightly they almost disappeared. Then, she pushed back from the table and turned off the music. "I cannot believe you like him!" She snatched her phone away from me. "He's such a jerk!"

I twisted my fingers together. "He's . . . *different* when he's not at school. I swear, he's not as obnoxious."

"Have you forgotten how he used to torture you?" Poppy demanded.

"That was a long time ago," I shot back. "Without Devon around, he's actually . . . nice."

"Once a jerk, always a jerk." She dropped her laptop into her backpack, zipped it shut, and headed for the hallway with her cookie tin. "I'm not gonna sit here and watch you get hurt by some spoiled-rich scumbag. I'm outta here."

"Wait!" I leapt up from the table and dug my fists into my hips, facing her. "Isn't this how changing the world works?

Martin Luther King, Gandhi, Ruth Bader Ginsburg . . . they all had help. What's the big deal? The more people collaborate, the better, right?"

"Oh, give it a rest." Poppy threw open the front door and walked straight into Squirrel.

"Poppy!" He wrapped his arms around her before she could escape.

"What's up, Squirrel?" she sighed. "How was school?"

"Good!" he exclaimed. "My friends saw me on their phones. I'm famous!"

"You sure are," she told him. "Today, social media. Tomorrow, *GQ*!"

He led her back into the hallway and kicked off his shoes and hung up his coat. "This weekend, me and my friends are gonna be in a commercial," he continued. He kissed me on the cheek in a blast of Old Spice, then picked up the piece of nankhatai I'd left next to the laptop and popped it into his mouth. "Any more cookies?"

Poppy handed him the gold tin. "Have a whole one," she said sweetly to Squirrel, ignoring me. "What commercial are you filming?"

Squirrel reached into his pocket and handed her a business card. "Alina gave this to me. Her friend's making the commercial. She told me to come to the college track on Saturday."

"Alina *Petrov*?" Poppy yelped. "OMG, Squirrel, you're on a first-name basis with Alina Petrov?"

I held out my hand for the business card and read it out loud. "Channel Islands Sports Drink. Sandra Johnson, President. Did you call this Sandra Johnson person?" I asked him.

Squirrel nodded. "She told me to bring all my friends. Even

Ricky's coming! He says he'll be in the commercial if I'm in it too."

"Ricky?" Poppy said.

"Miguel's cousin," I explained.

Poppy high-fived Squirrel. "Right on! OMG, what if Alina Petrov's there? Do they need volunteers?"

I spoke over her. "A *TV* commercial? Are you sure, Squirrel?"

"It's for a sports drink," he said. "I forgot to tell you."

I shook my head. "You can't be in a commercial. Mom and Dad will lose their marbles."

Poppy snorted. "Why? Sounds like Squirrel's already on YouTube and half a million social media sites."

"Mama and Daddy don't want me to be on TV?" My brother's eyes filled with tears. "They don't want me to be a celebrity?"

"It's not that—" I began.

"What is it?" The corners of his mouth turned down, and he slumped on a chair. "They don't think I'm handsome," he said. "No one does. Angelina said Billy is more good-looking than me."

"You're gorgeous!" I handed him another cookie. "Mom and Dad are just . . ." I remembered what Miguel had said on the lifeguard stand. "Not seeing you clearly."

"They treat me like a baby," he muttered.

I looked down at the flat spot on the right side of his head, flat because when he was an infant, he slept only on one side. I thought about how Miguel had said my parents were standing in the way of Squirrel's dreams. They were so busy they probably didn't even know what his dreams were.

"You know what, Squirrel?" I said slowly. "You're doing that commercial. I'll go with you Saturday and help out."

"Me too," Poppy said. "I'm going to ask if they need volunteers." She took out her phone and dialed the number on the business card.

"Yes, good afternoon," she said in the British accent we perfected when we were obsessed with Percy Jackson. "This is Ms. Poppy Banjaree calling with regard to filming a . . . um . . . TV commercial for Channel Islands Sports Drink this Saturday."

She listened to the person on the other end of the line. "No, I'm not the parent of a Special Olympian," she said, still in her fake British accent. "But I have his sister right here." She held out the phone.

I frowned and shook my head.

"Take it!" she hissed.

I smacked my palm against my forehead and took the phone. "This is Daisy Woodward," I said in my normal voice. "My brother's a Special Olympics athlete. Apparently, Alina Petrov gave him your business card and told him about a commercial you're filming."

A woman's voice replied, friendly, with a New York accent. "Sorrel and I spoke a few days ago. We're filming on the community college track this Saturday. We just need a signed consent form from a legal guardian. I can email it to your parents."

"Great," I said. "Can you send it right now?"

My mind raced. I'd already forged their signatures on Squirrel's model release; I might as well do it again. I'd get the consent form off their email and delete it before they could see it. And then on Saturday, I'd bring one of Dad's cameras and take photos and shoot video to post on YouTube—for Squirrel's channel *and* Miguel's. My brother would get a bunch of new YouTube followers before the commercial even aired.

I gave the woman my parents' email address. "When will the commercial be on TV?" I asked her.

"Right," Sandra Johnson said. "So we're a new business, and we don't have a lot of money. Ad time's expensive, so our commercial will run at midnight. It's not ideal, but it's something."

Perfect, I thought. Mom and Dad went to bed by nine. They'd never even see the commercial.

"We'll see you on Saturday," I said into the phone.

"Ask her about volunteers!" Poppy stage-whispered, socking me in the arm.

I rolled my eyes. "Um . . . do you need any volunteers?"

"We do," Sandra Johnson said. "That would be splendid!"

"Great. I'll bring my best friend." I hung up and turned to Squirrel. "You really are going to be on TV."

He studied himself in the mirror above the bookshelf. "Should I part my hair on the left or the right for the commercial?"

"You're asking me?" I said. "I almost never take mine out of a ponytail."

Poppy's eyes got a dreamy, faraway look. "What if Alina Petrov's there Saturday? What if we all end up having lunch together, and she casts me in the sequel to *Beetle Boy*?"

"Holy crickets," I sighed. "My parents are going to kill me."

She passed me the tin of cookies. "Have two!"

She grinned like she hadn't almost stormed out of the house, furious with me.

"Whiplash much?" I asked her. "I thought you were outta here."

"That was before we were poised on the precipice of fame!"

she shot back. "Listen up, people. We've got to make plans!" She pulled out her phone to take notes.

Squirrel dropped into the chair beside her. "Start with the most important thing of all," he told us like it was a life or death decision. "What are we gonna wear?"

21

I never thought I'd be happy to hear the Poop Fairy pickup rumble down the street before dawn on a Saturday, but the instant Mom and Dad left to scoop poop at some Humane Society 10K, I cranked up "The Time of Your Life" from *A Bug's Life*, scooped up Gregor and Samsa, and danced around my room in my pajamas.

A professional entomologist would probably tell you that Madagascar hissing cockroaches don't like to dance, but Gregor and Samsa waved their antennae like they were getting down with the beat. Even my millipedes seemed to crawl across their branches faster than usual, like they knew today was TV Commercial Day—the day that would help turn Squirrel into a celebrity.

Poppy texted right as the song ended.

Ready when you are!

I texted her back.

You're actually awake???

Still, it made sense that she was ready to go half an hour before we'd agreed to meet. She'd convinced herself that Alina Petrov (aka, the love of her life) was going to be there to help out with the commercial.

"A crush is a powerful thing," I told my cockroaches. I thought of Miguel—how his hand, when it touched mine, sent electricity through me like a firefly's chemical reaction. My brain got all foggy, and I wanted to hang out with him even more. *Big yikes.*

Crushing on Miguel was *not* an option, I told myself. We had too much work to do, and anyhow, he'd never be into me. I was Daisy Woodworm, only interesting because of my brother and Summer Games.

"Daisy! You up?" Squirrel called from downstairs.

"There in five!" I yelled, and pulled on a sweatshirt and shorts.

My brother sat at the table in his blue-and-yellow Special Olympics T-shirt and running shorts. He'd made me a peanut butter sandwich and filled two water bottles. "Sunscreen, sister!" He tossed me a tube.

"Bossy," I said, but the fact that he wasn't holed up reeking in his room with country music made me break into a full-on booty swing.

"Good one!" he cried, and swung me under his arm, then dipped me.

We walked out the front door laughing and jogged to Poppy's house. She met us in the front yard. Squirrel gasped. "Poppy! You look beautiful."

She'd piled her curls on top of her head and put on mascara and lipstick and dangly silver earrings with a black sweater and jeans. "Just in case they need extras for the commercial," she told me, and grabbed her thermos of coffee.

I'd never understand Squirrel's and Poppy's love of the spotlight. After I won second in girls' cross-country at

Regionals, reporters stuck cameras in my face the minute I crossed the finish line. I talked to them, sweaty and panting, but I wouldn't watch any of the videos or look at the pictures. Why torture myself?

We jogged to the community college wrapped in a chilly fog that drifted in off the ocean. Adults stood around the track in coats and hats, hands wrapped around steaming mugs. Some were setting up cameras and lights and microphones on tall poles. Others arranged folding chairs and cases full of brushes and hairspray and makeup. A blond-haired kid in a blue-and-yellow T-shirt sat in one of the chairs with his back to us. He stretched out his legs and cradled his hands behind his head like he was an A-list movie star.

"Well, if it isn't Billy, the girlfriend stealer," Poppy said loudly.

"Pops, chill," I said automatically.

"Hey!" she said. "Just because you never tell people what you're really feeling . . ."

Before we could get into it, Billy spotted us and leapt out of his chair and loped over to Squirrel. "Buddy!" he yelled, wrapping his arms around Squirrel and thumping him on the back like he hadn't stabbed him in the very spot he was slapping. "I missed you. Ready to be famous?"

Squirrel stood rigid for an instant, his face over Billy's shoulder frozen with a mixture of shock and excitement. I watched him weigh his options: he could hold a grudge and be angry, or he could forgive Billy and spend the day having a blast.

He broke into a wide smile and patted Billy on the back, then ruffled up his hair with his best Three Stooges laugh. "I missed you too," he said, and they walked off toward the track with their arms around each other.

Poppy rolled her eyes at me. "Forgiveness. Pass it on," she muttered.

I will, I thought. If Squirrel could forgive Billy for stealing his girlfriend, I could forgive Miguel for making fun of me all those years ago.

It was harder to forgive Angelina. She walked across the field toward Poppy and me in her black puffy coat, yellow rubber boots, and the yellow scarf Squirrel had given her two birthdays ago. "Hi, girls! Are you volunteering too?" She walked up and threw her arms around me like she hadn't betrayed my brother on the dance floor in front of all of their friends.

"You've gotta be kidding," Poppy said.

I shot her the Evil Eye.

"Fine," she muttered. "I'm gonna go look for Alina." She stalked away with her curls bouncing around her head.

I thought about what she'd said—how I never told people what I was really feeling. I pulled out of Angelina's grasp and looked at her. "You know," I said, "you really hurt my brother. It wasn't his fault that girl—what's her name, Megan?—kissed him. He only loves you."

She gazed at me, and her green eyes filled with tears. "I miss Squirrel," she admitted. "Billy wants to be the star of everything. I don't like being his girlfriend."

I didn't know what to say to that. But at least I'd said *something*.

Angelina flashed me a mischievous smile. "At practice, I threw Megan's swimsuit in the dumpster."

I made myself sound stern. "I think you owe my brother an apology."

Angelina's smile vanished. "I know," she said. "I have to say I'm sorry right now."

She jogged over to Squirrel and Billy by the track. She said something to Billy and shook his hand, then spoke to Squirrel. He broke into a huge smile and threw his arms around her.

"Forgiveness," I whispered. "Pass it on."

Squirrel's friend Sam ran over to me. He'd pinned his fluffy brown tail to the back of his running shorts. "We're gonna be famous!" he exclaimed. "Me and Squirrel and all the guys!"

There were five Special Olympics runners in the commercial—Sam, Squirrel, their friend Kia, Miguel's cousin Ricky, and Billy, who stood in front of a full-length mirror on the field, preening like a house fly grooming its antennae.

Ricky loped past me and onto the track. "Sorry I'm late!" he hollered to the other boys. "My cuz overslept. I had to wait for him to eat his oatmeal!"

"Well, that's embarrassing." Miguel walked toward me, rubbing his eyes and yawning. "My tío took us to the Lakers game in Los Angeles last night," he said in a voice still rusty with sleep. "We didn't get home until one in the morning."

"You eat oatmeal for breakfast too?" I squeaked. But Miguel only laughed—and not in a mean way—so I laughed too. The moment gave me courage.

"You know," I said, "I really don't appreciate you posting my photo on your website without my permission."

I lisped all the S-words and looked down at my shoes, half expecting him to make fun of me the way he used to. But he dug the toe of his running shoe into the grass, and when I glanced back up at him, his face was flushed.

"I'm sorry," he told me. "You're absolutely right. I just got so excited about the website, and I wanted people to know that you're helping to save Summer Games too."

It was my turn to blush. Miguel was okay with letting people know we were partners?

Before I could say anything else, a tall woman walked up to us, in a calf-length coat that looked like it was made out of flowered black carpet. "I'm Sandra Johnson," she said to Miguel and me, and smiled with super-white teeth. "We could use some volunteers at the finish line to hand out sports drinks to the athletes. Interested? You might even make it into the commercial and get paid!"

Miguel and I looked at each other. "I could use that money!" he said, and grabbed my hand. "It'll be fun!" He pulled me toward the finish line.

"I don't do cameras! Poppy can have my spot."

"Already here!" She'd planted herself in the middle of the finish line with her arms full of blue and red sports drinks. "Alina's not coming, but I'm gonna be on TV!"

She stared at Miguel, still holding my hand. "For real?" She sneered and jabbed the bottles into a giant tub of ice.

I dropped Miguel's hand. A man in tight plaid pants and a checkered jacket walked up and dabbed at his face with powder. "Cuts down on glare," he explained, and turned to me with his enormous pink puff. "Love your ponytail."

I blocked my face with one hand. "Sorry. I'm not in the commercial."

"Why not?" The man pushed his sunglasses up over his hair,

moussed three inches high. "You're gorgeous, sweetheart," he told me. "Look at those cheekbones!"

"Yeah, sweetheart." Miguel elbowed me in the side, laughing. "What he said."

My cheeks flamed. Was he making fun of me?

Poppy snorted and closed her eyes so the makeup artist could apply powder. She looked like she'd been sitting still for makeup artists her whole life, poised and ravenous for the spotlight.

I thought it would take half an hour to film a fifteen-second commercial. But three hours later, everyone's coats and sweatshirts lay in a pile on the field, and I squinted against the hot sun while the athletes ran and stopped and ran again. In the script, they were supposed to sprint the 100-yard dash. Then, Miguel and Poppy were supposed to hand them sports drinks at the finish line. Totally basic.

But Sandra Johnson and the director—a short, round woman with long locks—asked them to do take after take, until sweat glistened on their foreheads and the man in the plaid pants worked overtime with his powder puff.

On the millionth take, the director yelled, "On your mark, get set, go!" and the runners took off again. Billy elbowed his way to the front of the pack like he'd done every single take, only this time, he tripped and went flying. He landed beside a man with a microphone dangling on a pole.

The other boys raced toward the finish line. But Squirrel stopped in the middle of the track and looked back. I could tell he'd forgotten he was in a commercial. He thought he was running a real race.

"Keep going!" I yelled on the field. But he gave his head a little shake, and then ran back to Billy.

"You gotta finish," he said. "Please go for your dreams." He pulled Billy up to his feet, and they ran to the finish line with their arms around each other's shoulders.

Sandra Johnson's eyes got huge. Her mouth fell open in a surprised O. She rushed over to Squirrel and Billy. The director ran too. I got there just in time to hear her say, "That was perfect!" and then, "Can you do that one more time?"

Billy's face wrinkled up in confusion. "You want me to fall again?"

"I do," the director said, "but gently. Don't hurt yourself. And Sorrel, you run back to help him up, and say *exactly* what you said before, okay?"

"Okay . . ." Squirrel said, like he wasn't sure what had just happened.

"Okay?" Billy said. "But I'm still the star, right?"

Sandra smiled with her gleaming white teeth. "You're all stars."

We watched from the finish line as the runners took off again. Billy fell perfectly, sprawled out on the track. Just as he had before, Squirrel ran back, helped him up, and said his line. Poppy and Miguel handed the front runners their sports drinks as Squirrel and Billy jogged in with their arms around each other.

The director looked into her camera. The rest of us looked at her. At last, she gave us a thumbs-up. "And that's a wrap!" she said.

"Great job, everyone!" Sandra Johnson hugged all the runners. "Sorrel, you rocked it!"

"I did too." Billy wiped his face on a towel.

"You did indeed." Sandra climbed up on a step stool with a megaphone in her hand. "Don't forget to pick up a case of sports drinks and your paycheck before you leave!" she told the athletes. "Unless you had a speaking part. We'll send those checks within the next two weeks."

"Paycheck?" I repeated. "They got *paid* for this commercial?"

"And they earn extra for speaking parts," Poppy told me. "Squirrel just made serious bank for saying eight words."

I looked across the field to where my brother stood surrounded by his friends. Angelina literally hung onto his arm while Billy scowled outside the circle. How much money had Squirrel earned, I wondered. Enough to help with groceries and bills? More than that?

Miguel ran over to me. "Hey! I asked Sandra if she'd donate to our Save Summer Games campaign. She's gonna give us two hundred dollars and a case of sports drinks! We're up to almost three thousand, Daisy!"

Poppy wrapped her hands around her throat and gagged. "That sports drink is nasty. Believe me, I tried all the flavors. It's gross."

Miguel pressed his lips together and shook his head. "Who cares what they taste like? She's giving these guys a spotlight. She even got donations from restaurants plus a free banquet room in a hotel so she can throw them a party." He narrowed his eyes at Poppy. "We should support her, not trash her."

Poppy stared at him. She opened her mouth.

I pressed my fist against my stomach, bracing myself for her words. I desperately wanted Poppy and Miguel to like each other. They got me. And they got Squirrel. But they'd never be friends.

She narrowed her eyes at me. "Please?" I mouthed.

Maybe she saw how desperate I was and decided to take pity on me. "Know what, Miguelito?" she began, and then she actually smiled. "Daisy's right. Without Devon, you're not so bad."

Heat rushed to my cheeks, but Miguel only rolled his eyes. "Thanks. You know, I do have other friends. I barely ever see Dev except at school and track."

Sandra walked over to us. "The director says the commercial will be ready to air in a week. You're all invited to the wrap party. We've got a great venue, and Beto's on the Beach has donated a beautiful buffet. Gonzalez's Panaderia is making us a cake. Wait'll you see the design—it's sensational!"

Behind her, Angelina said something in Squirrel's ear. He laughed and put his arm around her. Billy rushed over to them, and Squirrel put his other arm around Billy.

"Holy crickets." I smacked my forehead with my palm. But even my brother's romantic drama—added to the fact that I was going to have to wear a dress—couldn't dim my happiness. I'd helped my brother move one step closer to his dream. I'd stood up to Miguel Santos, the most popular boy in school, and we were still friends.

I walked home with him and Squirrel and Poppy and taught them the words to "The Time of Your Life." We linked arms and sang over the rush of cars and Saturday afternoon lawn mowers. When people honked at us, we sang even louder.

For the rest of the day, I forgot about my Change the World project and the oral report and Devon. I forgot about Mom and Dad picking up dog poop at the Humane Society 10K. I even forgot about what they'd say if they found out Squirrel was the star of a Special Olympics sports drink commercial. For just one afternoon, none of it mattered.

For one afternoon, my life felt perfect.

Mom washed the dinner dishes that night, and I dried. "Squirrel seems unusually happy," she said as she scrubbed out the big blue soup pot.

"I guess." I looked sideways at her blue-and-white flowered apron tied around a Poop Fairy T-shirt and flannel pajama bottoms decorated with dogs.

"It's just odd," she continued. "Angelina broke up with him, and Summer Games is canceled, but he's dancing around the house like he won the lottery. It can't be just because I'm taking him to the new Pixar, right?"

I twisted the damp dish towel around my hand. "Um . . . maybe he's got a new girlfriend?" I said, but an icy chill ripped through my body.

In the Middle Ages, a vineyard owner had tried a plague of weevils in court for ruining his grapes, and the judge had ordered the insects to leave . . . or else.

We might be more evolved now, but if my parents found out what Squirrel and I had been up to, we'd get the weevil treatment, for sure.

Mom scrubbed at a spot of baked-on potato. "Squirrel would tell us if he had a new girlfriend. Billy's mom called this morning and didn't leave a message. If I get a spare minute, I'll see if she knows what's up."

My insides trembled. Marlena knew exactly what was up.

I'd seen her Prius in the parking lot when the athletes had finished their commercial. She'd stepped out of the car and waved to me and Squirrel, and then Billy had rushed toward her with a case of sports drinks held over his head like a trophy.

"Aw, Mom, don't call Marlena," I grumbled, way more casual than I felt. "She just wants to brag about Billy and Angelina being a couple." I grabbed a knife from the dish rack and held it like Billy's mom holding her cigarette. "Oh my *god*, I just *had* to tell you!" I mimicked her Valley Girl voice. "They're planning a June wedding. I'm totes sorry my son's a little beast, but you're *all* invited to the ceremony!"

"Oh, Daisy. That's not . . ." Mom's shoulders shook with laughter. "You really should be an actress."

I stuck the knife back into the dish rack. "Who ever heard of an actress with a lisp?"

"There are several actresses with lisps." Mom ticked them off on soapy fingers. "That woman who does voice-over on *Bob's Burgers*, the actress in *Little Shop of Horrors*, that little girl in *E.T.* . . ."

"Drew Barrymore?" I yelped. "Mom, she's like, fifty years old!"

"Wow. She's *ancient*," Mom said, and grew serious. "We can find you a new therapist, someone who specializes in lateral lisps."

But she couldn't. Not now. Even if I wanted to spend hours a week practicing S- and Z-words in the mirror like I had when I was little, we didn't have the money to pay for therapy.

"I'm fine," I told her. And actually, I was. So I lisped. Maybe I didn't need to fix it. Maybe it made me unique, in a good way.

Mom washed the three jam jars we used as water glasses and set them in the drying rack. "How's track practice?"

"Okay," I replied. "I'm not sure our new coach knows what he's doing. Ms. Bravo made us run six days a week. But Coach Lipinsky only wants us to run four, and then do weights and bike or swim. He says cross-training's gonna keep us from getting hurt. And he wants to teach us to meditate."

For once, Mom listened with her full attention. "I've been meditating before bed. It helps with sleep. I can see how it would help with running too."

I nodded. "There's a practice meet next Saturday. But you're probably busy."

"Write it on the calendar. Dad and I would love to go if we're not working." She paused with the sponge in the blender and stared out the window into the dark backyard. "We're missing so much of your life," she murmured.

I bumped her with one shoulder. "You okay?"

She closed her eyes. "I'm just tired," she said through a yawn. "Sometimes, I miss the old nine-to-five days. The steady paycheck too." She finished scrubbing the blender, dried off her hands, and wrapped her arms around me.

"Are we . . . are we really broke?" I mumbled. I thought of the girl I'd met at Thanksgiving, the one who lived in her car and wore shorts and flip-flops even though it was fifty degrees outside.

"Broke?" Mom rested her chin on top of my head. "No. But we really should figure out a way to spend less on groceries. This family eats like a herd of buffalo."

I thought of the pint of Ben & Jerry's I'd tossed into the cart last time I went shopping. Even though it was on sale, it cost two dollars more than the store brand. "I can get free lunch at school," I said. "And I'll research bean and rice recipes. There's a bunch on the internet."

"What would I do without you?" she said, and a single sob escaped her. I felt it against my chest. "I know how much you've sacrificed. Dad and I just need to work a little harder to build up a base of regular clients, and then we'll have money for extras again."

I reached into my pocket and rubbed the pewter ladybug charm Mom had given me years ago. "We're fine," I said. "Anyhow, it's not just our family that's on a tight budget. Poppy's and Miguel's parents are too."

"Miguel?" Mom pulled away. "The kid who was so mean to you in third grade?"

"We're friends now. I mean, sort of."

She nodded and picked up a sponge. "I'm sorry for whining."

"You're not whining." I swallowed against the tears that thickened my throat. "You work your butt off, Mom."

My phone buzzed in my back pocket. Miguel.

Check the comments on Summer Games YouTube!

My stomach churned. "I'll be back in a minute to finish drying," I promised Mom, and ran up the stairs. I locked my bedroom door and clicked on the channel. Three people had commented.

Please, no haters, I prayed. But the comments were nice . . . *more* than nice.

TTodd: Looking good!

DSMAMA: Stellar!

TeenModelAgency: Love this! So handsome!!

Teen Model Agency?

I texted Miguel.

TeenModelAgency? Is it legit?

He texted right back.

I checked it out. It's legit.

Maybe they want S to model!

I texted Poppy.

Check the comments on Summer Games YouTube!

She wrote back a minute later.

Modeling = killer! Hike Lone Pine Sunday to celebrate?

I danced around with my millipedes for a minute, then reached for my phone.

Sure. Okay to invite Squirrel?

Poppy sent me a happy face. I texted her again.

Okay to invite Miguel?

She didn't answer. I thought, after the commercial, she'd at least be civil toward him. He really cared about saving Summer Games. And he cared about Squirrel.

But maybe that didn't matter. Maybe she was still mad that we'd become friends. Or maybe Bestie Intuition told her I wanted to be more than friends with Miguel.

Romance = ick. For years, I'd believed that. But now, I thought of Miguel's hand in mine when he'd pulled me to the finish line on the track, the excitement in his eyes when he told me Sandra Johnson was going to donate two hundred dollars to our Summer Games campaign. *Our*, as in his and mine.

So maybe romance = ick unless it involved Miguel. Or maybe I was totally ridiculous, thinking the most popular boy in class could ever be attracted to Daisy Woodworm.

I turned off my phone and dropped it into my backpack. I did my math homework, read a chapter of *The Hate U Give* for English class, and went out to tell Mom, Dad, and Squirrel good night. Then, I climbed into bed and tried to fall asleep. But I tossed and turned for hours, worrying about my parents and money and whether Poppy would still be my best friend if I stayed friends with Miguel.

Finally, I got up and turned on my phone to check the time. Poppy had texted me at midnight. The message flashed blue in the dark.

Fine. Miguel can come.

23

The next morning, I walked into Squirrel's bedroom and threw open his curtains. "Wake up! We're going on a hike!"

I thought he'd hurl his pillow at my head. Instead, he threw off his covers and reached for his robe. "Let's go!"

Downstairs, our parents sat with coffee and *The Times* spread out on the table. Hasenpfeffer stretched out on my father's lap, getting white fur all over his black sweatpants. Mom took off her reading glasses and looked at Squirrel's khaki shorts and red polo shirt. He wore a red baseball cap and white crew socks.

"Why on earth are you up so early?" she asked him. "You look so stylish!"

"Daisy and I are going hiking," Squirrel said. He filled a bowl with oatmeal from the pot on the stove and added a handful of blueberries, then sat down at the table.

Dad looked up from the newspaper. "We'll go with you. We actually have a day off. Can you believe it?"

"Um . . ." I turned to fill my bowl. Mom and Dad could *not* come hiking with us. Not with Miguel there—that would be too weird. I pulled a banana from the bunch and sliced it into my oatmeal, thinking hard.

"Shall we go now?" Mom's voice interrupted my thoughts.

"You're tired from work." I sat down beside Squirrel with my oatmeal. "You and Dad should just stay here and chill."

"We're not that tired." Mom sat up straight and shook out her hair. "It's a gorgeous morning."

Dad stood up and went to the stove. "How 'bout this, kids? I'll make us all blueberry pancakes if you're not too full from oatmeal and then we can head up to Lone Pine."

Squirrel looked at me with longing in his eyes. He adored blueberry pancakes.

But I shook my head. "We're meeting Poppy and another friend from school. It's . . . it's kind of a kids' hike, you know?"

"But Sundays are *family* days," Mom said. "We always used to hike Lone Pine on Sundays, remember?"

I remembered. Almost every weekend, the four of us had hiked together, laughing at Dad's silly songs and bribing Squirrel to the top with M&M's that I hid on the trail. Dad would pull out his camera at Lone Pine while Mom told us fun facts about plants and animals. She'd use a blade of grass to point out the heads, thoraxes, and abdomens of ladybugs, flies, and stink bugs.

"It doesn't matter what kind of bug it is," she'd told us. "They all have these three parts."

Because of her—because she showed us the beauty of insects instead of slapping them away—I wanted to be an entomologist. But that didn't mean I wanted her on my hike with Miguel and Poppy.

I reached across the table and squeezed her hand. "Squirrel and I'll be fine. You deserve a day off."

"We're not kids anymore," Squirrel said over his oatmeal bowl. "We have our own lives."

Mom's hand flew to her mouth, and her eyes filled with

tears. Dad took off his glasses and ran them under the faucet with soap, then dried them on the dish towel.

"Squirrel," he said at last. "That wasn't kind."

But it's true, I thought.

"We'll hike with you this afternoon," I promised. "It's just that . . ."

"This morning is a celebration," Squirrel finished.

"Oh yeah?" Dad's eyebrows leapt for the ceiling. "A celebration of what?"

"A celebration of siblings!" I said before Squirrel could say anything else. "We have brother-sister stuff to discuss. We can have a family picnic up at Lone Pine later today."

"But Squirrel hates hiking." Mom wiped her eyes with her napkin and turned to my brother. "You're going to go *twice* in one day?"

Dad sat back down beside Mom. "Let the kids go, sweetie. Daisy's right. We can hike with them later." He winked at Squirrel. "I'll even bake my special picnic cake."

Squirrel clapped his hands. "Yeah! With little marshmallows and chocolate chips and brown sugar?"

"You got it," Dad said. "Been a while since I fired up the old cooking torch."

Dad fist-bumped Squirrel, and everything should have been okay again. We said goodbye and walked out the door. But I couldn't get Mom's sad eyes out of my head. Was this what it meant to follow your dreams—to keep secrets, hide the truth, and deceive the people you loved most in the world?

Poppy met us in our driveway, bouncing with excitement and caffeine. "There's Squirrel, the social media star and soon-to-be YouTube celebrity!"

"Why, thank you!" Squirrel beamed at her.

"What's wrong, woman?" She put her hands on my shoulders and looked into my face. "You look like you're going to a funeral—not on a hike with your bestie and your new boyfriend. Where *is* Miguelito?"

"He's meeting us at the trailhead." I pulled out of her grasp. "And he's not my boyfriend."

Poppy pursed her lips. "Hmm. Well, if he brings Devon, I'm not responsible for what happens at the top of the hill. Squirrel!" she added. "Did you bathe in Old Spice?"

"I don't want to smell sweaty like you."

"Ooh, burn!" She struck a pretend match on her palm and made a sizzling sound.

I grabbed their hands and pulled them down the sidewalk. "C'mon, you two. Can we just go already?"

We jogged to the park and headed for the trailhead under a grove of oak trees. Rain the night before had turned the ground soggy, and the spiky leaves under our shoes had lost their crunch. Miguel waved from the trailhead in shorts and a T-shirt, wearing a fanny pack that somehow made him look rugged instead of ridiculous. "Hey!" he said. "Looking good, Squirrel."

Miguel reached into his pack and handed us each a sandwich bag full of M&M's and almonds. "I brought trail snacks."

Poppy tossed the bag back to him. "I brought my own."

I'd packed trail mix, as well, and my homemade sports

drink in a jar, but I kept the bag Miguel had given me. Squirrel was already crunching the M&M's.

Miguel held out his phone, open to Instagram. "Check out this comment from one of your fans!" he said.

I read over Squirrel's shoulder.

DavysMom: I showed your picture to my son who has Down syndrome, and he wants to model too. Thanks for the inspiration!

"Whoa! Squirrel's an influencer!" Poppy cried.

My brother's forehead wrinkled in confusion. "An *influenza*?"

Miguel and I cracked up. Poppy shot us a dirty look. "An *influencer*," she said. "You know, someone who shows the rest of the world what's trending."

"Oh." Squirrel nodded. "Like Michael Jackson."

"Um . . . if you say so," she said. "Though I don't think he's gonna trend anytime soon."

"Hopefully, you'll persuade people that Summer Games is trending," Miguel told Squirrel. "We still need a bunch of money to make it happen."

Poppy tossed her ponytail. "Can we save the business meeting for later and go hiking, already?"

"Yes, ma'am!" he said.

"Come on!" I grabbed Poppy's hand and headed up the trail. Miguel followed.

Squirrel fell behind us almost immediately. "I forgot, sister," he panted. "I *hate* hiking."

"We're not turning back now." I handed him a handful of M&M's from my bag. "It'll be worth it at the top, I promise."

The trees began to thin out, and the dirt path turned to

mud. My boots squished each time I took a step. I stopped to scrape them off on a boulder.

"I feel like I'm hiking with an extra ten pounds on each foot." Miguel scraped his boots too. "Coach Wu would definitely count this as a workout."

"Good thing you're not wearing your new running shoes." Poppy sneered.

Miguel looked at me from under his eyebrows, and the corners of his mouth twitched. I knew the truth about how hard he'd worked for those shoes.

Poppy kicked out one foot, trying to fling mud off her boot. A clump went flying and hit me in the back. "Ow!" I yelped. "That hurt!"

"Sorry," she said, not sounding sorry at all.

Squirrel kicked out his foot and a clump of mud hit her in the head. "Ouch!" she shrieked, and then, she smiled. "Mud war!"

Suddenly, we were all kicking out our legs, flinging mud at each other. Squirrel hurled a big chunk toward Miguel's face. "Look out!" I yelped.

Miguel caught the clump in one hand. "Good aim. Summer Games should have competitive mud-flinging. You'd definitely get the gold."

Squirrel brushed mud off my face. "Don't worry, sister. You're still beautiful."

"Truce," Poppy said, shaking mud from her ponytail. "Let's go. It's getting hot."

We headed for Lone Pine and stopped in the shade to share my sports drink. Squirrel took a handkerchief from his pocket and wiped his face. Miguel pulled out his phone. "Okay to get a couple of photos of you for Save Summer Games?" he asked him.

"But I'm all sweaty," Squirrel said.

Miguel shrugged. "You look like an athlete." He turned to me. "Is that okay with you? I'd post the best ones to Instagram and Facebook . . ."

I nodded. "It's fine," I said. "Thanks for asking."

"Let's do it!" Squirrel ducked under a tree limb and posed with his arms folded on top of it.

"Perfect." Miguel held up his phone camera.

"You should sit on the branch and lean against the trunk, then look off toward the islands," Poppy suggested. "You know, like you're contemplating life."

Miguel nodded. "Good idea!"

I linked my fingers into a step so Squirrel could put his boot into them, then boosted him up to the limb. He leaned against the trunk with his legs stretched out. "You look like royalty," Miguel said.

"All hail King Squirrel!" Poppy bowed and dropped to one knee.

Miguel copied her. "Hail to King Squirrel, Ruler of Lone Pine!" he cried. "Your turn, Daisy."

I rolled my eyes, but I played along. "Hail King Squirrel!" I said, and knelt beside Miguel.

From his tree-limb throne, Squirrel gave us a royal wave. "Why, thank you," he said, and for the second time in a week, happiness flowed through me, thick and sweet as honey.

"I'm gonna post your picture right now." Miguel bent over his phone. "Wait. Hold on. Look at this new comment!"

He held the phone up to Squirrel, who squinted at it, trying to read the words. I read them for him.

RunnerSarah: You are cute. Would you like to go on a date with me?

"Ew!" Poppy cringed and leapt to her feet. "Stalker!"

"Hey, it could be legit," Miguel said. "How 'bout it, Squirrel?"

He shook his head. "I already have a girlfriend. She's Angelina."

Poppy and I exchanged a look. "But Billy—" I began.

"Nope, Angelina is mine again. She said she was sorry, and she threw Megan's swimsuit into the trash can!" He bent over, cracking up.

"Are you sure?" I asked. "I don't want you to get hurt again."

"She loves me!" Squirrel said. "We're going to the Special Olympics Valentine's Dance next Saturday!"

"Huh." Miguel nodded. "That's the same day as our first practice meet. We should volunteer at the dance," he told me.

"You're gonna bring Angelina to my Indian dance benefit, right?" Poppy asked Squirrel.

"Maybe she can star in one of our Save Summer Games videos," Miguel added.

"Yes and yes!" Squirrel spread his arms wide. He looked out over the city, and at the ocean stretched beyond. "I love this world!" he hollered.

"That's a heck of a power pose." Miguel stepped up beside Squirrel and threw out his own arms. "I love this world!" he echoed.

Poppy and I looked at each other. She shrugged. "I will if you will," she said.

We stepped up beside Squirrel and Miguel, and all four

of us spread out our arms. “We love this world!” we all yelled together.

Our shouts seemed to fill the whole sky. And all at once, I understood what Coach Lipinsky had been trying to tell us for months:

One kid—or a bunch of them, working together—could actually change the world.

24

"My friends, we've reached the Actions section of BARAT!" Coach Lipinsky greeted us in social studies on Monday with big blank pieces of paper and thick colored markers. "Use the next five minutes to write down all the actions you've taken so far to ensure that you're changing the world," he told us. "Myself, I need to go see a man about a horse."

He strode out the door, leaving us with John Lennon's song "Imagine" on his phone. Devon snorted. Poppy and I looked across the room at each other and rolled our eyes. Miguel chose purple and blue markers and started a bullet list. Then he stopped, looked at me, and handed me red and orange markers. "You've got this," he told me.

"If you say so," I whispered, and bent over my paper to start a list.

"Poor Daisy Woodworm. Your project's gonna fail." Across the room, Devon tilted back in his chair and clucked his tongue against his teeth. "I read online that insects are disappearing. Tough luck for your project."

Poppy bugged out her eyes at him. "You can *read*?"

"Insects are disappearing?" Kristen exclaimed. "That's horrible!"

Devon folded his hands behind his head and smiled at me. "The woodworms are going extinct."

I opened my mouth, but no words came out. Poppy and Miguel had my back.

"Shut up, Devon," Poppy snapped, and threw her pencil at him.

Miguel looked up from his list. "For your information, Daisy's project doesn't involve insects." He nudged me with his elbow and tapped his pen against his paper. At the top, he'd written

SAVE SUMMER GAMES.

Miguel Santos & Daisy Woodward, Partners

I felt like an African mantis under a blazing red heat lamp. "Actually," I told Devon, bolder than I'd ever felt around him, "you should be worried about insects dying off. Without butterflies and bees, there aren't as many pollinators for fruit and vegetables. Did you ever think of that?"

"Me meat eater." Devon slapped his chest with both hands. "Cows don't need some stinkin' pollinator to make my hamburgers."

"How are you gonna get your pickles and onions, your ketchup and mustard?" I asked him. "Your buns?"

Kristen giggled. I kept talking. "Those all come from plants that need pollinators . . . or didn't you realize ketchup's made from tomatoes?"

Poppy widened her eyes at me. "What about coffee? Tell me we'll still have coffee even if the bugs disappear!"

I shook my head. "Not much. Coffee's made from coffee

cherries, which come from flowers," I explained. "They can pollinate themselves, but bees increase cherry production. In a world without insects, coffee would be an endangered species."

"*Thpeetheeth*." Devon sneered, but everyone ignored him.

Poppy fell across her desk. "I don't want to live in a world without coffee!"

Coach Lipinsky walked back into the room and stopped in front of her. "Is there a problem, Ms. Banjaree?"

"I'll say," she wailed.

"Let's hope it doesn't involve your semester project."

She sat up and held out a big piece of paper decorated with a border of hearts and stars and colored in with blue and yellow markers. She'd written a bullet list of actions, and colored the bullets blue and yellow too.

"How'd you do that in five minutes?" Devon demanded.

She smirked. "Did it last night. Way ahead of you, Coach," she said, and handed him her paper.

He skimmed it. "Ah, so you volunteered for a commercial to help Miguel's and Daisy's projects, and they're going to assist with your dance benefit. That's some fine cross-pollination you've got going."

"Cross-pollination?" Devon made a farting sound with his lips. "Sounds more like cheating to me. I thought we had to do these projects ourselves."

Miguel raised his hand. "What's cross-pollination? Is that like cross-cancellation in fractions?"

Coach Lipinsky turned to me. "Ms. Woodward? Care to explain?"

I didn't care to explain. I'd already talked too much in class that morning. Devon glared across the room, daring me to say another S-word. My confidence trickled into a puddle at my feet.

"We're waiting." Coach Lipinsky pinned me with the same expression he had when I'd run seven quarter-mile repeats and he insisted on one more.

I twisted my fingers together on my desk. "Um . . . cross-pollination—" I began.

"Croth," Devon said, looking innocently up at the ceiling.

"*Mr. Smalley.*" Coach Lipinsky whipped around. "One more instance of disrespect in this classroom, and I'll suspend you from Saturday's practice meet."

"You can't do that," Devon countered. "Coach Wu won't let you."

"We've already discussed it," Coach Lipinsky said. "He's in complete agreement."

That wiped the smirk off Devon's face. I glanced at Poppy. One hand covered her mouth, but her eyes crinkled up with laughter. "Go on, Ms. Woodward," Coach Lipinsky said.

I stared at the poster of Jane Goodall and Greta Thunberg smiling grimly at each other above the whiteboard. "Well . . . cross-pollination happens when an insect . . . like a bee . . . drinks nectar from one type of flower and then transfers its pollen to another flower. Pollinators help plants survive. Sometimes, they even create a new type of plant."

"Wonderful!" Kristen said. Devon's mouth stretched in an exaggerated yawn.

Coach Lipinsky nodded at me. "See the analogy now, my friends? Miguel's project pollinates Daisy's project, and hers pollinates his, and Poppy's in on the collaboration, as well."

He raised his eyebrows at Miguel and me. "I assume you'll do everything you can to help with her dance benefit?"

"Absolutely." Miguel nodded. "Heck, I'll even put on a sari and dance."

Poppy laughed. "The audience would pay good money to see *that*."

"Likely. But try to resist the temptation." Coach Lipinsky pulled out his stopwatch, lifted his whistle to his lips, and blew a shrill blast. "You have exactly two minutes to list the actions you still need to take to ensure the success of your project. Go!"

I bent over my paper and wrote.

•Make and post videos of Squirrel giving fashion advice.

•Help Miguel with his fundraising car wash.

•Make Squirrel business cards with his YouTube website to pass out at the sports drink party.

Coach Lipinsky's stopwatch beeped. I scribbled my name on my paper and handed it in. He glanced at it.

"Looking good, Ms. Woodward," he said. "I'm eager to hear your presentation."

Miguel bumped my foot with the side of his shoe. Devon coughed. "Loser!"

I stared down at my desk. All the friends and action plans in the world couldn't make me feel better about standing in front of the class with everyone's eyes on me while I lisped my way through a five-minute oral report.

To: dwoodward@gmail.com
Subject: Your Attendance is Requested!

You're invited to celebrate the release of Channel Islands Sports Drink's inaugural commercial, featuring athletes from the Special Olympics Track and Field Team.

Light supper and dessert provided. Semiformal attire.

We look forward to seeing you!

Sincerely,

Sandra Johnson, CEO, Channel Islands Sports Drink

25

The buffet table at the Channel Islands Sports Drink party took up the entire back wall of the banquet hall. Silver trays on white tablecloths held more appetizers than I'd seen in my life. Poppy and I stood beside it salivating like dogs over the fried food Beto's had donated.

"Mozzarella sticks with marinara!" I wriggled my shoulders, trying to get comfortable. I'd swiped Mom's black dress, little black purse, and ridiculous heels from her closet. She and Dad were picking up dog poop at an evening dog show at the fairgrounds.

Poppy bounced up and down beside me in her red flowered dress and gold sandals. "Jalapeño poppers and ranch dressing! Pigs in a blanket!"

We looked around to see if anyone else was eating yet. People gathered in little groups across the hall. Some swayed to the music thumping over the speakers. Others gazed up at an enormous screen where the sports drink commercial played over and over without sound.

Squirrel appeared on the screen, larger than life. In shorts and running shoes, he ran to Billy, who was facedown on the track, and held out his hand, and they crossed the finish line with their arms around each other. People watched and smiled and dabbed at the corners of their eyes with paper napkins. I reached into Mom's purse to make sure I still had the stack of business cards I'd made for Squirrel.

He walked over to the buffet table in his suit and tie. Sam ran over with his tail swinging on the back of his tuxedo pants. "Cheese popcorn!" Squirrel scooped up a bowl and handed it to Sam, then filled another for himself.

"Wings and barbecue sauce!" Sam cried. "This is the best party ever!"

Poppy and I eyed the tortilla chips arranged around a bowl of cheese dip warmed over a burner. In the middle of the table, a chocolate fountain cascaded above trays of cut-up fruit and cookies. Silver ice buckets held bottles of Channel Islands Sports Drink. Squirrel opened one and poured it into a long-stemmed glass.

"Strawberry's so pretty!" He held his glass of pink sports drink up to the light.

"So's peach!" I toasted him with my glass full of pale orange liquid. "Really, it's not that bad," I told Poppy.

"No thanks. I'll stick with coffee." She opened her purse to reveal a bottle of Starbucks mocha.

Sandra Johnson appeared beside us in a short turquoise dress and yellow high-heeled sandals with velvet straps criss-crossing up her calves. Big pink hoop earrings swung against her neck. She looked like one of her sports drinks. "I'm so glad you could make it!"

I handed her one of the cards from Mom's purse. "Here's Squirrel's business card, in case you want to see his YouTube videos. We'll be posting the first one next week."

If we can get Mom and Dad out of the house for a day, I thought.

"Fabulous!" Sandra tucked the card into the belt of her

dress and nodded toward the buffet table. "You athletes need to keep up your strength. Eat! Eat!"

But Squirrel drifted away from the table toward a girl who'd just walked into the room—Angelina, in a bright green dress with white rosebuds woven into her hair. She threw her arms around Squirrel and kissed his cheek.

Poppy shook her head. "Love the one you're with, I guess. Where's Billy?"

I looked around at the athletes and their parents and the adults I thought I recognized from the day Squirrel had filmed the commercial. "I don't see him or his mom. And Ricky and Miguel aren't here either."

Poppy dropped two jalapeño poppers onto her plate and added two pigs in a blanket. "More food for us," she said. "You heard Sandra. Let's chow down!"

I grabbed a couple of mozzarella sticks and poured melted cheese over a pile of tortilla chips. "Not a word about this to Coach. He'll make us drink kale smoothies for a year."

The party seemed to be mostly about eating and trying to hear what people were saying in a room as loud and crowded as a honeybee hive. Squirrel's commercial played over and over. Someone had turned the volume on low. On the big screen, the athletes lined up, and Billy insisted he was going to win. The starter held a whistle to her lips. Then, Billy fell in slow motion, and Squirrel ran back to him.

"Please go for your dreams," he said again and again. Up close on the screen, I saw real concern in his eyes. I knew he wasn't acting. Squirrel was the kind of person who would stop for a friend even if the guy had stolen his girlfriend and vowed to beat him in a race.

The other guests at the party must have realized this, as well. They treated him like a celebrity, crowding around him and Angelina with questions.

"Are you really an athlete, or are you a professional actor like Lauren Potter from *Glee*?" a woman asked him.

Squirrel handed her a business card, just like I'd told him to. "I'm a YouTube celebrity. And I'm part of Save Summer Games. We need money for Special Olympics sports. Go to our website to donate."

"That's wonderful!" The woman pulled a twenty-dollar bill from her purse and handed it to Squirrel. "Please accept my donation."

"Whoa. Thank you!" He waved the bill over his head. "We're rich!"

Angelina and Sam giggled.

"He'll make sure it gets to the director of Save Summer Games," I told the woman. "That's Miguel Santos."

"Where *is* Miguel?" Poppy wondered. "He should be here with Ricky."

And so should my parents, I thought. Sam's mother and father stood across the room laughing and talking with Angelina's parents. Maybe if Mom and Dad were here to see Squirrel surrounded by his adoring fans, they'd realize how overprotective they were.

Maybe they'd even thank me for helping him go for his dreams.

"Yo, Squirrel!" a voice yelled. "Party on!" A blond boy with a fedora tilted over one eye strode into the room.

"Billy," Poppy groaned.

"Billy," I echoed. "He'd better keep his drama to himself."

We stood back and watched as Billy ran up and fist-bumped my brother. He spread his arms out to hug Angelina, but she pushed him. "Go away, Billy," we heard her say. "You brag too much."

Poppy laughed. Billy's smile faded, replaced by an angry scowl.

"Yikes," I muttered. "This could get ugly."

Marlena walked over to me in a shimmery gold pantsuit and big gold hoop earrings. "I haven't seen you in so long!" She hugged me in a cloud of cigarette smoke and perfume. "How's your mother? She never returns my calls. I guess she's incredibly swamped with that new business of hers."

"Look! It's the guy who fell!" A man in a striped suit pointed at Billy, and guests crowded around him to shake his hand.

"How many times did you have to fall?" someone asked. "Did you hurt yourself?"

Billy adjusted his fedora and shook his head. "I never hurt myself. I'm a professional."

Marlena crossed her arms. "Good heavens, I've created a monster," she whispered. "He said in the car that he was going to sign a hundred autographs tonight. I'd better go find him a pen."

A side door opened, and two women in white coats carried an enormous cake over to the buffet table. Gonzalez's Panaderia had decorated it to look like a track surrounded by palm trees, with plastic figures of boys crossing a finish line. Miniature bottles read "Channel Islands Sports Drink" in tiny letters, scattered around the track. Red icing spelled out *Congratulations, Special Olympics Athletes!*

Sandra Johnson climbed up on a chair and held up a wine glass filled with pink sports drink. "Three cheers for the

Special Olympics track team!" Around us, people cheered and clinked their glasses together. "Don't forget to take a gift bag on your way out!" Sandra added. "Inside, you'll find coupons for Channel Islands Sports Drink plus a commemorative CD of our commercial."

"So what did I miss?" Miguel appeared beside me in jeans and his brick-red shirt, hair pulled back in his Lin-Manuel Miranda ponytail.

"*Hamilton* much?" I asked him.

"Where were you, Miguelito?" Poppy handed him a plate with the piece of cake she'd just taken from the buffet table.

I gaped at her sudden change of heart.

"What?" She laughed at the surprise on my face and went back for another piece of cake. "I can be nice," she said over her shoulder.

"I'm a little worried," Miguel told me. "The Special Olympics staff gave up their Summer Games weekend at the university, and there are no dates left. We've got to figure out another place to hold the event, somewhere with a track and a pool and all that."

Then, he looked at me. *Really* looked, with eyes that saw my dress and shoes and the hour I'd spent with Mom's curling iron. "Looking good!"

I blushed and turned away to hand Squirrel a stack of business cards. But inside, I glowed. *Looking good.* I heard his words over and over in my head, like a song.

In that moment, I didn't have a clue that things were about to start looking really, really bad.

26

I knew something horrible had happened before I even walked into the house on Monday afternoon. It was 4:30, right after track practice, but the Poop Fairy pickup stood in the driveway. Mom and Dad hadn't beat me home in months.

The doors and windows were shut even though sunlight streamed across the lawn. The house felt tense, like it was waiting for something. When I kicked off my shoes and walked into the hall, I realized what it was waiting for: me.

Mom stood in the kitchen staring down at a tea bag in her mug. On the front, Tinkerbell knelt to pick up a tiny plastic poop bag tied in a knot—my father had drawn the bag with black Sharpie, as a joke.

I hated that mug.

"You're home early," I said, and peeled off my sweaty socks in the doorway.

"Meet me in the living room," Mom said in a low, stern voice, and handed me another mug of tea. It was Earl Grey, my favorite, and I could tell from the first sip that she'd added cream and sugar the way I liked it. Still, I shivered at the chill in her voice and wrapped my hands around the mug.

"Is . . . is everyone okay?" I asked. "Did . . . did one of the grandparents die?"

"Everyone's fine." Her back was rigid, and her shoulders tensed up toward her ears.

"Then is it okay if I shower first?" I ask. "I'm freezing, and I reek."

"*Later.*" Dad's voice rang out from the dim living room. I knew that tone—it meant the poop had hit the fan.

I peeked around the doorway. Dad sat on the couch with his posture way too straight. Squirrel sat beside him with his eyes round and scared.

"What's going on?" I said, but the instant I saw the TV screen, I knew.

Dad gripped the remote in one hand. He'd paused the video, stopping it on the frame that showed Squirrel reaching out to Billy and helping him up off the track on what I guessed was the commemorative CD from the Channel Islands Sports Drink party. Way in the background of the scene, so small you could barely see it, a figure stood with a ponytail and a purple Sea Urchins hoodie.

Me.

"Oh." I sat down on the arm of the couch. "That."

"*That,*" Mom echoed. "Imagine our surprise when a client canceled today, and we came home early to find your brother home early, too, and watching a commercial *in which he's the star.*"

"Sorry, sister," Squirrel mumbled.

I set my mug on the coffee table and twisted my fingers together so tightly that the tips of them flushed pink and red. "We were going to tell you," I began.

"Oh, really?" Mom set her mug down as well. It clattered against the ceramic coaster. "And exactly when were you going to tell us that your brother appeared in a television commercial without our permission?"

"He doesn't *need* your permission!" The words were out before I could stop them. "He's practically an adult!"

"Do you think I was born yesterday?" Mom said. "Minors can't appear on TV without parental approval on official forms. You forged our signatures, didn't you!"

I bit my lip and stared down at my feet. "I did."

Dad smacked his hands together. The sound cracked through the room. "I thought I'd been very clear, young lady, about how you were not to exploit your brother."

Anger flared through me, a wildfire flame. "I didn't exploit him! Starring in the commercial made Squirrel happy. He even got paid. Or he's going to, anyway."

Squirrel held up a slip of paper. "My paycheck came in the mail today."

"*Fifty* dollars." Dad snatched the check from his hand and shook it. "Fifty dollars, Daisy."

Fifty dollars, when I thought he'd earn thousands.

"Hey, it's something," I said in a small voice.

"And you've put him on YouTube!" Mom held out one of Squirrel's business cards. "I found this on his desk."

"He only did a few videos for Miguel's Summer Games fundraiser," I argued. *We never got to make a single one for Young Spice Squirrel Advice.*

Mom's face crumpled, and she leaned forward on the couch, her brown-and-gray hair covering her eyes and mouth like a curtain. "How could you?"

"A YouTube channel!" Dad bellowed. "With Squirrel's picture, and video after video with hashtags linking to . . . oh, I don't know . . . every social media site in the world!"

I couldn't help it—I rolled my eyes.

Dad was on me like a hornet on hamburger. "Did I, or did I not, forbid you to put your brother on social media?" he demanded.

"I was just trying to help," I shot back.

"Help *what*?" He leapt to his feet and paced the room, waving his arms in the air. Hasenpfeffer scampered into his cage and huddled in the corner. "Help make your brother more vulnerable than he already is? Help stalkers and haters find him? Or help *you* get an A on your social studies project? Honestly, what were you thinking?"

"I was thinking I could help Squirrel follow his dreams!" I yelled. "He wants to be a celebrity!"

"A celebrity." Dad spat the word. "You lied to us. You went behind our backs, and you lied."

I sprang off the arm of the couch and dug my hands into my hips. "Stop protecting him!" I yelled. "He deserves to do what he loves, just like everyone else. Only you're too busy to know what he loves! No one's stalking him, Dad. There aren't any haters."

"Oh, no?" Mom held out her phone in one trembling hand. "I found this photo of your brother on Instagram. Read the comment." She jabbed her finger at the screen.

Under Tía Tammy's photo of Squirrel, I read the comment from the girl asking Squirrel out on a date. Below it was a new comment, one that made my stomach flop and my head spin.

Your not handsome. Your not even cute.

#UglyBoy

"The same comment appears on his latest YouTube video," Dad said, "and on Facebook, and whatever other ridiculous sites you've been using."

Mom gazed at me, and her eyes glistened with fresh tears. "How could you put him in this position, Daisy?"

Squirrel slumped on the couch. "UglyBoy," he whispered. "I'm ugly."

I whipped around to face my parents. "Why do you always, *always* focus on the bad stuff? What about the fact that Squirrel's the star of a commercial? What about the fact that he's helping Miguel raise thousands of dollars for Summer Games? Why can't you focus on the good stuff instead of making him feel bad?"

Mom and Dad stood frozen, their eyes wide. I stalked around the couch and knelt down beside my brother. "How's this any different from a couple of trolls saying you'd never get a date?" I demanded. "Sandra Johnson chose you to be her star for a reason. You're handsome and kind and . . ."

Squirrel stuck his fingers in his ears and shut his eyes. "I can't hear you! I'm ugly! Ugly! Ugly!"

"Daisy!" my mother snapped. "Leave your brother alone!"

"If you're concerned that someone's making him feel bad," my father said in a cold, clipped voice, "you might look in the mirror."

My eyes burned, and I started to shake. My shoulders, arms, knees, legs—everything trembled. My teeth chattered, and I wrapped my arms around my body. My entire family glared at me, oblivious to the fact that I was about to pass out right there on the carpet. "I just thought . . ." I said, and stopped.

Everything that had seemed so clear in the last few weeks went cold and cloudy in my head. Did I honestly think Squirrel could become a YouTube celebrity? Who was I kidding?

Only myself . . . and my brother.

Hot tears seeped from my eyes and slid down my cheeks. "I'm sorry," I choked, and ran upstairs to my room.

"I want Squirrel's photo off all social media, and that YouTube channel canceled immediately!" Dad yelled after me.

"Fine!" I slammed my bedroom door and reached for my phone to text Miguel two words.

Delete Squirrel.

Then, I threw myself down on the bed and cried into my pillow until my nose ran and my head throbbed.

My parents didn't come up to check on me, but I heard a rustling under my door and sat up. Squirrel had slipped a piece of computer paper into my room. On it, he'd drawn a giant heart and a picture of us holding hands inside it. I read the words he'd scrawled at the top—I LOVE YOU, SISTER.

He'd slid something else under the door too—two Oreos. I had no idea where he'd gotten them. We couldn't afford anything but generic sandwich cookies.

I inhaled a ragged breath and set his drawing and the cookies beside a framed photo of us beside my cockroach terrarium. In the photo, I was five and he was eight. We stood on the beach path, both of us wearing roller skates. I stood up straight, proud that I could balance on the wheels. But Squirrel looked nervous. He hunched over, shoulders tense. I had my arm around him, holding him up, and he had his eyes locked on mine like if he just kept me in his vision, he'd be safe.

He'd always trusted me not to let him fall down. But I'd failed him.

My phone buzzed. I scrubbed at my eyes with the palms of my hands and read the text from Miguel.

SaveSummerGames is a bust. No place to hold the event.

We're too late.

Too late.

Out my bedroom window, afternoon darkened into evening. I heard the clink of plates and glasses downstairs, smelled fried onions and garlic and oregano, so that I knew Dad had made Spanish rice, but I went to bed without supper.

That night, Miguel's words spun over and over in my head as I tossed and turned in bed with my stomach growling.

Too late.

Too late for Miguel to change his semester project. Too late for me to change mine. Too late to save Summer Games.

Too late to save Squirrel.

27

When I was a seventh grader, track and field practice meets felt like a party. Long orange buses pulled up at dawn on the street beside our school's track, and kids from other cities stumbled sleepily through the gate wearing sweatpants in their teams' colors. Volunteers at the snack bar sold hot chocolate, cookies, and coffee. Poppy always bought a small hot chocolate to pour into her thermos with her coffee, and I got a hot chocolate with whipped cream.

Our team claimed the cement pad whenever we hosted a meet. We sat in a circle and stretched, talking and laughing, super jittery. One by one, we ran our races, waving at parents and friends who sat clutching their coffee cups on the cold metal bleachers. They cheered for us, and we cheered for each other even though our wins didn't count for anything official. Practice meets were celebrations.

But not this year.

On Saturday morning at dawn, I pulled on my singlet and shorts, and then my black-and-purple sweatpants and sweatshirt. I tiptoed down the stairs so I wouldn't wake my parents and Squirrel. Last year, Dad had left a good luck poem on the refrigerator before my first track meet, and Mom had left a note saying "Break a leg . . . okay, not really." But this morning, the door was just the usual jumble of pictures and flyers and coupons held down by Poop Fairy promo magnets.

My heart clenched like a fist in my chest. My parents wanted nothing to do with me. I was a liar, an exploiter. I slapped together a peanut butter and banana sandwich and bolted from the house.

The sky was still dark as I tied my running shoes and headed down the street. Fog drifted around the streetlights, and tree branches dangled ghostly and cold. Poppy staggered across her front yard like a zombie. "I don't do mornings," she muttered just like she did every time we had a track meet at dawn. "Yikes. Neither do you." She grimaced at me. "You look awful, woman."

I told her what Miguel had said about Summer Games being a bust.

"That sucks. You and Miguel and Squirrel worked so hard."

"Yeah," I mumbled. And then I told her about #UglyBoy.

Her head shot up, and she clenched her fists. "Who would write such a thing? We can't let some loser troll stop Squirrel. Tell him to ignore it, Daisy. He's gotta keep going with his videos!"

I shook my head. "Miguel already deleted them all."

"But why?" Poppy stomped along the sidewalk next to me. "Don't let one jerk ruin his dreams and your projects!"

"Easy for you to say. Your moms support everything you do. My parents practically kicked me out of the house when they found out about Squirrel on social media."

"It's not their call! He's freakin' seventeen years old!"

"I can't talk about this anymore." I pulled my sweatshirt hood up over my head and hunched my shoulders against the cold. "Let's just get to the track."

We jogged to school in silence, the slap of our feet on wet pavement the only sound aside from an occasional car. Since our school was hosting the track meet, we had to put out hurdles, get the snack bar ready, and make sure the locker rooms were not a "putrid cesspool of horror," as Coach Lipinsky called them.

"I'll set up the starting blocks." Poppy slogged across the wet grass beside me. "Last year, Kristen put some of them down on the track backwards."

I looked around for something to do. Coach Wu and Coach Lipinsky were dragging the big blue high-jump cushion over to a spot beside the long-jump pit. Miguel stood alone in the one-room snack bar, arranging granola bars in a basket with his head hung low. He looked nothing like the happy guy who'd put chocolate peppermint brownies on a plate at the Moonlight Ball.

I stepped into the snack bar. "Hey," I said, and reached for a pair of blue rubber gloves.

"Hey," Miguel grunted. We'd barely talked since I'd asked him to delete Squirrel. I could tell, every time I looked at him, that he felt as bad as I did. Not only had we'd failed to change the world—we'd failed our family and friends.

I helped him stack cookies and energy drinks on the shelf below the window, and we poured buckets of ice into the soda machine. "So . . . what exactly happened with Summer Games?" I asked.

Miguel looked up from pouring half-and-half into a pitcher. "Special Olympics gave up their reservation at the college where they usually hold the Games, and there are no dates left. Any other place we could use has been booked for a year."

He shook his head and shoved the half-and-half carton into the crammed-full refrigerator. "We need a basketball court, a baseball field, a swimming pool, a track, a long-jump pit, and bleachers," he reminded me. "Not many places have all that."

"So even though you raised all that money . . . ?"

"Even though *we* raised all that money," he corrected me, "the director said to save it for next year's Games. This year stays canceled."

"That's just wrong."

"Tell me about it. I told Ricky, and he bawled like a first grader." Miguel blew out a sigh. "My parents said they'd take us camping on Anacapa Island that weekend instead, but he's still miserable."

I nodded. "Squirrel's crying too." Ever since #UglyBoy, Squirrel had gone straight to his room after work. He stayed in there all evening with no music and refused to come out for dinner.

Who wrote that comment? I wondered for the thousandth time. Billy, mad that Squirrel and Angelina were back together? Devon, furious at me because I'd been hanging out with Miguel? Or some anonymous hater who thought it was fun to ruin other people's lives?

Two runners from another school walked up to the counter, shivering in hats and gloves. "Hot chocolate and cookies," they ordered, and their breath made smoke in the air. Miguel and I got to work.

Kristen's grandmother appeared in the doorway with a bright orange jacket zipped up to her chin. "Go warm up, you two," she told us. "I'll take it from here."

"Thanks," I said. Miguel and I pulled off our rubber gloves and jogged over to the cement pad to stretch with the rest of our teammates.

Coach Wu stood studying a clipboard in his purple sweats and black jacket. Coach Lipinsky wore a purple Sea Urchins sweatshirt and enormous rainbow-knitted gloves. Drops of water from the fog glistened in his beard. "Welcome, friends!" he greeted us. "I expect great things from you today. Let us support each other with our whole hearts and souls."

He looked at Devon, who sat with his hood pulled up tight around his face and his eyes closed like maybe he was still asleep. I wanted to grab him by the shoulders and ask if he was responsible for #UglyBoy. Instead, I pulled the bottoms of my feet together into a butterfly stretch and focused on loosening my hips.

"First race is the girls' four hundred!" Coach Lipinsky said. "Ms. Banjaree. You ready?"

Poppy huddled in her coat and hat looking like a frozen mushroom with steam from her thermos drifting up around her face. "Sure, Coach," she said, dripping sarcasm. "I just *love* racing at the butt crack of dawn."

Kristen giggled. Coach Lipinsky pointed a rainbow finger toward the track, where girls from other schools were stretching and jogging. "Go warm up."

Poppy groaned and pulled off her coat and hat. "Coach, you're sadistic."

I dragged myself off the cement pad and walked with her to the starting line. People cheered from the home bleachers—her moms, standing up with a big white sign that read "WE LOVE YOU, POPPY!" in purple letters. I saw Miguel's parents, too, and Devon's. I recognized Kristen's from their food truck. But my parents weren't there.

I wasn't really surprised. For a week, my parents had quietly asked me about my day and thanked me for doing laundry and making dinner and washing the dishes. But their voices were sad, and they wouldn't meet my eyes.

The worst had been last night—the first Friday in years that we didn't have Pizza-Movie Night. "Tell Poppy we're just not feeling up to it," Mom had said, staring out the kitchen window as she peeled carrots for a salad. "We shouldn't be spending money on pizza anyhow. It's cheaper to make it at home."

But we didn't have homemade pizza that night. Mom, Dad, and I ate salad, rice, and beans at the table without Squirrel, and then I washed the dishes and hid out all evening in my bedroom with my millipedes and cockroaches.

"Girls' four hundred!" The announcer's voice crackled over the loudspeaker. Poppy bounced on her toes, then braced her feet in the starting blocks and crouched, tense and waiting.

"On your mark . . . get set . . ." The starter fired her gun in the air beside me, and Poppy and the other runners took off in a flash of purple, pink, green, and yellow shorts. She broke ahead early, first by a good two seconds. And then, a girl in orange and white sprinted by her.

"Get that girl! Get her!" Beside me, Coach Lipinsky leapt into the air, waving his arms and screaming. "Pick up your pace, Banjaree! Kick it in . . . now!"

I stared at him. He'd gone feral, practically frothing at the mouth.

But Poppy didn't seem to hear him. She kept her eyes on the track, never breaking her stride. Right as it looked like the girl in orange would win, she stretched out her legs and sprinted down the final straightaway in a flash of Sea Urchins purple.

"First place!" Coach Lipinsky tossed his rainbow gloves into the air and did a victory dance on the wet grass. "Way to go!"

The other coaches looked at him sideways like they weren't quite sure what planet he'd come from. I jogged toward Poppy bent over at the side of the track. She held up a warning hand. "I swear . . . I'm gonna . . . hurl," she panted.

I jumped back. "Good job!"

She spoke with her head upside down. "Coach . . . needs . . . to . . . chill."

"He's out of control," I agreed. "Here come your moms. I'm gonna go stretch."

I walked back toward the cement pad. Miguel and Devon were lining up for the 1600 meter with the guys from other schools. I stopped to watch. Miguel placed his spikes in the third lane starting blocks and stared at a spot in front of him. He looked focused and lock jawed, way too tense.

The starter fired her gun, and the boys took off on the first of four laps around the track. Miguel settled in behind the lead runner, his arms and legs pumping with energy that seemed angry, even from where I stood.

"Go, Miguel! Go!" his mother yelled from the bleachers with a purple-and-white blanket wrapped around her shoulders. His father stood up and shook a purple-and-white pompom.

"Go!" I whispered. "You can do it."

"Ready for your sixteen hundred, Ms. Woodward?" Coach Lipinsky looked into my eyes. "You feeling okay?"

I pictured myself yelling, *No, I'm not feeling okay! Before you go telling kids to change the world, you need to tell them how cruel it is!*

Instead, I mumbled, "Yeah, Coach. I'm ready."

"Well, go warm up," he said. "You race after the girls' three thousand."

I walked back to the cement pad and pulled my track spikes from my backpack. They, at least, weren't a total disaster. I'd only worn them in races last year, so the spikes still gripped the track, even if the shoes were so small that my toes threatened to burst through the top. I tested each spike to make sure it was screwed in tightly. Then I pulled off my sweats. I had my head stuck inside my sweatshirt when I heard Kristen's voice. "Oh, no!" she cried. "What's he doing?"

I tore off my sweatshirt and searched the track. Miguel had drifted back—far back—almost in last place.

Coach Lipinsky stood motionless, watching. Apparently, he reserved shouting for the girls' team. Coach Wu stood at the finish line, congratulating Devon, who'd sprinted ahead of everyone else to come in first.

Miguel practically limped the last straightaway, followed by a boy in green shorts who half jogged and half limped to the finish line.

Poppy and I rushed to Miguel. He shrank into the shadows behind the snack bar, and we followed him. "What happened?" Poppy demanded. "Cramp? Shin splints?"

He stayed bent over, not looking at us.

"It's because of Summer Games," I said quietly. "You're distracted."

He nodded like even that little bit of movement was too much. "I thought it would be easy," he muttered. "Just raise the money and everything would fall into place."

"I get it," I said. And then I did something I never thought

I'd do. I put my hand on Miguel's shoulder and squeezed it, just a little.

"What the . . . ?" Poppy began, but I shot her a look and she closed her mouth.

"I can't believe I came in second to last," he said, and shrugged my hand off his shoulder. "I'm such a loser."

"Miguelito, it's *one* race." Poppy put her hands on her hips. "You've gotta get a grip."

Miguel stood up straight. Then he turned away from us without another word and jogged off to the boys' restroom. Poppy looked after him and shook her head. "I didn't have the heart to point out that his expensive new shoes failed him."

"Good," I told her.

We watched the girls' 3000 meter, and then it was time for my race. I looked again at the home bleachers. Parents and kids from our school filled the stands, but Mom and Dad weren't among them. Even Squirrel hadn't made it. But when I stuffed my windbreaker into my backpack, I found another one of his notes. This time, he'd drawn a picture of a running shoe, the words GOOD LUCK, and a tiny, lopsided heart.

A lump formed in the middle of my chest like a black beach pebble. I walked to the starting line with my molars clenched and my eyes burning. Kristen stood on one side of me. A girl in an orange-and-white singlet crouched on the other side. Coach Lipinsky popped up beside me. "Remember to pace yourself . . ." he began.

"Coach?" I held up a hand. "I need to concentrate."

The starter held up her gun. "Coaches off the track!" she commanded. "On your mark . . . get set . . . go!"

Adrenaline shot through me, and I ran. The 1600 meter

was my favorite race—it was long enough to maintain some serious speed, and short enough not to get boring. I liked to be the front runner in the first lap, then fall back into second or third, saving energy to sprint the final lap.

But this time, when I fell back, I stayed there—not in second or third place, but fourth, and then fifth.

"Move, Woodward!" Coach Lipinsky shook his fist in the air. "Use those legs! Run!"

But the pebble in my chest dropped down to my stomach, heavy as a boulder, and my legs refused to sprint.

Squirrel's face appeared through the fog in my brain. "I'm ugly!" he sobbed. Mom and Dad appeared too—their faces full of shock and anger and sadness.

No wonder they aren't here to see me race, I thought. *I betrayed them all.*

And then, I was glad they weren't there because I came in last. *Last*, when I'd been second in the county for cross-country just a few months before. I felt people watching me from the bleachers. My teammates glanced at me from the field, and then looked away.

Coach Lipinsky met me on the graveled path near the snack bar. "What the heck?! Half a minute slower than practice last week! What happened, Woodward?"

I blinked at him through my fog and burst into tears.

Poppy and Miguel ran toward me. "Coach?" Poppy pulled me away by one hand. "I think you need to go take a chill pill." She handed me my sweatshirt and a bottle of Gatorade.

Miguel nodded. "We've got this." He handed me a wad of napkins from the snack bar. I turned away and blew my nose and wiped my eyes, gasping for breath. Poppy made worried chicken noises, and Miguel punted a rock so hard that it cracked against the side of the snack stand.

Coach Lipinsky watched us without a word. He coughed, then cleared his throat and patted my shoulder with his big, rainbow-gloved hand. "What's up, Daisy?" he said in his normal, gentle social studies teacher voice. "Did something happen at home? And you, Miguel. Something's not right. Poppy, tell me what's going on?"

Poppy looked at Miguel and me for permission. Miguel shrugged. I nodded. She sucked in a deep breath and told Coach Lipinsky about Summer Games being canceled. Then, she told him about #UglyBoy.

He stroked his beard and took off his hat, looking inside like he was searching for a solution. "Anonymous comments are the work of cowards and bullies," he began.

"We know," Miguel said, "but that doesn't make Daisy's brother feel any better."

He nodded. "I get it. I'm guessing Summer Games would have cheered him up."

Miguel shook his head. "Sure. But there's no place to hold them, so they're canceled."

"I see." Coach Lipinsky drew a square in the gravel with the toe of one ancient running shoe, then drew an arrow shooting out of it. "You've got to think outside the box," he told us. "With apologies to my cat, there's more than one way to skin one."

"Gross," Poppy groaned.

I stared down at the box in the dirt. To me, it looked like a cage—a cage I was locked in, with no hope of finding a key.

Coach Lipinsky bent and looked into my eyes again. "Don't

give up on your dreams or Squirrel's. Not yet. For now, stay in the moment, please. You've got another race today, all of you."

He stood up straight and pointed sternly toward the track. "There's a time for everything, friends," he told us. "Right now, it's time to run."

On Monday, I slept through my alarm. My muscles still ached from the 1600 and the 800, which I also bombed. When I finally woke up, my parents and Squirrel were gone. The house was silent except for the sound of rain pelting the roof and Hasenpfeffer rattling wooden toys around in his wire pen.

"Holy crickets!" I yelled. "You guys could've woken me up!"

Downstairs, I found a basket of pumpkin chocolate chip muffins from the batch Dad had baked on Sunday, but no note, and definitely no poem.

I ran to school through fat rain drops, trying to eat and brush my teeth at the same time. I showed up halfway through social studies soaking wet, covered in toothpaste and chocolate.

"Why, if it isn't Daisy Wood—" Devon began.

"Mr. Smalley!" Coach Lipinsky said. He pushed the button to lower the projector screen, and I dropped into my seat.

Poppy gave me a worried look. Miguel nudged my foot with his. "What's up?" he whispered.

What was up was that my family had apparently disowned me, and now I sat wet and shivering while Devon smirked at me from across the room in new board shorts and a Patagonia shirt that probably cost more than my parents earned in a month.

I slumped down in my seat and stared blankly at my desk covered with paperclip-scratched graffiti. Outside, raindrops pounded the cement. The bottlebrush tree and the palm trees trembled in the wind. Coach Lipinsky opened his laptop and turned on his projector.

"Not another PowerPoint," Poppy groaned.

"Is there a problem, Ms. Banjaree?" he asked.

"Actually, Coach, there is," Miguel said.

I turned toward him. He looked as exhausted as I felt—dark circles under his eyes and hair uncombed. "Changing the world is *hard*," he said. "There are so many roadblocks."

"And rules!" Kristen tugged on the end of her braid. "I mean, who knew starting a math club would be so complicated? I have to sign all the kids in and out, and they're all jumping around all the time so I can't tell who's in and who's out, and half the kids are just there for the free snacks. Plus, adults keep barging in and telling me how to run the club."

"Adults have all the control," I muttered.

Devon whistled. "Daisy Woodworm grows a backbone! But wait . . ." He put a finger to his lips and widened his eyes. "Insects don't have backbones."

"Shut up, Devon," Miguel said.

"Troglodyte," Poppy added.

Coach Lipinsky pointed toward the open door. "Mr. Smalley," he said. "*Principal.*"

Devon folded his hands on his desk. "I'll be good, Coach."

The finger stayed pointed. "I said, *principal.*"

Devon snorted. He choked out a half laugh. "You can't be serious."

"I assure you, I am," Coach Lipinsky told him.

Slowly, Devon stood up. He grabbed his backpack, yanked the zipper closed, and stomped outside.

"Now, back to our regularly scheduled program." Coach

Lipinsky reached into the tall cabinet behind his desk and took out four large bags of cheese popcorn and a stack of paper bowls. He tore the bags open and passed them around. "Share!" he commanded.

"Popcorn for breakfast?" Poppy toasted him with her thermos. "Sweet!"

"Pay attention," he said, and clicked his remote. A title slide appeared on the projector screen—big black letters on a blue background.

Teens who Overcame Roadblocks to Change the World!

"D'you have an entire *library* of these things?" Miguel asked.

"I do." Coach Lipinsky clicked to the next slide. A girl with long brown hair and black glasses stood with her hands on her hips in a school hallway beside lockers. She wore lacy fingerless gloves and colorful bracelets.

"Dawn Loggins grew up in poverty," he told us. "In middle school, she owned two dresses. Mostly, she survived on noodles. Kids made fun of her because she never washed her hair, but she had no running water at her house. Then, her parents abandoned her, and she became homeless."

"That's criminal!" Kristen cried.

Devon looked over at her, but for once, he kept his mouth shut.

"It *is* criminal," Coach Lipinsky agreed. "But Dawn didn't let it stop her. She found places to sleep. She studied by candlelight. Then, a friend's mom invited her to live with them, and a school counselor helped her work on college applications. Dawn worked as a janitor at her high school and took AP classes. Kids still made fun of her. But now, she's going to Harvard."

"*The* Harvard?" Kristen said. "That's almost as impressive as Cambridge."

"*The* Harvard." Coach Lipinsky tapped the screen with his pen. "While she's there, she's volunteering to help homeless students in her city."

"Great," Poppy said. "But she's the exception. I mean, she's like a superhero."

"Interesting." Coach Lipinsky clicked to the next slide. "Joey Kemmerling." He read the name below a picture of a brown-haired guy in a T-shirt that read *I won't stand for harassment.*

"Joey came out as gay in the eighth grade," Coach Lipinsky said. "Kids started taunting him. One boy brought a knife to school and threatened to kill him. Joey changed schools, but he was still bullied, both at school and online. He couldn't walk home without someone threatening him."

"That's some serious shade," Poppy said.

"Joey knew that," Coach Lipinsky replied. "But instead of holing up in his house and hiding out from the world, he got help from the national Gay Straight Student Alliance. Then, he started a Facebook nonprofit called Equality Project. It helps people who've been bullied because of their gender or sexual orientation. Joey's in law school now," Coach told us. "He didn't let a knife threat stop him from doing his part to change the world."

"All right, all right," Miguel said. "I see where you're going with all this."

I put my head down on my desk. I was too tired to care, too

tired to think. If Coach Lipinsky's motivational lectures and PowerPoints worked on Miguel, fine. But I was done. Done lying to my parents, done going behind their backs, done hoping I'd pass my social studies class.

When the bell rang, I stood up and staggered to my locker. "What's wrong with you?" Poppy demanded. "Is this about Squirrel and your parents, or did something else happen?"

"I'm going to the nurse," I mumbled, and headed down the hall.

Devon sat waiting in a chair outside the principal's office. The health center was next door. If I had any chance of getting sent home, I'd have to walk past him to the nurse.

I stopped in the hallway beside a gutter spewing water into the grass. His eyes drilled into mine, and his mouth opened like he was about to spew new, hateful words in my direction.

If he teases me, I'm going to pass out or punch him, I thought.

I walked past the office door, out of school, and down the street toward my house without telling anyone I'd gone.

The driveway was empty when I got home, and the house was dark. I let myself in and took out a freezer bag of vegetable broth to thaw for lentil soup, then sat down at the laptop to make sure Miguel really had deleted all Squirrel's photos on social media.

Above me, Squirrel's bedroom door clicked shut. In a moment, a country singer began to wail.

I walked up the stairs, opened the door without knocking, and stood in his doorway. "What are you doing home? Are you sick?"

My brother lay in bed with the covers pulled over his head. "I got a note from the school nurse," he mumbled.

"You're smarter than me. I just left." I opened his curtains to let in the cold, bright morning light and turned down the music. "Guess we're both ditching school today."

He stayed under his bedspread, silent. I sat on the edge of the bed. "Want to go take pictures at the beach?" I asked. "It's stopped raining. The sky's all full of pink clouds."

Now that I was home, I wanted to be somewhere else, somewhere that didn't remind me of Dad yelling, Mom in tears. But Squirrel wouldn't budge.

"No pictures ever again!" The bedspread muffled his voice, but I could hear how sad he was. "I'm ugly, remember? Ugly!" He buried his head under his pillow. "Go away!"

"Squirrel!" Tears rushed to my eyes. He'd never told me to go away before. We'd always been each other's cheerleaders. After #EligibleBachelor, I'd told him jokes every day until he gave in and laughed, and when my favorite stick insect died, he'd blasted an old David Bowie song called "Uncle Arthur" and bounced into my room slapping his knees and elbows like a German folk dancer until I cracked up.

We could always pull each other out of a bad mood. But not today. And my heart felt ripped in two.

I walked into my room and sat down at my desk with my head in my hands. *How do you overcome a roadblock when you have a broken heart?* I wondered.

I'd told my parents to focus on the good stuff in Squirrel's life instead of the bad. "Maybe I should take my own advice," I muttered to my cockroaches.

I reached into my desk drawer for a sheet of paper and a handful of markers. Coach Lipinsky had told Miguel and me to think outside the box about our Change the World projects. What did that even mean?

I drew a box in the middle of my paper. Inside, I wrote: Squirrel = YouTube celebrity.

But how? I wondered. Mom and Dad had forbidden it . . . twice.

I dropped my chin into my hands and stared into my terrariums. The stick insects perched on their twigs, motionless. The millipedes walked up and down the new bamboo I'd given them with their little legs waving. I reached into the cockroach terrarium and picked up Gregor. His black-and-brown shell felt cool between my fingers and thumb. His bent antenna didn't move, but the other one rotated around like he was trying to tell me something.

Insects were capable of amazing things. Scientists called Madagascar hissing cockroaches "living fossils" because they looked like the cockroaches that lived on Earth with the dinosaurs. Their species could survive almost anything.

I thought of the Darwin's bark spider, able to spin a web twenty-five times stronger than steel. I thought of dung beetles that could pull over one thousand times their own body weight in poop.

If insects could overcome roadblocks like being small or terrifying or gross, if they could defy rolled-up newspapers and the bottoms of people's shoes, then couldn't I fulfill Squirrel's dream and change the world for him?

I had no idea how . . . but I had to try.

YOUTUBE VIDEO #1
DAISY WOODWORM CHANGES THE WORLD
Length: 30 Seconds

VIDEO	**AUDIO**
FADE-UP ON: 1.MADAGASCAR HISSING COCKROACHES IN TERRARIUM	FADE-UP ON: MUSIC: "THE TIME OF YOUR LIFE" FROM A BUG'S LIFE
CUT TO:	
2.CLOSE-UP OF DAISY TALKING	DAISY: I'm Daisy Woodworm, future entomologist, here to tell you about why insects are awesome. A lot of people see a bug on the ground or in the air and freak out. But the world needs insects. They're capable of amazing feats of speed and strength.
3.CLOSE-UP OF GREGOR ON DAISY'S ARM 4.CLOSE-UP OF DAISY'S DRAWING OF ROACHES HEAD-BUTTING	Take Gregor. He's a Madagascar hissing cockroach. His wild relatives eat leaf litter in forests, helping to break it down into soil so plants can grow. Males butt each other with their horns to defend territory, and the winner stands up on his back toes!
5.CLOSE-UP OF DAISY TALKING	It's so easy to walk right by insects without stopping to notice that they're awesome. It reminds me of how people walk right by my brother and his friends without saying hi, just because they have intellectual disabilities.

6.CLOSE-UP OF GREGOR STANDING ON TOP OF SAMSA, "BUGGING" HIM

Even though my brother can really bug me—I mean, he's my brother, right?—he and his friends are super cool. They're athletes, capable of amazing things.

Still, everyone needs a little help now and then. Cockroaches need leaf litter to eat. Pollinators need nectar in flowers to thrive. And my brother and his friends need donations for their Special Olympics Summer Games. So bee cool and donate at www.savesummergames.com.

7.CLOSE-UP OF DAISY'S DRAWING OF A HONEYBEE AND THE WORDS "SAVE SUMMER GAMES!"

DISSOLVE TO:

8.STICK INSECTS IN TERRARIUM

Follow my YouTube channel for fascinating facts about insects!

FADE OUT

MUSIC: *FADE OUT "THE TIME OF YOUR LIFE" FROM A BUG'S LIFE*

29

On Friday morning, Mom walked into the kitchen in her Poop Fairy tee and rubber boots. "We have to work late tonight at a Humane Society benefit," she told me. "Are you okay to stay with Squirrel?"

"Of course," I mumbled, biting my tongue so I wouldn't point out that we'd be skipping yet another Pizza-Movie Night. I could tell from Mom's slumped shoulders and sad eyes that sharing a Beto's Pie of the Day was the last thing she wanted to do with me.

"Keep moving forward," Coach Lipinsky said in my head.

I texted Poppy and Miguel.

Emergency meeting after track practice—my house.

That afternoon, we met in my bedroom with lemonade I'd made from our trees and the gold tin full of nankhatai. Poppy sat cross-legged on the floor hugging my pillow, as far as she could get from my terrariums while still staying in the room. Squirrel sat in my desk chair with his arms crossed tight over his chest and his mouth turned down. I'd had to bribe him out of his room with cookies and the promise to clean Hasenpfeffer's litter box three days in a row.

Miguel sat on my bed watching one of my millipedes crawl up his arm. "Wait," he said. "Is this Millie or Pete?"

"Flip it over." I held up my magnifying glass and peered at the seventh segment of its body. "That's Pete. See those two tiny bumps where the legs should be?" I pointed. "The seventh segment on a female has another set of legs—no bumps."

"Impressive." Miguel lifted his eyebrows. "It's not everyone who can tell you the gender of a millipede."

Poppy snorted and threw my pillow at my head. "Weirdo."

"We'll see who's weird when I'm a famous entomologist," I shot back.

Squirrel said nothing at all.

"Anyway, I invited you all over today to show you something." I opened my laptop. "I made a YouTube video."

"What?" Poppy said. "Why?"

"You'll see." I pushed play, and then there I was, talking about insects and Squirrel and Save Summer Games while my cockroaches crawled around on camera. I lisped a lot. But suddenly, that didn't matter as much as getting my message out into the world.

"Should I publish it?" I asked my friends.

They nodded. "Absolutely," Miguel said.

"Go for it." The corners of Squirrel's mouth turned upward just a little. "You did great, sister."

"It's killer," Poppy agreed. "But what about your parents?"

"They never said *I* couldn't be on social media." I clicked the blue square that read *publish*. "Phones out, people," I said. "We've gotta share the link everywhere."

We all bent over our phones for a while. "Moving forward," I said when we'd sent the video to everyone we could think of, "we need to talk about the Summer Games car wash."

Poppy and Miguel stared at me. I didn't blame them for

being surprised—I barely recognized myself. *Daisy Woodworm, Influencer*, I thought.

"I thought you'd canceled the car wash, Miguelito," Poppy said. "Why bother doing it if you don't have a place to hold Summer Games?"

"I can't cancel," Miguel explained. "I already told all the athletes and posted flyers all over town. And Beto's is letting us use their parking lot." He reached for his phone to make notes. "Daisy's right. We've got to get organized."

"First up, we need some awesome signs." I reached behind my desk for the giant pieces of neon posterboard I'd stashed there the night before. I handed them around with pencils and wide black markers. "Drivers need to be able to read these from the street. Write *Special Olympics Car Wash*, and make it big."

"Okay!" Poppy and Squirrel bent over a piece of orange posterboard and sketched out letters.

Miguel looked up from a piece of lime-green posterboard. "Thanks," he told me. "I was so bummed that I almost gave up. I'm glad we're partners."

For once, Poppy let it go. Squirrel raised his eyebrows at me like he knew my heart had just done the high jump in my chest.

"No problem," I said, like me taking charge was the most natural thing in the world.

On Saturday morning, we met in the parking lot of Beto's. The athletes were already there with buckets and rags and newspapers for polishing car windows.

"Here's the donation jar!" Miguel reached into his backpack

and pulled out the coffee can we'd decorated with photos of Squirrel and his friends.

"Right on!" Sam dropped two quarters through the slot in the plastic lid. "We're gonna be rich!"

Poppy set a stack of her dance flyers on a bench beside the donation can. She helped Angelina separate sheets of newspaper while Sam filled buckets with soapy water, and Ricky and Squirrel swept the parking lot. "I'm glad Billy's camping," I said quietly to Miguel. "We don't need his drama today."

"Agreed." He clapped his hands together, Coach Lipinsky–style. "Okay, people, circle up!" He draped his arms around Poppy's and my shoulders, and we huddled close with the athletes. "Tell me what you like best about Summer Games, so that we can tell customers at the car wash."

"Basketball!" Sam leapt up into the air and pretended to sink a hook shot with his tail swinging behind him.

"Swimming!" Angelina cried.

Ricky flexed his biceps beneath his Special Olympics T-shirt. "Weight lifting. And hot dogs."

"Hot dogs?" Miguel frowned. "What're you talking about, cuz?"

"At the Summer Games barbecue," Ricky explained. "And the beans."

Sam's face wrinkled up. "Beans make me fart."

"Fart!" Squirrel and Angelina doubled over with laughter. Ricky and Sam cracked up, too, slapping each other's shoulders. Poppy and Miguel rolled their eyes at each other and burst out laughing.

"Stay focused," I told them. "We've got three buckets, five

sponges, two hoses, and a ton of newspaper. I brought speakers for music too. What should we play?"

"Michael Jackson!" the athletes yelled.

Poppy grinned at me. "You had to ask?"

Miguel cranked up "Don't Stop 'Til You Get Enough" on his phone. Music thumped across the parking lot. "Let's party!" Squirrel cried. He spun on one foot and did the moonwalk. His friends cheered.

"Grab the signs!" I pointed to the pieces of posterboard propped against Beto's front wall. "We've gotta spread out on both sides of the road so drivers can see us from all directions."

"Good idea," Poppy told me. "You and I can stand across the street."

Already, customers were pulling into the parking lot—someone in a blue Jeep, and a man and a German shepherd in a big white truck. I crossed the street with Poppy, and we stood on the sidewalk with our signs held high. Miguel said something to the athletes across from us. They pumped their fists in the air and cheered.

"Miguel Santos," Poppy said. "He's actually an okay dude."

"I told you," I said, with my face on fire.

She bumped me with her shoulder. "Looks like you've got a date for eighth-grade prom."

"As if I'd even go," I scoffed. "C'mon! We've gotta keep moving!"

We danced up and down the sidewalk with our signs. A few drivers honked at us. Two made U-turns and headed back to the car wash. "I'm kind of feeling Coach this morning," Poppy said. "We're changing the world just a little, right?"

"Right," I said. Across the street, Squirrel and Angelina

danced as they scrubbed the Jeep. Ricky and Sam did hook shots with their sponges, scrubbing the top of the truck. My phone buzzed. I pulled it out of my pocket and showed Poppy the text.

Honda driver donated $10.

Truck driver gave Ricky $20!!!

I texted Miguel a thumbs-up. The rest of the day, he and Poppy and I took turns holding signs and washing cars. Right before three, we were cleaning up the soggy wads of newspaper and dumping out buckets when a car rolled into the parking lot. "What the . . ." Miguel began.

Blue-and-green painted peacock feathers gleamed on every inch of the car. A blue ceramic peacock decorated the hood. The door opened, and the driver stepped out in running shorts, a Sea Urchins T-shirt, and a wide straw hat. Coach Lipinsky, with a scruffy white dog in his arms.

"This is April," he said, like we weren't standing there staring with our mouths open. "One car wash, please. What?" he added. "Haven't you seen an art car before?"

Squirrel's forehead furrowed into a worried frown. "I don't think you're allowed to paint your car."

"Sure you are!" Coach Lipinsky said. "There are thousands of art cars all over the country!"

"It's beautiful!" Angelina stroked the peacock hood ornament with one finger.

"Paint it yourself, Coach?" Miguel asked.

"I did," he replied. "How's it going? Making lots of money for Summer Games?"

"We're up to almost four thousand dollars. But we've got

to save it for next year since we still don't have a place to hold them."

"Ah, but you do." Coach Lipinsky smiled, and his eyes crinkled up behind his glasses.

"We don't," Miguel said. "We're too late."

"Mr. Santos," Coach said kindly. "Where is your characteristic optimism?"

"The project failed," Miguel reminded him. "We couldn't make it happen."

Coach Lipinsky put one hand on his shoulder and one on mine. "You just need a little help."

"We're supposed to be able to change the world *without* help!" Miguel said. "That's the whole point!"

Coach shook his head. "I think you misunderstood me. Those kids on my PowerPoints? They all had help from parents, teachers, counselors, business owners."

He addressed all of us now—the athletes and me and Poppy and Miguel. "At our faculty meeting last Friday, I told my colleagues about your predicament. They agreed that you could hold Summer Games at our school. We'll work with Special Olympics to include as many athletes as possible in the space."

For a moment, there was silence. Miguel looked at me. I looked at Poppy. And then, we started screaming, jumping up and down in the soapy puddles and laughing. "Are you serious?" Miguel cried. "That's epic!"

He grabbed my hands and danced around in the soapsuds with Coach Lipinsky's dog barking at our heels. "It's happening, Daisy! We did it!"

Squirrel tackled me from behind, soaking wet. "Summer

Games is happening!" Sam high-fived Ricky and then chest-bumped him.

Only Angelina looked concerned. "What about a pool?" she demanded. "I'm a swimmer."

Poppy's eyes widened. "She's right. Our school doesn't have a pool. How're the swimmers gonna compete?"

Coach Lipinsky walked over to Angelina. "We've got you covered. I called up the manager of the public pool, and she said we could use it for Summer Games."

"Coach!" Miguel hollered. "You're the best!"

"Indeed." He stuck a bill in the donation jar and helped Angelina polish his car windows.

"You're like a fairy godmother," she told him. "You even have a royal chariot."

"Coach is better than a fairy godmother," Poppy said.

Miguel nodded. "He's the real deal."

"Enough!" Coach Lipinsky scooped up his dog. "Keep it up, and I'll think you're pandering for good grades. By the way, Ms. Woodward," he added, "nice work on your YouTube video."

I looked up from polishing the peacock hood ornament. "You . . . you saw it?"

"A hundred and seventeen people saw it, last time I checked. Haven't you read the comments?"

I winced. "I try not to read those."

"I want to read them!" Poppy bent over her phone. "Whoa! Some woman saw your video and made a donation to Summer Games!"

"'I love your enthusiasm for insects.'" Miguel read another comment over her shoulder. "'Your brother sounds great. I sent ten dollars to help with the Games.'"

"It's actually working!" I cried.

"Listen to this comment!" Poppy held up her phone. "A guy says 'Your video's great, but I want to hear from your brother. Let him speak for himself!'"

Squirrel and I frowned. We knew the truth: our parents wouldn't *let* him speak for himself.

"My dad told me I can't be on social media," my brother said to Coach Lipinsky.

Coach nodded and scratched his dog behind the ears. "In the words of that esteemed philosopher Taylor Swift, 'haters gonna hate.' When you put yourself out there, you're going to get a whole lot of love and a little bit of grief."

Poppy fist-bumped Miguel. "Truth."

"I'm okay with a little bit of grief," my brother said slowly. "Some strangers are mean on the computer, but Sam showed me how to block them. I want to make 'Young Spice Squirrel Advice' videos. People need my fashion tips." He turned to me. "I don't care about UglyBoy. I'm gonna be a star!"

"That's the stuff," Coach Lipinsky said.

"Tell that to our parents," I muttered.

Coach scrawled a phone number on one of Poppy's dance flyers. "Have them call me. I'll bet I can help them see your project in a new light."

He told us all goodbye, then drove off in his peacock car. We threw the newspapers into the trash, overturned the rest of the buckets, and squeezed out the rags. Then we sat down on the curb. "I'm exhausted," Sam groaned.

Poppy clutched her stomach. "I'm starving!"

Angelina nodded. "Me too."

Miguel reached for the donation can and started counting

money. "You two count the change." He slid a pile of coins over to Poppy and me. "I'll deal with the bills."

He unfolded a bill and let out a yelp. Ricky leapt to his feet. "What is it?" he shrieked. "Spider?"

I jumped up too. "Let me see it!"

But it wasn't a spider. It was another pink sticky note folded around two twenty dollar bills.

Miguel held it up. "From Coach," he said, and read the words out loud:

For the teens who are brave enough to change
the world, hot fudge sundaes—my treat.

30

Miguel and I met at the Buddhist temple to help Poppy decorate for her dance benefit. A hundred folding chairs stood in rows on the wooden floor. Big red and gold satin bows decorated the end chairs.

Poppy and her mothers and sisters were walking around barefoot in their red-and-gold saris, with their hair pulled back in jeweled headbands and dozens of red and gold bracelets on their arms. They'd painted their hands and the tops of their feet with henna. Poppy's mothers each wore a silver ring in one nostril. They looked gorgeous. *Everyone* looked gorgeous. Especially my best friend.

"I'm so glad you're here!" She ran over with her curls bouncing and her eyes wide so I knew she'd downed a double-shot latte after track practice. "This concert's out of control. We sold the last tickets just now, and we don't have enough coffee or dessert!"

"Put us to work," I said.

"How can we help?" Miguel asked at the same time.

Poppy pushed a fistful of bills into his hands. "Go to the market across the street and buy four bags of Oreos and shortbread, and a big jar of instant coffee, plus a quart of half-and-half."

"On it!" Miguel headed out the door.

"You!" Poppy pointed to a table full of red and yellow tulips and glass vases. "Fill these with water, and do something with all those flowers!"

"Got it." I picked up two vases and headed for the sink at the back of the temple.

Poppy took each vase as soon as I'd finished arranging the tulips and placed them at the front of the temple on a low wooden stage. Jealousy burned in my chest. Her dance benefit had sold out, and she'd be able to send a bunch of money to India, just like she'd planned.

And now, thanks to Coach Lipinsky, Miguel had saved Summer Games, just as he'd planned.

I was the only one who'd failed. My YouTube video had 216 views and we'd gotten a few five-dollar and ten-dollar donations to Save Summer Games, but Squirrel's chances of becoming a celebrity looked grim. When we got home from the car wash, we handed our parents the piece of paper with Coach Lipinsky's phone number on it.

"My social studies teacher," I'd explained. "He wants to talk to you about our YouTube project."

"I told you, Daisy, I do not want Squirrel on YouTube," Dad had said, automatic as a robot.

Mom had nodded. "I have to agree. This family can't handle any more internet trolls."

I clenched my molars and walked over to Poppy, who stood frozen in the middle of the stage, staring out at the rows of empty chairs.

"Stage fright?" I asked her.

She nodded. "This is big. The biggest thing I've ever done."

I touched her tightly folded hands. "Let go. You'll ruin your henna. Everything looks beautiful." I pointed at the posters she'd propped up on easels—pictures of people and buildings half-submerged in flood water. "Think about why you're having this concert. This night's not about you. It's about your relatives and friends in India."

She blinked and gave her head a little shake. "You're right." And then, she laughed. "I've never had stage fright before. Now I know how you feel."

But she didn't, not really. She'd changed the world, and next week in social studies, she'd tell us all about it without lisping in front of Devon.

Miguel pushed through the door with his arms full of cookies and coffee. "Get this!" He dumped the bags on a table covered with a red cloth. "I talked to the market manager who's a friend of my mom's, and she said they'd donate refreshments for Summer Games—cookies and vegetable trays and a huge cake!"

"No way!" I forced excitement into my voice. "That's amazing!"

"Killer." Poppy tore open a bag of shortbread and popped a cookie into her mouth. "There's gonna be a ton of Channel Islands Sports Drinks too."

Sandra Johnson had donated a dozen cases to Summer Games, just like she'd promised. And Miguel had gotten a local printer to give him a discount on T-shirts and hats for the athletes. "We're up to seventy-two athletes!" he said. "And more keep registering. Ricky's been lifting weights three hours a day to get ready."

"Squirrel too," I said. "All he talks about is Summer Games."

An alarm rang on Poppy's phone. "It's time! Miguelito, open the doors!"

Miguel pushed open the heavy wooden doors, and people began to pour into the room. Kristen sat down with other girls from our track team. Most of our classmates showed up too. My parents were there with Squirrel and Angelina. Mom looked around at the temple, at the bows and the tulips and the refreshment table, and the chairs slowly filling with people.

"*Poppy* organized all this?" she asked me.

I nodded. "Miguel and I helped a little, but it was mostly her."

"Incredible." Mom nudged Dad, who had his best camera slung over one shoulder. "Look at what Poppy's done!"

He glanced around the room and adjusted his tripod. "I promised her moms I'd take pictures of the event," he said, and headed for the front row and the chair they'd reserved for him.

Squirrel sat down beside me in a red shirt and a red-and-gold tie. "I called Poppy so we could color coordinate!" he told me. Angelina sat next to him in her green satin dress, holding his hand like their palms were superglued together.

For the third time in four months, I was wearing a dress. I'd used part of my new shoe fund and bought it for ten dollars at Poppy's favorite used clothing store. It was brown and pink and sleeveless, and it looked great with the brown suede sandals she'd loaned me.

"That's a great outfit, Daisy!" Miguel dropped down to the empty chair next to me and rested his arm on the back of my chair. "Hey, Squirrel! Hey, Angelina!"

Mom looked at him. "It's Miguel, right? I remember you from track meets, back when I used to have time to go to them."

Miguel shook her hand. "Nice to see you again, Mrs.

Woodward. It's been great working with Daisy on Save Summer Games."

"Sorry?" Mom's eyes went from him to me. "Squirrel told me they're back on, but I wasn't aware that Daisy . . ."

"Miguel's the reason Summer Games are happening," I interrupted. "It's because of him and our social studies teacher, who's letting us use the school."

"And because of you." Miguel shook his head. "Honestly, Mrs. Woodward, without Daisy, there'd be no Summer Games. She's amazing."

Heat rushed to my face. Mom gave me a long look, and her lips twitched upward into a smile. "Amazing," she echoed. "So *this* is why you've been so happy lately."

"Shh!" Squirrel said. "It's starting!"

Poppy dimmed the lights and moved to the center of the stage. She stood in the spotlight in her red-and-gold sari and looked out at the crowd.

"Wow!" Squirrel whispered. "Poppy's beautiful!"

"Hey!" Angelina cried, and socked him in the arm.

Someone giggled. Poppy covered her mouth with one hand, and her eyes crinkled up with laughter.

"I'm beautiful too," Angelina whispered.

Squirrel put his arm around her and pulled her close. "Don't be jealous," he murmured. "You're the only girl for me."

Poppy spoke over the sound of stringed instruments. "This event is a benefit for my family and their friends in Kerala, India, which was partly destroyed by floods. The money you've donated will help them rebuild their houses and schools."

People broke into applause. Dad sat down beside Mom and took her hand. Poppy pressed her palms into prayer position and bowed. "Thank you," she said. One of her mothers turned the music up, and she began to dance.

I'd seen her perform before, at Asian festivals and show-and-tell at school. Tonight was different. Alone on stage, Poppy danced the story of the mythical Indian enchantress Mohini so dramatically that I forgot to breathe.

"She's really good!" Miguel exclaimed when the dance had ended and the audience applauded again.

"She is," I agreed. *Go away, jealousy,* I thought. *Don't ruin this night.*

"I'm so proud of Poppy!" Mom cried, blinking back tears. "To do all this . . ." She pointed at the refreshments and the flowers and the chairs packed with people. "Did you help with this, too, Daisy?"

"Miguel and I both helped to set up," I said. "It was fun."

She nodded and nudged my father. "Our kids," she said, and wiped her eyes on the tissue he handed her.

Dad blinked behind his glasses. "I had no idea this social studies project was such a big deal. You've devoted the whole term to it?"

I nodded. And then Poppy took the stage again to dance with her sisters.

At intermission, people crowded the dessert table piled with nankhatai and store-bought cookies. Coach Lipinsky walked over to Poppy and her moms. "Spectacular work," he said, and shook Poppy's hand, and her mothers' hands too. "I never dreamed, when I assigned this project, that the students would rise to the occasion this spectacularly. You must be very proud."

"She's quite a kid." Poppy's mom smiled at her.

Her mama clasped Coach Lipinsky's hand between her own hands. "You've helped these kids to achieve amazing things," she said. "Thank you."

"Big yikes." Poppy pulled me toward the coffee station. "That's enough emotion for one night!"

Sweat glistened on her forehead. She pressed down on the red bindi between her eyebrows, making sure it didn't fall off. "Wait'll you see the dance we're doing for the finale," she told me. "It's called Kathakali. Usually, men perform it in costumes and masks and makeup, but this time, it's all women!"

"Sounds cool," I said.

"What's wrong, woman?" She peered into my face, so close that the tip of her nose touched mine.

I waved her away. "I'm fine." I shoved my jealousy down into the pit of my stomach. "This is the best concert ever."

"Unless I fall off the stage in the second act," Poppy said.

Her mama dimmed the lights again. Her sisters danced, and then her mothers danced. Finally, all five of them got up on stage, whirling and twisting like flowers in their spinning skirts and colorful masks.

Then, the concert was over, and Poppy stood alone once more in a circle of light.

"Thanks to you," she told the audience, "we've raised almost two thousand dollars to send to India."

Again, people cheered and applauded. Squirrel jumped up on his chair and pumped his fist in the air. "Pop-py! Pop-py!" he chanted. She motioned him down.

"We're not finished yet," she said with a sly smile. "I've got an encore for you, just in case you've still got a few dollars burning a hole in your pocket."

One of her sisters carried a screen to the center of the stage. The other turned on a projector and laptop. Poppy picked up a remote, and suddenly, there was picture of Miguel and me on the beach—the photo Tía Tammy had taken that morning in January.

"What?!" Miguel yelped, and grabbed my hand.

"I have no idea," I whispered. "What's she *doing*?"

"I want to tell you about another project that's changing the world," Poppy said, and grinned at me and Miguel. "Each year, Special Olympics teams from around the world hold Summer Games, a lot like the Olympics we watch on TV. Only this year, our region ran out of funds and had to cancel. But two of my classmates didn't think that was fair. They got together with a bunch of the athletes and raised enough money to save the Games." She pointed at Miguel and me.

Squirrel and Angelina cheered. Mom and Dad stared at me. "I barely did anything," I whispered.

Still, Miguel pulled me to my feet. "Take a bow, Daisy! You deserve it."

I sort of bobbed my head and sat down fast. But Poppy wasn't finished. "Squirrel! Angelina! You two also helped raise money to save Summer Games. People, these are two of the athletes who'll be competing in June."

Squirrel and Angelina stood up and waved. My parents frowned at each other, and Mom reached out toward my brother to get him to sit down. But the applause grew louder, and my father's mouth fell open. He and Mom looked at all the smiling faces—not a hater among them. Gradually, they began to smile too. They clapped for Squirrel and Angelina, and Dad put his fingers in his mouth and did his loudest whistle while Mom cried fresh tears.

Poppy reached behind a cabinet for a bouquet of sunflowers. "Before we leave, I want to recognize someone who inspired all of us. He believed in our projects even when we hit roadblocks. Coach Lipinsky!" she called. "Will you come up here, please?"

Our teacher stood up from the back of the room, shaking his head in embarrassment. He walked to the stage in his tie-dyed shirt and fleece vest as people clapped and hollered. "Ms. Banjaree, is this really necessary?" I heard him say, but she ignored him and pushed the bouquet of sunflowers into his arms.

"You showed us we really could change the world," she told him. "Thank you."

And then she was crying, and he was wiping his eyes with a rainbow handkerchief, and Mom and Dad were hugging me and Squirrel. "I'm so sorry," my mother told us both. "We were just trying to protect you. We had no idea . . ."

Dad wiped his eyes with the back of his hand and gave a mighty sniff that should have embarrassed me in front of my friends, but didn't. "I'm sorry, too, kiddos," he said. "You two are absolutely brilliant. The world needs you."

Squirrel beamed at Angelina. "My father said I'm brilliant!" he told her.

She tossed her red curls over one shoulder. "I know that," she said to my brother. "Duh!"

We all laughed, and then someone put on Bollywood music and people began to dance. Miguel and Kristen folded up chairs and stacked them against the wall, creating more space.

"C'mon, Daisy!" Miguel waved me over. "Let's boogie."

I shook my head. "I don't dance."

He laughed. "You danced just fine at the Moonlight Ball!"

"That was just goofing around with Squirrel," I protested, but he put one arm around my waist and took my other hand. Then, he spun me out like some Broadway dancer. For an instant, I almost felt graceful. But before he could spin me back toward him, Poppy ran up with Squirrel and Angelina. She threw her arms around Miguel's shoulders and mine. "We're changing the world!"

Near us, Coach Lipinsky was talking with my father. "That's your dog truck outside? Fantastic! You've got to see my peacock car!"

Mom walked over to us. "Pizza-Movie Night at our house this Friday. You're all invited," she said, looking straight at Miguel.

He nodded. "Thanks, Mrs. Woodward! I'd love to come over."

I should have been happy. Everyone around me was talking and laughing and eating. But I was miserable. When no one was looking, I slipped outside and headed for home. Poppy had plenty of people to help her clean up, I reasoned, and I needed a few minutes alone to figure out how I was going to tell my entire class next week that I'd failed my project.

At home, I cut up an apple to share with Hasenpfeffer, then sat down at the laptop. I opened it and logged onto my YouTube channel. There were the three videos I'd made, with photos of my millipedes and stick insects and cockroaches. There was my username—Daisy Woodworm—and my profile picture, a not-too-buggy selfie of me with my magnifying glass around my neck.

There were two new comments below my last video. I read the first one.

Hi, Daisy! I'm the president of our high school science club. We're looking forward to meeting you in September. In the meantime, keep up the good work!

The second comment read:

Because of your videos, I made a donation to SaveSummerGames. Your brother sounds amazing. Thanks for making the world a better place, Daisy Woodworm!

I read that last sentence over and over, until it felt like part of my heartbeat. *Thanks for making the world a better place.*

So Squirrel hadn't become a YouTube celebrity—not in the way I'd imagined—but people knew about him thanks to Miguel's project, and the sports drink commercial, and Poppy's dance concert, and my videos. They knew about him, and they admired him.

In some small way, maybe I'd succeeded, after all.

31

On the third Saturday in April, I woke before dawn for a big track meet east of Los Angeles. I pulled my sweatpants and sweatshirt over my shorts and singlet and stumbled downstairs to grab a banana for the cold, dark walk to school.

A box sat on the kitchen counter, wrapped in brown paper. I rubbed my eyes and bent over to read the note on top in Dad's handwriting.

A gift for a girl full of speed and smiles.
We hope these will help you fly miles and miles.
Love, Mom and Dad

I unwrapped the box and lifted the lid.

White-and-purple running shoes—specifically, track spikes in my size. I pressed them against my chest.

Beside the fruit bowl, Dad had left two of his giant pumpkin chocolate chip muffins in a bag. "One for Poppy," he'd written on a sticky note. "XOXO." I tucked the bag into my backpack and slipped out the front door. Through the fog, I smelled the ocean mixed with jasmine from my neighbor's bushes.

"I'm not awake," Poppy mumbled at her gate. We jogged to school in silence and boarded the long orange bus outside the office. I handed her one of Dad's muffins. She reached into her backpack and froze. "I forgot my coffee."

"There's a snack bar at the meet," I reminded her.

She shook her head. "They don't serve coffee—they serve brown water. My day is ruined," she moaned. "Wake me when we get there." She leaned against the window and closed her eyes.

Our other teammates fell asleep or listened to music in their earbuds as the bus sped down the freeway. The driver dimmed the lights, and even Coach Lipinsky and Coach Wu closed their eyes.

Across the aisle, Miguel had scored a seat to himself. He curled up on the ripped black vinyl to sleep. But I was wide awake. I had a million ideas for my YouTube channel. I pulled a notebook from my backpack and started a bullet list.

•Fruit flies! 1st living animals sent to space!
•Carnivorous insects—Big Yikes!
•People in Africa use army ants to stitch together open wounds!

I'd written down a dozen ideas by the time the bus driver pulled up to Mt. San Antonio College. I followed my teammates off the bus, and we headed for the football field as the sun began to rise. Poppy and I spread an enormous blue tarp on the damp grass, so the girls' team could stretch without getting soaked. Miguel and Devon did the same for the boys. Coach Lipinsky cranked up music on his phone: Justin Timberlake's "Can't Stop the Feeling."

"What feeling would that be, Coach?" Poppy groaned. "The

feeling of wanting to go back to bed and sleep for twelve more hours?"

"What's your plan for the four hundred?" he asked, pulling a bottle of Starbucks mocha from his backpack and passing it over to her.

She looked at the bottle like he'd handed her a bar of gold. "For real?" she breathed, and narrowed her eyes. "Did you put kale in this coffee?"

"It's pure caffeine," he assured her. "Plus milk and *way* too much sugar."

She popped off the lid and took a long drink. "Ah, the elixir of life."

I stretched out my legs on the tarp and reached for the tops of my new track spikes. "Love the shoes!" Poppy bent to examine them. "Sea Urchin colors. You finally earned enough to buy them."

I shook my head. "My parents left them on the table for me this morning."

"Awesome. Hey, I think Miguelito's trying to get your attention over at the snack bar." She pointed to where he stood in line waving at me. "Go." She pushed a crumpled bill into my hand. "Get us a couple hot chocolates."

"He's not gonna believe all my YouTube ideas!" I said, and grabbed my notebook and jogged over to Miguel. Around us, other runners bounced up on their toes and bent over to stretch their hamstrings, or sprinted up and down the track. "What's up?" I said.

"Cool shoes." He looked down at my feet.

"It's not just about the equipment," I began, smiling as I mimicked what he always said.

"But it helps," we finished together, and laughed.

Miguel got serious. "Hey, I know it's early in the morning, and maybe you're not totally awake, but—"

"I *am* awake!" I opened my notebook and held it out to him. "And I have so many ideas for my YouTube channel!"

But he didn't even look at them. "The thing is, I mean, I know you'll probably say no, but—"

"Spit it out," I commanded. "We've gotta go watch Poppy race!"

Across the field, the starter got into position. Poppy and other runners jogged toward the track, kicking up their knees and stretching their arms overhead.

"Girls' four hundred in five minutes," a woman announced over the loudspeaker.

I tapped my foot against the gravel path. Miguel's cheeks flushed the color of the Red Vines in the tub on the snack bar shelf. "The thing is," he repeated. "I . . . uh . . . well, I wondered if you'd go to the eighth-grade prom with me."

The words rushed out of him so fast that I thought I hadn't heard right. "Did you just invite me to the prom?" I asked.

"Um . . . yeah."

I looked around for Devon. Was he snickering in a corner, cracking up over Miguel's joke? Or was he filming me?

"I don't dance, remember?" I stepped up to the counter and handed the volunteer Poppy's five-dollar bill. "Two hot chocolates, please."

Miguel nudged my shoulder with his own. "Please? It'll be fun."

"You're not joking." I looked at his flushed face and anxious eyes. "Are you . . . are you asking me out on a date?!"

He nodded. "I am. As Angelina would say, 'duh.'"

A smile tugged at the corners of my mouth. I tried to bite it back, but it spread until it took over my entire face. "Okay," I said. "I'll go."

"Epic! Hey, want to go cheer for Poppy? Her race is starting."

"Absolutely," I said.

When we traveled to track meets, we had to work extra hard to be each other's cheerleaders. Most of our families didn't make the long drive, so the away bleachers stood almost empty while local parents and students packed the home bleachers. Still, there were Miguel's parents, walking up to the top bench with a silver heart-shaped balloon. Poppy's moms showed up, too, with a big sign that read "Go Sea Urchins!!!" in purple glittery letters.

I wondered where my parents were picking up dog poop that morning, and what Squirrel was doing.

The starter's gun interrupted my thoughts. Poppy burst out of the starting blocks and sprinted with her ponytail flying out behind her. She left everyone else in the dust.

"Fifty-nine o' six!" Coach Lipinsky tossed his hat into the air as she shot past the finish line. "Incredible!"

"Poppy's a superstar," Miguel said beside me.

For an instant, I was jealous. But I was the one he'd asked to the eighth-grade prom. *Me.*

Coach Lipinsky strode over to me. "Girls sixteen hundred in ten. You ready, Ms. Woodward?"

I bit the tip of my tongue, remembering the disastrous practice meet. "I'll go visualize being ready," I told him, and walked off to shed my sweats.

This meet was important. University coaches wrote down

the names of the kids they'd keep an eye on in high school—kids who might be worthy of a full scholarship. I had to come in first or second in my two races.

I needed that scholarship.

I put on my new track spikes and walked toward the track. At the starting line, I crouched in the blocks and stared at a spot in front of me. I was vaguely aware of Miguel and Poppy and Coach Lipinsky watching from the sidelines. Girls from other schools got into position around me, and the starter raised his gun.

"On your mark . . ." he began. "Get set . . . go!"

I took off fast and forced my breathing into a rhythm with the pounding of my feet. "Go! Go!" Coach Lipinsky yelled as I ran the first straightaway.

"Get it, woman!" Poppy hollered.

I kept my eyes on the girl in orange and white in front of me, the girl who had beat me during the practice meet. My heartbeat hammered in my head. Air rushed in and out of my lungs.

The first two laps were easy—I hung out in second place, saving my energy. The third lap was harder. I'd started too quickly, and a cramp pinched my side. I fell back into third place, trying to catch my breath.

For an instant, I remembered how I'd failed at the practice meet. And then I thought of how Miguel had looked when he asked me to the prom, and happiness shot through my body. My leg muscles felt new again, fresh, and I sprinted the final lap.

"Go, Daisy! Go!" a voice cried from the bleachers. "Kick it in!"

I flew down the final straightaway, past a girl in purple and half a second behind the runner in the orange-and-white jersey.

"Second place!" Coach Lipinsky met me at the finish line with a bottle of water and an enormous smile. "Well done, Ms. Woodward!"

I stared at him, my chest heaving. "You're not . . . mad . . . about second . . . place?" I panted.

"Not at all. Gives you something to work for in the eight hundred later today."

I bent over to catch my breath. Upside down between my legs, I saw Poppy and Miguel on the field. They waved and called to someone in the away bleachers.

"Walk it off!" Coach Lipinsky commanded. "And hydrate." He pushed the water bottle into my hand.

I nodded and began to walk toward the field.

"Yay, sister!"

I stopped in my tracks at the sound of Squirrel's voice and spun around. My brother stood up on the metal bleachers with Angelina beside him, shaking a purple-and-white pompom. Mom and Dad stood next to them.

Mom waved to me. "Good work, Daisy!" she called into her cupped hands.

Dad held up his camera. "Got some great photos of you," he yelled. "Nice shoes!"

Mom said something in his ear. He nodded and clattered down the bleachers toward me. In front of everyone, he hugged me. "I'm so proud of you. You're the best kid I know."

My heart fluttered like it was about to fly out of my chest and swoop around the track. "Thanks, Dad." I pulled out of his grasp, embarrassed. "I'm all sweaty and gross."

But he wasn't finished with me yet.

"I talked with your coach about Squirrel's YouTube idea. Interesting guy. A little odd, but a heck of a teacher."

"Coach is right, you know." I pressed my hands against my chest in case my heart made a break for it. "Squirrel deserves a voice. He deserves to go for his dream."

Dad put his hands on my shoulders and looked into my face. "I've never seen either of you so happy. You've put so much work into this project, and Squirrel's obviously thrilled to be on YouTube."

"So?" I prompted.

"So how can Mom and I help with your project?" he asked.

"Really?!"

"Really," he said. "Now go get a towel. You're sweating all over my camera."

I ran to the tarp to put on my sweatshirt. Coach Lipinsky stood nearby. "What'd you tell my dad about Squirrel's YouTube channel?"

He shook his head. "It's not what I told him, Daisy. It's what he saw in you and Squirrel that changed his mind."

"Yeah, but you must have told him something," I persisted. "I saw you two talking at Poppy's dance benefit."

Coach Lipinsky shrugged. "I told him the two of you were runnin' down a dream. Good thing he's a Tom Petty fan."

I laughed and headed for the bathroom in the girls' locker room. I retied my ponytail and smeared on more sunscreen. As I washed my hands at the sink, I met my eyes in the mirror.

"Thank you," I whispered to myself, to Daisy Woodworm.

For the first time in my life, I knew she could do anything.

32

On the morning of our Change the World reports, the classroom buzzed like we'd been invaded by locusts. Maybe not the 12 trillion locusts that once flew over the Midwest for five straight days, but trust me, the room was *loud*.

Almost everyone had dressed up. Kristen wore heels and lipstick. Poppy wore her sari with gold sandals, gold hoop earrings, and a bunch of bracelets, plus an anklet with bells that jingled every time she crossed her legs.

Miguel wore his blue-and-yellow Summer Games T-shirt with "VOLUNTEER" on the back. Coach Lipinsky wore a suit—an actual *suit*, gray with a white shirt and a blue tie dotted with little gold stars. I knew Squirrel would approve.

"Looking good, Coach!" Devon slouched in wearing his usual shorts and running shoes.

"Nice of you to dress for the occasion, Mr. Smalley," Coach Lipinsky said with just enough sarcasm that I was glad I'd put on my pink-and-brown dress and borrowed Poppy's sandals again. Coach drew a big purple T on the whiteboard and turned to us. "Greetings, friends. We have reached the end of BARAT. The time has come for you to *triumph*!"

Kristen cheered. Miguel stomped his feet, and Poppy banged her thermos on her desk. I stared down at my hands, so tightly folded that my knuckles were white.

I'd thought about calling in sick, getting the secretary to tell

Coach Lipinsky I'd gotten the plague from a rogue rat flea. But Squirrel wouldn't let me. He'd set his alarm for 6:00 a.m. , burst into my room, and dragged me out of bed. "Today, we change the world!" he'd hollered, dancing around and singing until Mom and Dad appeared and told him to get ready for school and leave me to prepare in peace.

"Good luck," Dad said at the door before they left for work. He handed me a little bag of gingerbread bunnies frosted white and decorated with purple sprinkles. "Found them in the back of the freezer and thought you could use them," he said. "Break a leg today, kiddo. You and Squirrel worked your butts off on your project."

I'd practiced my oral report in front of him and Mom and Squirrel the night before. Still, in the classroom now, my stomach churned. Devon slouched in his chair like a spider waiting to paralyze me with poisonous fangs.

I reached for my social studies folder and sketched a picture of me reaching for the sky in front of a firing squad of hornets. Miguel looked sideways at my drawing. "Relax," he whispered. "You're gonna do great."

Coach Lipinsky cleared his throat. "It's been my privilege to inspire and guide you through the process of realizing that you . . . yes, you," he said solemnly, and looked at each one of us in turn, "*you* can change the world for the better." He moved his stool in front of the open door and sat down. "So no one can escape." He chuckled, and his silver curls shook. "Who wants to go first?"

"Might as well get it over with." Poppy shot to her feet and propped her posterboards on the metal whiteboard tray at the front of the room. "My family raised two thousand dollars to send to India. My ammachi and achachan are flying to Kerala so they can personally deliver the money to my aunties. And . . ." She paused dramatically. "I get to go with them and stay for a month this summer!"

"Wow! That's incredible!" Kristen exclaimed. "World travel is so fulfilling."

Miguel nudged me with his elbow, a little smile on his lips. I sighed quietly, already missing Poppy. She kept going with her report, holding up a picture of a red-roofed building half-full of water and people outside wading up to their waists in the street. She showed us another picture of five Indian kids smiling and holding up a sign that read in English, *Thank you, Poppy's friends!*

"The money we raised will help my aunties and uncles and their friends rebuild their houses, schools, and stores that got damaged in the flood," Poppy explained.

"Spectacular!" Coach Lipinsky clapped his hands together. "What's the most important lesson you learned from this project, Ms. Banjaree?"

She had an instant answer. "I didn't believe you when you said one kid could change the world. I still don't."

Everyone laughed. Coach Lipinsky folded his arms across his chest. "Go on."

"I mean, sure, I helped raise the money," Poppy continued, "but so did my moms and sisters, and Daisy and Miguel, and everyone who came to watch the performance." She pointed at the purple T on the whiteboard. "It wasn't just me. We *all* triumphed."

"Good point," Coach Lipinsky said. "But the inspiration started with you. *You* took the steps to make it happen."

"BARAT!" Poppy said.

"BARAT!" Coach Lipinsky echoed. "Choose someone to go next."

She looked around the room. *Not me,* I pleaded silently. Her eyes drifted past me and settled on Devon's face. "Mr. Smalley," she said sweetly.

Devon snorted and sauntered to the front of the room. He didn't have a posterboard or even a piece of paper to read from. He flipped his blond bangs out of his eyes and stared down at his feet. "My project started out kind of selfish," he admitted. "I wanted to improve my time in the fifteen hundred so I'd win State this year."

"How does that change the world?" Poppy demanded.

He shrugged. "I thought I could be a role model for other kids. You know, share my training tips online, and inspire other guys to train harder and run faster."

"*Guys?*" Poppy said.

He scowled at her. "Girls too. You know . . . everyone. So . . . I started waking up really early and going to the high school track to train before school."

"Impressive." Miguel whistled. Kristen gazed at Devon like Hasenpfeffer drooling over a graham cracker.

Devon continued. "On the track that early, it was just me and this group of old people. At first, I didn't take them seriously. All they did was walk around the track and talk. But then, they started to run."

"And?" Poppy splayed her fingers in the air. "Get to the point, already!"

"Ms. Banjaree?" Coach said. "Chill."

"And they were really, really fast," Devon said. "They're Masters runners—people over forty."

"Ah. Old people." Coach Lipinsky smiled.

"Yeah. And some of them were almost as fast as me." Devon reached into his pocket and pulled out a thumb drive. "Can I use the laptop?"

"Be my guest," Coach Lipinsky told him.

Devon stuck the thumb drive into the computer and pushed the button to lower the projector screen. His first photo showed a van with words painted on the windows that read "Go Team!" and "Senior Games or Bust!" Six men and women, hair in different shades of silver and white and gray, stood in front of the van wearing matching red shorts and white shirts and running shoes.

"They're part of the Masters team," Devon explained. "They drove down to compete in the Senior Olympics . . . you know, for people older than fifty. They needed a timekeeper and someone to keep track of statistics, and pass out water and snacks and first aid—someone to get people bandages or ibuprofen, or whatever. I said I'd do it."

He clicked to the next slide—a picture of himself in a Sea Urchins sweatshirt wrapping an older man's ankle with an ACE bandage while people in the background raced around a track. Another photo showed him standing beside a long-jump pit with a clipboard, in a spray of sand from a woman in silver braids who'd just landed.

Coach Lipinsky's smile got a whole lot wider when he saw those photos. "So what did you learn from your project, Mr. Smalley?" he asked.

"What'd I learn?" Devon squeezed his eyes shut, thinking.

"Um . . . I guess I learned I'm not bad at first aid. Blood and stuff doesn't scare me. Maybe I'd be a good sports doctor or something?"

Poppy tapped her foot, and her anklet bells jingled. "But how'd your project change the world?"

"It changed *me*," Devon said. "I mean, how I felt about old people, you know? I've been volunteering to be their timekeeper before school every day. I take videos of them so they can study their gait and prepare for races and stuff."

"That's cool!" Miguel said. Kristen swooned across her desk, looking ready to propose marriage on the spot.

Coach Lipinsky stood up from his stool. "Well done." He shook Devon's hand. "I'm proud of you."

Devon sat down, red-faced. "Miguel can go next," he muttered.

Miguel walked to the front of the room carrying a three-sided display board like the kind I made for science fairs. I'd helped him print out text and arrange pictures of the Special Olympics athletes, but I'd told him no way in H-E-double-hockey-sticks was I going to stand up and talk about Save Summer Games. One oral report was enough.

Still, he mentioned me in the very first sentence of his presentation. "Daisy and I raised five thousand dollars with help from the Special Olympics athletes," he told our class. "We saved five grand because the teachers are letting us hold Summer Games for free here at the school the first weekend in June, right before prom. Everyone's welcome to volunteer," he added, looking at Devon.

"I'll think about it," he grunted, and scribbled something on the front of his folder.

"What I learned from this project," Miguel continued, "is that if you know what your goal is, and you know how to ask for help in a way that makes people care, it doesn't matter how young you are. You really *can* change the world. But you've got to have help."

He pointed at me. "Daisy helped so much. She got her brother to model for our campaign and made videos of him for Save Summer Games. Check this out!"

He reached for the laptop and showed us one of Squirrel's YouTube videos, online again with my parents' approval. In the video, Squirrel told viewers how much he loved basketball, then showed off LeBron James's shoe.

Coach Lipinsky pressed his palms together. "Bravo!" He made a little bow in Miguel's direction.

Miguel pointed to the pictures on his display. "Now, I want to introduce you to a few of the athletes." There was Ricky in his basketball jersey at the Moonlight Ball, and Sam running on a track with his tail streaming behind him. Angelina stood poised to dive into the swimming pool, and Billy stretched on a field in his running clothes.

There were Squirrel and Angelina in front of Coach's peacock car with their arms around each other, and my brother at the TV commercial party surrounded by people toasting him with Channel Islands Sports Drink.

"Magnificent." Coach Lipinsky glanced at the clock. "Pick someone to go next."

"Daisy." Miguel sat down beside me. "You've got this," he said, his breath warm and minty in my ear.

"Me?" I squeaked.

Devon tipped back in his chair and grinned at me. "You."

The room spun. My face burned like I was back in second grade. Just as he had for years and years, Devon sat smirking, waiting for me to lisp an S-word.

"Ms. Woodward?" Coach Lipinsky walked over and put his hands on Devon's shoulders. "We're eager to hear what you have to say. Trust me."

Poppy crossed her eyes at me and stuck out her tongue.

"Go on!" Miguel said, and glared at Devon. "We've got your back."

I stood up and staggered to the front of the room. "The thing is . . ." I began.

My tongue lisped the S in "is." I glanced at Devon. He sat frozen, Coach's hands still on his shoulders, staring straight ahead like if he even breathed wrong, he'd be off the track team and banned from State.

"The thing is," I repeated, "my project almost failed. I wanted to help my brother to follow his dreams and become a YouTube fashion celebrity. But my parents were mad at me for putting him on social media because some troll left a comment that wrecked him."

"*#UglyBoy*." Poppy shot Devon the Evil Eye. "I wonder who would write such a thing?"

"Hey! I'm not *that* big of an ass," Devon said, and everyone laughed.

"Ms. Woodward?" Coach Lipinsky nodded at me with an encouraging smile. "Please continue."

I swallowed. My mouth felt full of sand. Every molecule in my body told me to sit down, to fake an emergency case of malaria. But then I thought about what dinner with my family would look like that night—how Mom and Dad and Squirrel would ask about my report, and I'd have to tell them about this exact moment.

I walked over to the computer and connected it to the projector. Then, I inhaled a deep breath through my nose. "Finally, my parents let me launch my brother's YouTube channel. It's called Young Spice Squirrel Advice."

I clicked play, and Squirrel appeared in his tuxedo with his hair perfectly styled and his face super-serious. "Today, I want to teach you all how to dress for the eighth-grade prom," he said into the camera.

"Good idea!" Kristen leaned forward, chewing on the end of her braid. "Your brother's so stylish, Daisy."

"Shh!" Poppy put a finger to her lips. "You've gotta hear this next part."

"It's important for you and your date to match," Squirrel told the camera. "For example, my cummerbund matches my date's dress."

On the video, I'd inserted a close-up of the emerald-green sash above Squirrel's waistband, and then a picture of him beside Angelina in her emerald-green dress at their junior prom in May.

"Spectacular," Coach Lipinsky said.

On the video, Squirrel moved on to hair. "This is me before."

I'd cut to a photo of him with his hair hanging shaggy over his eyes. "And this is me after I use my products!" He patted the top of his styled-up bangs. "It's important to smell any hairstyle product before you buy it. You're gonna be dancing close to your date, and you don't want to stink!"

My classmates laughed. "You know, he has a point," Miguel observed.

"Listen!" I turned up the volume on the video. "This is my favorite part."

"You've got to get your date a flower," Squirrel told the camera. "My love, Angelina, got me this one." He pointed to the pink rosebud in his lapel. "And I got her a big corsage! Watch how I pin it on!"

I'd panned the camera lens out to show Angelina in the frame, so people could watch Squirrel pin the corsage on her shoulder. "Be careful with the pin," he said, "or your date might *explode*!" He pushed the pin through the emerald-green material on her dress, and the balloon they'd hidden beneath it popped. On camera, they both burst out laughing.

In my classroom, everyone cracked up.

"Classic!" Devon pounded his fist on his desk. "I love this guy!"

"He's the best," Poppy said.

"A cool cat," Miguel agreed.

And then the video was over. I hovered the cursor under the number of views—564. "We're working on his next video about how to find designer labels in thrift stores. My dad's been driving us to places all over town."

"Gross," Devon said. "I'd never wear someone else's old clothes."

I shrugged. "I saw a Billabong shirt like the one you're wearing for seven dollars on a thrift store rack."

"I don't need to shop used," he scoffed.

Miguel looked at me and rolled his eyes.

"Tell them about that guy at Goodwill," Poppy said.

"Oh, yeah." I closed the laptop. "One of the thrift store

managers wants to use Squirrel as a model in his promo fliers. My dad actually said okay."

Coach Lipinsky lifted his eyebrows. "How about that? So how would you say your project changed the world?"

"Um . . . well, it changed *my* world." I thought of my new YouTube channel and the entomologist from Washington who'd emailed to ask if I'd make a video about mosquitoes, and then invited me up to intern with her for a couple of weeks. *I'll show you how we collect mosquitoes at the local wildlife refuge, and how to analyze them for species and test them for West Nile Virus*, she'd written.

And I thought of Miguel, how—thanks to our Change the World projects—we'd dug beneath each other's public personas and become friends. More than friends.

"How did my project change the rest of the world?" I said at last. "Well . . . my brother's so happy giving fashion advice. Every time he gets a new subscriber, he dances around like he's won a gold medal. Maybe his fashion videos, and the ones he made for Save Summer Games, are helping YouTube viewers think about people with Down syndrome in a new way. I mean, maybe his videos are changing *their* world. And . . ." I paused, not sure how much I should reveal.

Across the room, Miguel gave me a thumbs-up.

"You go, girl!" Poppy said.

"Well . . . the project changed my family too," I said. "My parents are finally giving my brother some freedom. They seem happier, even though, let's face it . . ." I glanced at Devon. "They do pick up dog poop for a living. And I . . . well, I've found my . . . my voice."

Coach Lipinsky clasped his hands over his heart. "Thank

you, Ms. Woodworm." He gave me a little bow, and his eyes shone with tears behind his glasses. "A-plus."

"Thanks," I mumbled, and started for my seat. But suddenly, Poppy and Miguel were applauding, clapping and stomping their feet and cheering. The rest of the class joined in, just like they had at Poppy's dance benefit. Even Devon drummed his hands on his desk.

"So what did you learn from this project?" Coach Lipinsky asked over the applause.

I thought for another long minute. I'd learned so many things—too many to put into words. But one stood out.

I walked back to the laptop and clicked on Miguel's Instagram feed so everyone could see the group shot I'd taken of Squirrel and his friends on the track while they were training for Summer Games. I pointed at the picture on the screen, and then to Poppy and Miguel. A smile pulled at the corners of my mouth, and happiness washed over me like a wave.

"What did I learn?" I repeated Coach Lipinsky's question, and then answered it in my best YouTuber voice. "If you want to change the world," I said, "cross-pollination is key!"

YOUTUBE VIDEO #8
DAISY WOODWORM CHANGES THE WORLD
Length: 30 Seconds

VIDEO	AUDIO
FADE-UP ON:	FADE-UP ON:
1.MILLIPEDES CRAWLING ACROSS PICTURE OF A RUNNING TRACK	MUSIC: "THE TIME OF YOUR LIFE" FROM A BUG'S LIFE
CUT TO:	
2.CLOSE-UP OF DAISY TALKING	*DAISY: I'm Daisy Woodworm, future entomologist. I'm just back from volunteering at Special Olympics Summer Games, so I thought I'd tell you about the fastest insects on land and in the skies. Heads up: They're not millipedes.*
3.CLOSE-UP OF AUSTRALIAN TIGER BEETLE DRAWING	*The Australian Tiger Beetle can run over five and a half miles per hour. It's the fastest land insect. By the way, my older brother just competed in Summer Games and got a gold medal for running the two hundred meter race. So cool!*
4.CLOSE-UP OF DRAGONFLY DRAWING	*My friend Sam killed it in the one hundred, and this guy Ricky flew across the basketball courts. My friend Angelina swam with the speed of a dragonfly—that's the fastest flying insect, by the way. They can zoom around at 35 miles an hour.*

5.CLOSE-UP OF DAISY TALKING	*That's all I have for you today because I have to get ready for the eighth-grade prom. Here's a peek at my dress!*
6.CLOSE-UP OF MADAGASCAR SUNSET MOTH	*Oops! That's a Madagascar Sunset Moth, the inspiration for my dress.*
7.CLOSE-UP OF DAISY IN GREEN, TURQUOISE, YELLOW & ORANGE DRESS & FRINGED HEADBAND	*Here's my dress, designed by my brother, and created by me and my dad.*
8. CLOSE-UP OF MOM	*MOM: Hey, I made the headband!*

<u>DISSOLVE TO:</u>

9.STICK INSECTS IN TERRARIUM WITH PROM HEADBAND DRAPED ACROSS THE TOP	*VOICE-OVER: Thanks, Mom! Follow my channel for fascinating facts about insects, Special Olympics, fashion, and more!*
<u>FADE OUT</u>	<u>MUSIC:</u> *FADE OUT "THE TIME OF YOUR LIFE"* FROM A BUG'S LIFE

Author's Note

I grew up in Southern California with my brother Mark, who has Down syndrome. My mother didn't treat us differently from one another; Mark was just my sibling—sometimes annoying when he woke me up at 6:00 a.m. on Saturday, and most of the time one of my very best friends. We loved singing and playing the guitar together, building tree houses in our backyard, and watching movie musicals with a big bowl of popcorn.

My brother is the inspiration for Squirrel in *Daisy Woodworm Changes the World*. He's always adored men's fashion and Special Olympics sports. His circle of friends shares his interests. Just like Squirrel and *his* friends, they take the bus to athletic competitions and formal dances together when they're not at work or hanging out at home.

People with Down syndrome are celebrities—think Lauren Potter from the TV show *Glee*, Zack Gottsagen from the movie *The Peanut Butter Falcon*, and model Madeline Stuart whom Daisy discovers on Instagram. People with Down syndrome are Ironman triathletes like Chris Nikic, disability advocates like Abigail Adams, and entrepreneurs like Allison Fogarty of Doggy Delights and Nate Simon of 21 Pineapples. They're university graduates like Pablo Pineda.

Because of their intellectual disabilities, they would need a great deal of assistance to write a novel. Since I grew up with my brother, and we continue to be close today, I felt confident that I could give readers a complex, true-to-life character who has Down syndrome. Squirrel, like the rest of us, longs to follow his dreams. Like the rest of us, he's not perfect. He gets into bad moods. He snaps at his sister and forgets to clean his rabbit's litter box.

We all have challenges of one sort or another. I speak with a slight lisp, especially when I'm tired and forget to articulate properly. Long ago, I realized what Daisy has to discover for herself in the novel—our challenges make us interesting. We can learn to work with them, and then forget about them as we focus on changing the world for the better.

Ideas for Further Research

Celebrities Who Have Down Syndrome

Madeline Stuart, fashion model

Abigail Adams, advocate, athlete, and entrepreneur

Chris Burke, *Life Goes On* actor and activist

Lauren Potter, actress

Jon Stoklosa, Special Olympics weight lifter and activist

Pablo Pineda, Spanish actor and teacher

Karen Gaffney, long-distance swimmer and activist

Zack Gottsagen, actor

Tommy Jessop, actor

Archie and Sevy Eicher, global ambassadors

Lucas Warren, the 2018 Gerber Baby

Allison Fogarty, chef at Doggy Delights

Chris Nikic, Ironman triathlete

Nate Simon, CEO of 21 Pineapples

Volunteer Opportunities

Special Olympics

www.specialolympics.org/

National Down Syndrome Congress

www.ndsccenter.org

National Down Syndrome Society Buddy Walk

www.ndss.org/play/national-buddy-walk-program/

Gigi's Playhouse Down Syndrome Achievement Centers
www.gigisplayhouse.org
The Arc
www.thearc.org

Entomology for Kids

The Bug Chicks, offering digital and in-person classes
www.thebugchicks.com
Entomology Today, part of the Entomological Society of America
www.entomologytoday.org/2020/03/27/learning-at-home-with-bugs/
Dr. Samuel Ramsey (aka "Dr. Sammy")
www.drsammy.online
Bugs for Breakfast: How Eating Insects Could Help Save the Planet, by Mary Boone. Chicago Review Press, 2022.
And check out **Picture Insect**, a free smartphone app that helps you identify insects!

Running Organizations for Kids

Girls on the Run
www.girlsontherun.org
Kids Run the Nation, a program of Road Runners Club of America
www.rrca.org/programs/kids-run-the-nation
The Morning Mile
www.morningmile.com

Acknowledgments

It takes some serious cross-pollination to write and publish a novel, and I'm deeply grateful to everyone who helped Daisy and Squirrel to flourish.

Big thanks to Jolly Fish Senior Editor Meg Gaertner for believing in my manuscript, and for her incredible patience as we debated the perfect size for the Madagascar hissing cockroach on the cover.

Speaking of that cockroach, I'm indebted to illustrator Elena Bia for a truly stunning book cover. She took my scattered Pinterest board ideas and turned them into art.

Thank you to copy editor Meredith Madyda and proofreader Jackie Dever for your eagle-eyed skills; I so appreciate your careful reading of the final draft of *Daisy*!

It's been marvelous to work with Heather McDonough and Taylor Kohn on publicity for *Daisy*; thank you for your supreme organization—your remarkable marketing spreadsheet kept all my ducks in a row.

I'm so grateful to journalist and author Amy Silverman, who has an adult daughter with Down syndrome and read the final draft of *Daisy* with a discerning eye and brilliant suggestions for giving Squirrel even more agency as a young adult. Thanks to the ARC of Ventura County and to Special Olympics Southern California Ventura region for all the love and care you lavished upon my brother, Mark Wilmot, for two decades, and the devotion you show to all your clients.

Thanks, too, to Sitara Carden, whose dance benefit for her relatives in Kerala inspired Poppy's Change the World project. Much gratitude to Dr. Priya Carden, who advised me on the classical Indian dance scene. Watching Priya, Sitara, and little sister Indu dancing on stage fills me with joy.

Enormous thanks to my agent, Jennifer Unter, who believed in this manuscript as fervently as she's believed in all my other manuscripts, and who always manages to calm my anxiety with her chill, witty vibe.

To my editor, Kelsy Thompson, you've been a joy to work with on *Daisy*, and your thoughtful and thorough editing notes deepened my characters and strengthened my story in ways that continue to amaze me. Your kind emails have endlessly brightened my days.

This book could not have been written without the unfailing support of my husband, Jonathan Smith. It's a privilege to write a novel, and he made sure I had as much time and space and chocolate as I needed in order to focus on this one. Thank you to my daughter, Maia, who keeps my memes fresh even if she refuses to look at my TikTok because "It's *so embarrassing*, Mom."

And especially, thanks to my younger brother Mark, the most fashionable man I know.

About the Author

Melissa Hart's writing is focused on kids and parents, with a particular interest in marginalized communities. She grew up in Southern California with her brother, who has Down syndrome, and spent a decade working as a special education teacher. She lives in Eugene, Oregon, with her husband and daughter, and teaches for the MFA Program in Creative Writing at Southern New Hampshire University with a focus on MG/YA Literature. She's the author of the middle grade novel *Avenging the Owl*, and her writing has appeared in the *New York Times*, *Washington Post*, *Real Simple*, *National Geographic Kids*, and numerous other publications. Learn more at www.melissahart.com.